James Rogers was educated at Christ's Hospital and Exeter College, Oxford, and lives in London. His previously published books are *War and Peace in Milton Keynes* and *Dog's Life*.

SAVAGE LIFE

James Rogers

Library of Congress Catalog Card Number: 94-68597

A CIP record for this book can be obtained from the British Library on request

First published in 1995 by
Serpent's Tail, 4 Blackstock Mews, London N4, and
401 West Broadway #1, New York, NY 10012

Set in 10½ Plantin by CentraCet Ltd, Cambridge
Printed in Great Britain by
Cox & Wyman Ltd, Reading, Berkshire

For Anthea Morton-Saner

CHAPTER ONE

GAZ HOSKINS WAS waking up. He was drifting up, like he was coming up through hot percolating water. Then he came violently awake. He jerked in the bed, rapidly surveyed the room. He was naked, drenched in sweat. The scrunched-up duvet was wrapped round his foot and trailing on the floor. The sun cut a bright dagger across the room, across the piles of rubbish and the picture of Norman Bellwether pinned to the wall.

He remembered the event horizon of his dreams, a red twilight world of burnt-out buildings and rotting bodies. Charles Bronson carried a gun. Gaz's mother, her face like an old chimpanzee, was kneeling, a wizened old man taking her from behind. He was seized with terror. Someone wanted to kill him, someone lurking in the cavernous shadows. He was running, but the ground was a treadmill. No matter how fast you ran you just stayed still.

The killer came out of the shadows, wearing a motorcycle helmet, was just raising the gun, then he always woke up. He wondered what happened if he didn't wake up at that bit: what happened if the guy shot him? Maybe he would just die in his sleep, and no one would ever know. It always fucking terrified him when he thought about that. So he tried to think of something else.

He settled back on the bed and thought hostile thoughts about his enemies, specifically about his sister's boyfriend Dave 'Dog' Barber who was at present Gaz Enemy # 1, no question about it. There was no extremity of human cruelty, no far-flung torture chamber of the imagination which Gaz would not happily have inflicted on Dog. For six months now Dog had been cohabiting with Christie. He was always there in the morning, his revolting fat red face hunched over the kitchen table while he ate his breakfast and whinged about his routine hangover.

Gaz wanted to kill him, badly wanted to kill him.

The only problem with this plan of action was that Dog was about five times as big as him and readily inclined to gratuitous displays of violence. Dog was something in the building trade, specifically a Cowboy. Gaz thought this probably accounted for his size: all that hefting hods up ladders and carrying bags of cement and stuff. This was probably why Dog was so disgustingly large.

His thoughts turned now to his trainers, three weeks old and showing signs of distress. He thought about superior trainers, in particular the pair of Yakasoto inflatable basketball boots (£179.95) he had yesterday espied upon the feet of a black guy standing on the Uxbridge Road outside Alabama Fried Chicken. He wanted a pair of those, he badly wanted a pair of those totally awesome bits of footwear.

As he got up he could hear his mother's TV through the wall, the indistinct throb of the *Wake Up!* show. He untangled the putrescent duvet from his foot, walked across the room and switched on his Toshiba. The fierce metallic reverberations of FYM (it was short for Fuck You Man) lashed out at the walls. He inspected his lean, pimply physique in the mirror which was propped against the wall (he had found it in a skip); the body had not grown any larger during the night, but seemed rather to have shrunk, to have become more pallid and spindly than ever before. He pulled his smalls on and started rootling round for the cleanest socks he could find.

His mother entered the room. 'You going down the shops?' she shouted over FYM.

'No,' he said blankly, refused to look at her.

'I need some ciggies.'

'Tell Christie to get them.'

'She's asleep.'

'Well I'm not fucking going, am I?' he said.

'I can't go with my agoraphobia,' his mother said.

'Leave your fucking agoraphobia behind then.' He thought this was incredibly funny and laughed.

'You're a bastard,' his mother told him, and slammed the door shut behind her.

In the kitchen he found his sister Christie, the porno queen, star of last month's *Slag Mega Melon Special*, making coffee for Dog who was recumbent upon her bed, slow death rattles of last night's vindaloo croaking in his guts, slow lager farts seeping from his arse like nuclear spillage. Gaz had heard him coming in about twelve last night, pissed and going on about some bloke he'd aimed in the Goose Green or the Stumbling Block or the Bald Pigeon or one of the pubs he spent half his life in, drinking, playing pool, getting into fights.

'Mum wants some ciggies,' Christie said.

'Why don't she get them then?' he said.

'She's not well. You haven't got no sympathy, have you?'

'What's wrong with her then?'

'It's her agoraphobia – you know that, dirt-box. You know perfectly fucking well. She gets sick if she goes out.'

'Why's it always me? Why don't no one else go?'

'I haven't got no clothes on, have I?'

'So what's new then?' Ha Ha.

'Don't you try and be funny with me, toe-rag. I've got a living to make. Why aren't you at school? Aren't you supposed to be at school?'

This was a point which invariably riled Gaz. He said, 'Fuck off,' and went down the stairs and out of the flat, slamming the door as hard as he could so as to announce his departure.

On Esterhazy Road crisp packets and Fanta cans and

McDonald's wrappings were piled in the gutters. The sun was already high in the sky, frazzling everything beneath it. A couple of car alarms were singing a morning duet, one high-pitched and staccato, the other a more sonorous howl lurching up and down like a dangerous fairground ride. A stereo blasted reggae somewhere down the street. Another blasted Country and Western. A disorientated blackbird tried to make itself heard against the background roar.

At the bottom of the road he stopped and loitered in the shade of a tree. His thoughts turned to burglary, and to the miserable failure of his own intended life of crime. I'm fourteen, he thought, and I still haven't knocked off a house. That's pathetic, that is, fucking pathetic. There were guys up on the White City who did their first VCR when they were six or seven. They were born with it, in their blood like. Out of the cradle, in through the window.

He knew the reason for his failure to perform this essential rite of passage: he'd bottled out. On numerous occasions now he had been presented with perfectly decent house-breaking opportunities, and he had failed to capitalize on them because he'd bottled out. He had performed only the most derisory of crimes – a couple of car radios, gear from the Paki shop, bicycles, a couple of mopeds for quick, breathtaking joy rides – all beginner's stuff, rubbish. Dog laughed at him: 'Nicked any bubble gum today then, cunt?' It was humiliating; it was demeaning.

The house he was inspecting with a view to his first proper burglary was No 51, a dwelling located on the corner of Esterhazy and Wilson Roads. It presented an ideal target: it was large, it did not appear to have a burglar alarm, it did not house a large, furious, yellow-eyed dog, and it afforded a number of points of potential access, one of which – a small, ground-floor window – was conveniently concealed behind some shrubbery. Best of all, it belonged to yuppies who drove round in a Series 3 BMW. Ergo there would be plenty of gear worth nicking.

For some weeks now he had been monitoring the activities of The Yuppies. There was Mr Yuppie, a smug-looking bastard who went out in his BMW every morning, dressed in a suit and chain-smoking cigarettes. There was Mrs Yuppie, an extremely tasty bird he reckoned was about in her mid-thirties. There were two Yuppie sprogs with billions of pounds' worth of toys which he wanted to incinerate with a flame-thrower.

He was rehearsing in his mind the forthcoming burglary. He was going to wait till they all went out; when it was dark he was going to force the small window behind the bush with a heavy screwdriver he had specially nicked for the purpose. He'd get the gear – video, CD, jewellery, cash, anything silver or gold – cram it all in his Head gymbag, and be out of the front door in three minutes dead. He'd leg it round the corner into Wilson Road, then saunter round the block and back home. Simple. Wicked. Awesome. It was just a matter of waiting until the Yuppies took the sprogs out one evening, waiting until he saw those Kidsafe safety seats going in the back of the motor, and he'd be in there like a shot. He'd be a proper burglar and get some fucking respect.

He shuffled off, not wishing to attract attention to his surveillance operations. He rounded the corner into Wilson, hung a left up Schenectady, came up on the Uxbridge Road, and proceeded towards the Green. Cars hummed in the ozone air. Brilliant red ribs turned slow revolutions in the window of Rib Shack. A mad black woman hopped down the street with a plastic bag over her head. A group of paddies swigging Wobbler Brew sheltered from the sun under the awning outside the Supernova Store. Two kids wove rollerskates between the columns of traffic. Waves of chip fat smell flowed slowly on the heavy air.

He hopped through the stationary traffic coiled round the Green and ID-ed the source of the congestion: a mini pile-up down by McDonald's, bus, motor bike, Montego. A crowd had gathered behind the police cordon to take in the action. An ambulance came sirening through the traffic.

The centre of attention seemed to be the guy from the bike. He was crashed out on the floor with a load of filth and ambulance guys round him blocking the view. Everyone was rubbernecking to get a better eyeball on him. The big question was this: was he dead?

Gaz pushed through the mêlée, watched until they stretchered him into the back of the ambulance, then went into McDonald's. Five minutes later he came out with a cheeseburger and a Coke and headed back up Uxbridge. In a rare display of public-spiritedness he turfed his burger container into a waste bin.

He was thinking.

No 51. No 51. My first big job. For the millionth time he rehearsed the details of the plan, picking through every possible eventuality, every potential pitfall. He experienced a rush of adrenalin, a hard jolt of excitement lodged deep in his thorax. Thinking about the burglary was even better than wanking, something of which he also did a great deal.

CHAPTER TWO

THE MERRY YEOMAN CARVERY was a redbrick construction behind a small sodium-lit car-park in the cleavage between the M4 and the M25. It occupied an area of grim scrubland where a 15-storey Holiday Inn servicing the needs of airport and motorway rose high above the exhausted gravel pits and the marina, the Heliodome Indoor Shopping Complex and the mini golf course.

It was ten o'clock on a hot, stagnant summer evening and Colin Nutter was feasting with his employer, Dorian Savage, in the Banqueting Hall, a part of the restaurant decorated with stags' heads, hunting horns and landscapes depicting carnage and debauchery in Merrie Olde England.

The entire Carvery was similarly themed: a bar called the Mead Hall boasted a reconstruction of a Viking longboat and a burbling video game called *Beer Wolf*. Grey-suited middle management were drinking as much lager as possible on their way home from the office to the western suburbs. To the rear, facing out over the gravel pits, was Mr Pickwick's Pantry where accounts clerks were hurling back the lagers, fisting peanuts and trying to pull secretaries.

When Colin had been bundling up his briefcase in the nearby offices of Savage Life, Dorian had strolled in and said, 'Fancy a drink, Col?' Colin had not fancied a drink. He had promised his wife he'd be home by eight for a dinner party. But when Dorian said 'Fancy a drink?' it was, as far as he was concerned, a divine edict.

'Yeah, sure,' he'd said. 'I'll just give the doris a bell, tell her I'm going to be a bit late.'

Now, two hours later, they had moved on from swigging lager in Mr Pickwick's Pantry to gourmandizing in the Banqueting Hall, and he had entirely forgotten the dinner party.

Dorian Savage was the Managing Director and Chairman of Savage Life, a small but successful insurance broking firm specializing in life assurance policies. Colin revered Dorian, who was not only his employer but also a far more successful salesman and a far more intelligent human being than himself.

Generally Colin disliked intelligence: intelligent people made him look stupid. With Dorian it was different though. Dorian didn't deploy his intelligence ostentatiously to fill in crosswords, speak French, answer the questions on *Mastermind* or do any of the other things intelligent people did which wound him up. Dorian used his intelligence to sell policies, to spank the client, give the punter a real tanning. And that was all right – that was what it was all about. It was all right to be intelligent if you were doing something straight-up and honest like that.

Colin had grudgingly admired Dorian since his first day at Savage Life when Dorian had pushed him across the room, called him a cunt, and then locked him in a dark cupboard with a telephone for the rest of the day, refusing to allow him out until he had succeeded in gaining interviews with three potential prospects. He had spent two days in the cupboard. Dorian's only concession had been to pass in an empty lager bottle into which he was permitted to piss. When he emerged – with red, sunken eyes, a mangy, uneven growth of beard, writhing pains in his bowels and breath like an anaconda's – Dorian insisted they share a bottle of Smirnoff to commend his sterling achievement. It was like being in the Army, Colin reasoned. Tough but rewarding.

Now, four years on, he felt that Dorian's harsh training

methods had made him the salesman he was, and for this he was incalculably indebted to Dorian. Dorian was a lion among insurance salesmen and he had been privileged to sit at his feet, snatching what scraps he could from the feast.

A waitress approached and was routinely subjected to the lagery gaze of both men.

'Colin?' Dorian said.

'T-bone, well done, chips and er – '

'Something to start with, sir?'

'Yeah.' He thought about it. Ideally, he would have liked to start with another T-bone, but that was out of the question. 'Pâté.'

'Salad?'

'Yeah.' He never ate the salad, it was just something which adorned the table. He stirred it round a bit with his fork, occasionally sampling a segment of tomato.

Dorian ordered mushroom soup, grilled trout, a green salad and a 1975 something-or-other, then said, 'You'll get mad cow disease, Col.'

Colin looked perplexed. 'That's all bullshit, isn't it?'

'Bull's brains, Col – brains, nerve tissue, offal. I don't eat much meat these days – you don't know what they've done to it. Very nasty. Course, you've got to be careful with fish too. Half of it's radioactive or covered with shit. I read this thing about the life-cycle of a turd: comes out your arse, toddles off down the sewer, floats out into the North Sea, gets eaten by a fish, ends up back on your plate before you know it. Not just your turds either: could be any bastard's. You're all right with trout cos they farm it. That bloke who used to be in The Who.'

'Keith Moon,' Colin said. He remembered Keith: a childhood hero. Smashing up hotel rooms, doing drugs, laying chicks. All the things young Colin had wanted to do.

'Daltrey,' Dorian said. 'The one that did the Amex ad.'

'Course.'

He swilled some lager and lit a Benson & Hedges. 'See the football last night then?' he asked.

'What was that then?'

'Arsenal.'

'No, I didn't see it, Colin.'

'Oh.' Sometimes there was no accounting for Dorian. Colin supposed his mentor had spent the evening sipping wine and listening to Brahms on his Bang & Olufsen. Funny guy.

The wine and starters arrived. He stared at the waitress's retreating rump, said, 'I could give her one.'

Dorian delicately unfolded his serviette and laid it on his knee. A gold ring glistened on his finger. 'I don't really care for football any more,' he said. 'It's not a proper sport nowadays.'

What? Football was something which inspired a virulent nationalism in Colin: he didn't know what it was, but whenever he thought about Our Boys out there engaging the foreign wooftah little hot tears welled up behind his eyes and his throat went hard with emotion, as though a loved one had just died.

'Bullfighting,' Dorian said, 'that's a sport. I always like to take in a bit of bullfighting when I'm in Spain. Or a good bit of middle-weight boxing, when two guys are really knocking shit out of each other. I like that.'

There was a snuffling sound as Colin dispatched his pâté in one mouthful. 'Good clean fight,' he said through half-masticated meat.

'No, Col. I like a really dirty fight myself.'

'Yeah, I mean, that's what I meant.'

'A metaphor for life,' Dorian said.

After a pause Colin said, 'Racing,' for no particular reason.

'Dog-racing,' Dorian said. 'I like greyhounds, whippets – very elegant creatures.'

'Right. Course, I don't hold with dog-fighting, things like that. No human involvement – no skills. I mean, it's not like racing, cos you've got trainers and jockeys involved. I saw this thing about this guy in the East End who fights Rottweilers, for money like. You know, has grudge fights with em.'

Dorian sipped at his soup. 'Fucking prat,' he said.

'Yeah.'

'As you know, Col, I'm really a man of the sea. A man pitted alone against the elements – that's my idea of sport.'

The main courses arrived. Colin ordered yet more lager, said, 'Lovely arse.'

Dorian meticulously dissected his trout. Then he said, 'Thing about mad cow disease, Col, is it's like AIDS. Don't know you've got it. You could have it for seven, eight – maybe ten years and not know about it. Then you're in the pub one evening, or at a dinner party – '

'Oh shit,' Colin interjected, remembering his prior engagement.

' – and your eyes go all funny, start rolling in your head, and you lose control of your limbs, start flailing round like some spastic, foaming at the mouth, pissing all over the place. Lose control of your arse and start crapping in your pants. Then you go mad. Not a pretty sight.'

The operation of Colin's mandibles upon his meat had grown gradually slower during this dissertation until it now came to a complete halt. His mouth hung ajar. 'Yeah, but this is steak, right? Comes from its arse. Nowhere near its brain, is it?'

'You seen an abattoir, Col? The way they mix all the bits up together.' Dorian's tone grew nostalgic. 'I remember when I was a kid. Used to watch the cows and the pigs going off to the abattoir. They knew what was happening. No question about it. Looked at you with these great big sad eyes, like they were saying, "You bastard. You betrayed me. I thought you was my friend." I've seen the inside of an abattoir, Col. Everything piled up in fucking heaps, like something out of the Holocaust.'

He sipped wine.

'And what about that Cornish pasty I saw you eating the other day? They put everything in there, you know, all the bits of gut and brains and hooves and the other stuff no one else wants. MRM – mechanically recovered meat. Why d'you think they're all so funny down in Cornwall? Ever been to Cornwall? I have. They're all round the fucking twist down there. People used to think it was the inbreeding, but I reckon it's mad cow disease. They've had it for years. Course, you've started now, so you might as well finish.' Dorian grinned.

Colin swilled some more lager, as though this might disinfect his innards.

'How much did you make last year, Col?' Dorian asked with his customary abruptness. Colin chewed cautiously at his steak.

'About forty,' he mumbled.

'And how many sprogs have you got now?'

'Two – Sylvester and Jessamy.' Dorian knew all this: he was angling for something. He didn't like it. Didn't like it one bit.

'That was planned, like, was it, Col? I mean, you wanted to have them?'

'Kate did.'

'You were trying for a while, weren't you?' Dorian feigned innocent curiosity.

'Well, sort of.'

'Didn't you have to go and see this doc and wank off into a test tube, to see if you was fertile, like?'

Words could not express how bitterly he regretted the occasion when he had got pissed with Dorian and let slip that little secret. Dorian had never ceased to remind him of it.

'I can just imagine you in this little cubicle with a copy of *Heave* or *Grunt* trying to point the end of your dick into a test tube.'

'It wasn't like that,' Colin protested angrily. 'It's scientific.'

'Get these sexy little nurses to come and help out, do they, Col?'

'No. But I'm just saying, you know, it's sort of medical, isn't it? Anyway, there was nothing wrong with my spunk. It was fine. Doctor said I was very potent, as a matter of fact.'

'Funny thing though, isn't it?' Dorian asked. 'Nature. Most of us spend the whole time trying *not* to have one, and there you were desperately trying to pop one in there. I was watching this programme about these wildebeest things in South Africa. The thing is, how incredibly stupid they are, these animals. Unbelievably stupid. Every year they have to cross this river that's flooded, and rather than walk up the river to where it's shallow enough for them to cross, they all pile into it, half of them drown, and the other half get eaten by these lions. All the lions have to do is just toddle down there and there's a banquet laid on for them. Now, you'd think the wildebeests would learn their lesson eventually – you know, survival of the fittest, natural selection and all that – but they don't. They do exactly the same every year, and the lions are just sitting there laughing at how easy it all is.'

Dorian peeled a last sliver of pink flesh off the trout's backbone and placed it in his mouth. Colin tried to puzzle out whether or not Dorian had once again succeeded in subtly belittling him. Was there some connection between the wildebeest's stupidity and his own efforts at procreation?

'And, of course, you've got quite a hefty mortgage on that place.'

'Yeah.'

'Kate not working at the moment?'

'She's doing a bit. Temping and stuff.'

'Not much in that, is there?'

'Well, no.'

Dorian's expression was solemn. 'School fees, Col. When are you going to start thinking about that? Haven't got for ever, you know. It's a mistake a lot of people make. Don't think about it till the last minute, then find they can't afford it. The arrow of time is whizzing by.'

It was unbelievable: the man was a miracle. It was a Friday night and Dorian was trying to sell a policy to his friend and longest-serving employee. That was the sort of persistence it took, the sort of unremitting dedication – that was why Dorian earned three? five? ten? times what he did. How much *did* he earn? It was a question Colin often pondered. 'There is never a situation where you can't sell something,' Dorian had once told him. 'Never. I sold two policies at my brother's funeral – one to his widow, the other to the vicar. Made fifteen hundred commission out of that funeral.' The man was a miracle.

'What I'm driving at, Col, is this. What kind of condition are your finances in at the moment?'

Suddenly he knew the motive behind this sojourn to the Merry Yeoman: Dorian was going to fire him. *Underperforming*. 'You're a cunt, and what's more you're a stupid cunt.' That was how it had been last time he sacked someone. Now it was his turn.

But Colin knew his stuff. He'd learnt from Dorian. Don't even blink. Lie through your teeth. 'Fine, Dorian. Very nice, no problems.' Don't go too far here – don't gild the lily. 'Why d'you ask?'

Dorian smiled and toyed with the stem of his wine glass. He liked to test his people out like this: if they could lie to him, they could lie to any bastard.

'Interest rates up again, Col,' he said. He'd been saying this every few weeks of late, reminding Colin of his ever greater mortgage overheads.

'Yeah,' he said, disgruntled.

'No, you see the thing is I've decided to upgrade on my boat – go for something a bit bigger – and I was wondering if you'd be interested in taking the *Dealer* off my hands. How about something else – some cognac?'

Colin was so happy still to have his job he readily agreed to the cognac, despite the strange disorientation the lager was now inducing.

Dorian continued: 'It's just that I know you were interested in getting a boat, so I thought I'd give you first whack at it. It's a nice boat, very good nick. I'll be sad to part with it, really. I had my first fuck with Rebecca on that boat. Come to think of it, I had my first fuck with Sarah on it too. Something about the sea air – makes me very horny. D'you know what I mean?'

'Yeah. Yeah, absolutely.'

Colin reflected that this was an arrant lie. The only thing the sea made him feel was sick. He had absolutely no interest in yachting, hated everything to do with the sea, water and boats. But that wasn't the point. The point was this: the marina where Dorian had the *Dealer* moored had a large number of big boats in it, belonging to some very rich people. Dorian did nearly half his business these days through contacts he had made down there. That was how you got results in this business – through socializing with the right class of punter.

'I'm interested,' he said. 'What sort of price are we looking at?'

'Not cheap, Col. Not cheap.'

(It was like the Stella ad: not at all cheap, but the real goods.)

'Yeah sure. Put a number on it.'

'Eighteen – I can't say fairer than that.'

'That sounds fine,' he said blithely. His brain snapped: where do I find eighteen grand? Borrow. *Borrow*. BORROW! This is an investment. 'Course, I'll have to get someone to give it a once-over, you know, just to make sure everything's all right.'

'Course, Col. You'd be a cunt if you didn't. I know a very

reasonable surveyor, but you'll probably want to get your own guy in.'

'Yeah,' he said.

'Well, you let me know when he wants to have a squint at the boat and I'll let you have the keys. Okay?'

'Fine.'

'Another drink?'

They had a few more cognacs. Colin drove home to Shepherd's Bush. It was one in the morning when he pulled the BMW up outside No 51 Esterhazy Road.

CHAPTER THREE

DOG WAS OUT, RUINING someone's central heating, nicking breezeblocks from the back of the builders' merchants, bodging someone's dry rot, playing pool in the Goose Green, ballsing-up an elementary bit of wiring, screwing Shireen who lived high up on one of the blocks on the Green, dismantling a dodgy motor, doing a line of speed in the Athenaeum Snooker Club, permanently disabling someone's sink disposal unit, fighting – whatever it was he was doing, it was sure to be destructive, sure to be adding to the general level of entropy in the universe.

Christie was in, tanning her melons under the sun lamp by way of preparation for the 'Mediterranean Orgy' in *Belgravia*. His mother was in, one of her daytime soaps unfurling – *The Parkers*, the one about the yuppies going round in Renaults taking their brat to school and setting up businesses, *Dominic and Judith*, the one where these two cunts drink coffee all day and go to New York and keep trying to get off with each other, *Bette and Friends*, the one about the revolting cow who talks on the phone all day. One of the fucking rubbish soaps she watched all day. They were all the same.

He chewed a Snickers bar, changed the music on the Toshiba. He was reading an interview in *Boot!* with his hero, Norman Bellwether, the QPR left back. He'd been at it for an hour now. This is what he'd read:

'My Dad was a big influence on me like. He was unemployed when I was a kid and we used to take a ball up to the Scrubs and he'd make me tackle him. He was a good dribbler. He could have been a pro if he'd got the breaks. At first I couldn't get nowhere near him. But I learnt quick and soon I was getting the ball off him quite often. As I got bigger I got the ball off him more often. Then the accident happened. I just went in a bit too hard. I was really cut up about it. I can still see him in that wheelchair – really, just like he was in front of me. Every time I think about it it really does me in. I think he forgave me before he died though. He never stopped encouraging me like. He was the real inspiration behind my game. I wasn't able to be with him when he died because it was during that semi-final against West Ham when I stopped Pete Mason inside the box. Mum said he died with a smile on his face.'

It had been a long slog, a real bulldoze of a read, but had been well worthwhile. It had made him think about something he'd never thought of before: who his dad was. He supposed he must have one. Everyone had one, didn't they? Even if they didn't know who it was. He resolved to interrogate his mother.

Later he went and skulked in the corner of her room, waiting for a suitable moment to try and inveigle some cash out of her. Then he broached the subject.

'Ooze my father then?'

Adeline didn't register the question.

On screen, Judith was flirting with yet another of the deliciously hunky men who kept her from the arms of Dominic (who was in NY today, on business). Judith poured some coffee and looked as though she was about to go down on the bloke.

'Why d'you suddenly wanna know that then?'

'Just do, don't I? I've got a right to know.'

His mother appeared unusually pensive, as though some process of recall were actually taking place in the bombed-out cavity of her brain. He scuffed at the floor with his trainers, his foot narrowly avoiding a plate.

'He wouldn't wanna know you,' she said.

'I din say he would did I? I just wanna know who he is like.'

'He was better than your sort – he had some brains and some manners.'

'Who is he then?'

'You don't wanna know.'

'I do. I just said I do, diden I?'

'It won't make no difference.'

Judith's hand caressed the rim of the man's coffee cup as she handed it to him, a subliminal hand-job. Outside a car alarm warbled.

'You don't know who it was,' he said, feeling, strangely, a sense of triumph.

'Course I do. Don't you talk to me like that.'

'Who is it then? I got a right to know.'

This was a vexed question between mother and son. Gaz was forever asserting supposed rights. When he felt any kind of grievance he insisted he had a right to this or that. His mother invariably denied that he had any such thing. He thought it was all extremely unfair. He had a right to have rights, didn't he?

'You haven't got a right to nuffin,' she said, predictably.

Next day standing close to the cover of the tree at the bottom of Esterhazy and monitoring his intended target (lights on; voices; BMW on road outside), he had an idea: his mother kept photographs, envelopes of old snapshots. Was it not a racing certainty that there would be a picture of his progenitor? And it was possible to date the time of his conception, was it not? He was born in February 77, so the pertinent fuck had taken place the previous summer. Detective work – logical deduction. It remained only to find an opportunity to have a recce at the photos.

Fortunately an opportunity presented itself the next morning. It was his mother's monthly pilgrimage to the doctor's to get her tranquillizer prescription renewed or – even better

– increased. Sometimes the doc had a new potion he was keen to try out, a refined elephant knock-out juice which totally disabled the head. She spent the morning whining about how her agoraphobia was terrible, then caught a cab to the doctor. Dog went out to put away Prairie Brew in the Goose Green. Christie went out to earn her living at the *Rump* studio. The coast was clear.

He entered his mother's room. The floor was covered in shit – magazines, clothes, an old Chinese take-out. Even with the window open the room smelt of dope, fags and his mother's musky smell.

After a swift search, he located the bundles of photographs in one of the drawers under the telly and rifled through them.

His first thought was: back in the old days everything had more colours. The sky was a more vivid blue; people's faces a glowing pink; grass a sinister green. Many people had bright red eyes, which was particularly weird. People wore fucking weird clothes too. Look at this one: a bloke and a chick standing outside a club called Downers. He's wearing massive flares and a tie nearly as thick as his chest. And take a shufty at those shoes. Jesus. People used to wear gear like that! History. And the chick: the chick's wearing a skirt so short you ought to be able to see her G-spot. Fluorescent dyed blonde hair and a skinty, sequined little top barely able to contain her bazoomkas. Who the hell is she? *Shit* – she's my fucking mother!

Never having experienced feelings remotely Oedipal before, he was disturbed by the photograph. In his memory, his mother seemed always to have been the raddled dinosaur who now occupied this room. He contemplated Time, and did not like what he saw.

Most of the photographs were conveniently labelled with dates which aided the task of detection. His mother and Kipper-tie was *Sept 72*. Way out. He moved forward through the archive, the colour of his mother's hair changing with disorientating rapidity. Kipper-tie was lost to sight, usurped by Gold Bracelet, then by Missing Tooth, then by Sloping Forehead, each coming in a swift succession which took us through to the end of 1972. There was evidence of a Christmas festivity that year: scenes of havoc in a large house, a man performing an obscene gesture with a spurting champagne bottle (it was pretty obvious where he planned shoving it later), a girl smoking a joint the size of a dachshund. This must be how they celebrated Christmas back in the Old Days.

It was Ancient History.

He progressed forward:

His mother topless on a white sand beach. Very decent tits in those days. Missing Tooth swigging bottle of Bacardi. 1973.

His mother showing signs of pregnancy. Was Missing Tooth Christie's father? Early 74.

A pub by a river somewhere in the country, blue Jaguar in background. A new face: Cro-Magnon Jaw. Mother heavily pregnant, guzzling gin, smoking fag. Mid 74.

Rear view of Cro-Magnon Jaw pissing in hedgerow.

Baby Christie sitting on floor with bunny rabbit. Unidentified male trousers in background.

Mass Murderer looking half-dead lying on bed; stubbly blue chin, bloodshot eyes, flaccid circumcised cock reposing on hairy thigh.

Mass Murderer jumping up out of bed, running at photographer with raised fist. Autumn 1975 – alarmingly close.

To his surprise, he recognized his father instantly he saw him. It was not Mass Murderer or Missing Tooth or any other of the nightmares his mother had shacked up with; it was, in fact, a man half decent-looking, dressed in a suit, a reasonably pleasant smile on his face which betrayed no obvious signs of his having recently coshed a granny or bitten the head off a chicken or molested someone's child.

There was absolutely no doubt about it: he looked right

and the dates fitted. The hot summer of 1976. There were four photographs of him in total, two of them good clear shots from which identification ought to be possible, even with the passage of the years. In one the man was standing alone in a kitchen (it must have been the kitchen when they lived up at White City) pouring from a bottle of scotch; in the other he had his hands wrapped round his mother's then thin waist, the fingers creeping up towards the tits under the orange and turquoise blouse.

Gaz had discovered his father. It was a momentous, massive moment.

BOOK THE THIRD
Chapter XII:
The Foundling Orphan, After Much Travail,
Discovers His Father, Lord Dundingley,
and Is Apprised of His Inheritance.

He remembered Norman Bellwether's words, and now he really understood. It was like a mysterious link, something you couldn't take away, something deep down inside you like. My Dad. My Father. A friend who has been waiting out there all these years.

He stared at the two photographs for a while, then pocketed them. He returned the rest to the drawer, roughly piling the envelopes on top of one another the way he had found them. There was no way his mother would know they were gone. He felt good inside.

Now all he had to do was discover who the guy was – get a name.

My Dad. My Father.

Little goose pimples trickled down his back.

CHAPTER FOUR

COLIN ARRIVED HOME at one, was attacked by a small dog when he set foot in the house, had a raging argument with Kate about the dog (which had been deposited on them by her mad sister Julia who was on a health farm), argued about his non-appearance at the dinner party, and wrapped the evening up with an argument about his excessive drinking, a charge he denied vehemently.

Other than to complain about the presence of the dog, an aggressive and malodorous Yorkshire terrier called Patrick, he did not speak to his wife on Saturday morning.

Before lunch he left for the Bradwell Marina where he met a marine surveyor who looked over the *Dealer*. He agreed to buy it for Dorian's asking price, got wrecked with Dorian in the evening and ended up staying in a hotel.

On Monday he had another argument with Kate, then they made up and he suggested they take the children to the seaside next weekend. She said she wouldn't let the children in the car if he was drinking. He promised he wouldn't touch a drop.

'And anyway,' he said, 'it's this hot weather – makes me thirsty.'

'Alcohol dehydrates you,' she said. 'You should be careful.'

This made no sense. He thought about it when he sat in the Crash Landing in Feltham on the way home from Savage Life the next day. It was true though: he was drinking too much. He didn't know how it was happening, but drinks seemed to be disappearing. He would get in from work, pour a scotch, sit on the settee, take a sip, put the glass on the table, read the TV page of the *Mail*, conclude there was nothing worth watching, reach for his drink and find it was empty. He knew he hadn't touched it.

He concluded he was going mad. His memory was blown-out. He had premature Alzheimer's. It was mad cow disease. Dorian had been right, as always.

Next day, sitting in the Merry Yeoman at lunch-time, he started crying. He conceived of himself as tragically doomed to an early grave, unable to look after his children, unable to see little Sylvester and little Jessamy grow to maturity. And all on account of one Cornish pasty.

The phenomenon recurred that evening. He poured a drink, had hardly looked at it, and then it disappeared.

All evening and the next day he worried about it. In every unoccupied moment he put in hard worrying time. He considered discussing it with Dorian, concluded you couldn't tell your boss you were suffering amnesia as a result of excessive drinking (he had now discounted mad cow disease as a possible cause).

He sat on the bog with knitted brow.

He woke up in the middle of the night gripped with anxiety.

He went to the Stumbling Block for some private worrying away from Kate's inquisitions. Drank six pints.

The worst of it was this: it was the worst of all possible things to be worrying about, because the one sure thing anxiety did to him was to make him drink even more than usual. And then he had cause for even more worrying.

Thursday morning. There was a conference in Birmingham, organized by the Association of Personal Financial Services Suppliers. There had been an alarming new development: politicians were talking about the ethics of cold calling, and threatening to outlaw it. The Association decided to convene a special two-day seminar intended to facilitate action to stave off this vicious attack on the livelihoods of honest, hard-working insurance salesmen.

He had been deputized by Dorian to attend, on behalf of Savage Life, this august gathering of professional men and women, or, as Dorian had put it, 'This complete fucking waste of everybody's time run by a bunch of cunts who couldn't piss straight in the Pacific Ocean.'

Over breakfast Colin outlined his view to the children:

'What about young guys trying to get established in the industry? Like I was four years ago. How are they going to get started? It's all right for people like me who've been in the industry for a while, had time to build up a client portfolio. But what about the young guy? It's an attack on fundamental human freedoms – creeping socialism. A bunch of militants who want to see initiative and enterprise destroyed. This is just the first straw. Then, before you know it, it'll be back to the winter of discontent before you can say "Ken Livingstone".'

He was rather proud of this speech which he had spent the last three days composing.

Kate said, 'I'm sure you're right, darling.' Kate wasn't terribly interested in the insurance business, a fact which rankled. She wiped a bit of muck off Jessamy's face and continued:

'You can see their point though. It's very irritating when you get people ringing up trying to flog you double glazing or something. I had three people last week. One of them got me out of the bath.'

It was all right. He was prepared for this.

'No no no,' he said, gesticulating like Mussolini. 'You're totally wrong. You're looking at this from the narrow perspective. Freedom of information is the key to our most basic, vital liberties. You stop people communicating information and the whole process of democracy breaks down. Which is what the socialists want, of course. Information is the vital commodity of modern market economies. You tell a guy he can't pick up a phone and tell someone about a range of financial services – or anything else; the principle applies to window cleaning just the same – and you're suppressing the flow of information, destroying the operation of the market. Next thing you won't be able to tell a guy in the pub what you think about the government. That's censorship. You're looking at Tin – Tian – shit. What's that place in China?'

'Tiananmen Square,' Kate said.

The BMW grumbled through traffic, air conditioning pumping and sucking at full whack. It crawled up on to the M25 and settled into the lethargic trail of vehicles. He made a few calls on the cellphone, but kept getting cut off by approaching bridges.

Older and frailer vehicles were breaking down in the intense heat, beached on the hard shoulder, bonnets open like gasping dogs. He knew Dorian would say something clever about it: a metaphor or something like that. Darwin: the survival of the fittest motor. He felt a sly contempt for these people: they should sort out a decent motor. Only got yourself to blame.

The *Origin of Species* was a book Colin had been meaning to get round to for some time. For about four years, in fact, since the first time he had heard Dorian talking about it. Darwin was evidently Dorian's favourite writer, a novelist from the same time as Charles Dickens and the guy who wrote *Tess*.

From what he had managed to glean it sounded like a cross between the first half of *2001* and *Quest for Fire*. (Colin's joke about *Quest for Fire*: driving round London after the pubs close looking for the hottest chicken vindaloo. Ha ha.) The plot concerned two rival packs of monkeys fighting it out to see who is strongest, fittest to survive. One troop are bigger and very nasty fighters, and they keep wiping out large numbers of the other troop. But Troop 2 wise up and grow bigger brains. They discover fire, invent primitive weapons, the wheel and things like that. With these technological advances, they blow away the other monkeys. They evolve into human beings.

He hit the M1, pointed his nose into the fast lane and drove. Signs along the side of the road indicated the interesting experiences he was missing out on. MODEL TOWN. TRADITIONAL NATURE RESERVE. NATURAL TRADITION PARK. SITE OF OLD CAR FACTORY. TEENAGE MUTANT HERITAGE PARK. He was in Birmingham two hours later.

The conference passed uneventfully enough, without his speaking. In the evening he fell in with some salesmen from Bristol and got catastrophically drunk. They proceeded anon to a French restaurant with a picturesque view of the Bullring Centre and threw bread rolls at each other. He returned in the early hours to his hotel.

He got out of the cab and hurriedly paid the driver.

He scanned the half-empty car-park and saw a giant hippopotamus in the sodium light. He ran across the tarmac and plunged his head into its jaw. A torrent of lager and wine and cognac and food shot into the hippo's throat. The hippo spoke: 'Thank you for caring for your environment.' Each time he retched it repeated the message.

In the reception lobby he tried to find some cigarettes. He ordered a large scotch, sat down and read the front page of the *Star*. The text turned slow circles before him, forcing him gently to rotate his head in an attempt at keeping up with it. He was about to fall off his chair into a rubber plant when the smirking doorman approached. 'Is sir alone tonight?'

'Yes.'

'Would sir, perhaps . . . rather not be alone?'

'Er . . . yeah.'

'Perhaps sir would like . . . some company?'

'Yeah. Why not?'

'Room 412, is it sir?'

'Don't know . . .'

'If sir looks at the key in his hand I think he'll confirm that it is.'

He looked at the key. It was 412.

'A young lady will join sir in a short while, if that is agreeable to sir. 412 is on the left when sir gets out of the lift on the fourth floor.'

Sir proceeded to his room having forgotten to bring the scotch he ordered earlier. He plundered the cabinet of miniatures in the room and fixed a lukewarm g-and-t. He removed his jacket, went into the bathroom for a piss and missed spectacularly; splashed cold water on his face and felt considerably revived. He fixed another g-and-t.

He gazed out over the desolate skyline – orange-lit motorways, yellow speckles of bleak motels, distant lights of the airport. He was suddenly enraptured by the taut loneliness of hotel rooms in unfamiliar towns; he enjoyed the calm anticipation of the girl's arrival. He lit a Dunhill International; a bird fluttered in his soul.

There came the quiet knock on the door.

He never knew her name. She sat on the bed, flare of peroxide atop her young, crudely made-up face.

'D'you want me to take my clothes off?' Flat, nasal brummie.

He sat back in the chair, sipped at his drink, drew on the Dunhill and watched proprietorially as she hastily divested herself of garments. Her breasts were largish, slightly pendulous, her cunt a small thicket of dull mouse brown.

She came forward and knelt in front of him; grappled with the catch of his trousers, peeling the zip down. He wriggled his buttocks free of the trousers. She caressed a Durex on to his cock.

After a lengthy, barely pleasurable blow-job, he fumbled in his wallet for a fifty. The girl left without a word; he crashlanded on the bed, trousers still around his ankles, one shoe dangling from his foot.

*

Next morning he remained in bed till midday and missed the rest of the conference. He rang room service for every pharmaceutical product they had in the house. After spending twenty minutes curled up on the floor of the shower unit, he stumbled down to the lobby where the doorman smirked at him. Temporarily forgetting the existence of a reverse gear he drove the BMW into one of the bushes which decorated the car-park. Pulling on to the slip road he glanced at the speaking litter-bin hippo and recalled last night with a vivid shock.

He lunched in the Delirious Gobbler by the side of the motorway, a platter of Classic English Fried Foods.

By three he was back in the Savage Life office.

'Not looking very well, Col,' people kept shouting at him.

'Not looking too bright, Col!'

Everybody laughed a great deal.

'Didn't get pissed, did you Col?' Dorian enquired, as though this were the most unimaginable eventuality.

'What was her name?' Tony Cotterell shouted.

'Do it differently in Birmingham do they, Col?'

He left the office at three-fifteen.

'Home early,' Kate said. 'Good conference?'

He sat stoically in an armchair and remained motionless, a bust of Plato contemplating the universe. Sylvester, his frail frame dwarfed by an LA RAIDERS baseball suit and cap, played silently in the corner of the room, seemingly oblivious of his father's presence.

'Say hello to Daddy?' he suggested.

'Hello Daddy.'

'Give Daddy a hug?'

Obediently the boy stood and came to the chair. Colin wrapped his hands round him and picked him up.

'What you been doing today then?'

'Playing.'

'Playing with what?'

'Lego.'

'What did you make?'

'House.'

Sylvester was not a loquacious child.

The evening passed slowly. Kate was making a vegetarian lasagne; Colin glanced at some earnestly tedious programme about the rain forests; Patrick sat bolt upright in the doorway snarling and glaring at him with unalleviated hatred.

He looked at the low, smoked-glass coffee table where his g-and-t was empty, despite his certainty that he had taken no more than two sips. This was now quite customary. He looked at the dog. A thought suddenly hit him.

He went to the sideboard where the drinks were kept, poured another drink, returned to the settee, placing the glass at the far edge of the coffee table where it would be physically impossible for him to touch it without actually getting up. He sat down and pretended to read the newspaper.

Sure enough. The dog slunk silently across the carpet, glanced up to ensure that it was unobserved, placed its tiny paws on the steel rim of the table and buried its snout.

He was about to call out to Kate to come and witness this extraordinary phenomenon. Then a better idea occurred to him and he kept quiet.

A minute later the dog had finished the drink and curled up behind a chair.

He smiled inwardly, full of Zen calm.

On Saturday morning Kate arranged the children preparatory to the trip to Bradwell and Southend. He secretly filled a glass with Black Label and placed it before the dog. Then another. The dog wobbled a bit, collapsed behind the settee.

'Can you put Patrick's bed in the car, darling?' Kate called out.

'He's asleep. Perhaps we'd better leave him.'

'He can't be left. Julia says he howls.'

'Well I can't seem to wake him up.'

'Give him a shake.'

'I've tried that.'

'Shake him harder.'

'I am. Come and look if you don't believe me. I'm nearly pulling his tail off – he just won't budge. Looks like we'll have to leave him.'

Kate came in. After ten minutes of shaking the comatose animal she was forced to agree.

CHAPTER FIVE

FROM HIS POSITION OF subtle concealment, lurking behind a Transit on the far side of the road thirty yards distant, Gaz watched as the Yuppie secured the Yuppie sprogs in the rear seat of the BMW. Watched as various bags and Yuppie sprogs' plastic bucket and spade were inserted into the boot. Watched the tasty Mrs Yuppie – whom he sometimes thought about when he wanked – fussing round to ensure the security of the infants, and then climbing into the front passenger seat. Watched Mr Y locking the front door, lighting a cigarette, checking his trouser pockets, entering automobile, and pulling away round the corner into Wilson Road.

He knew that his hour of destiny was upon him.

His senses were keen, alert, heightened.

He repaired to his own less salubrious dwelling at the other end of the road, there to finalize plans. As he climbed the stairs, he could hear Dog's voice from the kitchen. He was arguing with Christie, but took time out to abuse Gaz as he passed by the door:

'And don't you fucking look at me, toe-rag,' he said.

'Yeah, piss off, dirt-box,' Christie concurred.

He said nothing as he continued up the stairs to his lair where he shut the door and pulled his tools – the tools of his new trade – from under the pile of clothing where they were concealed. He laid the heavy screwdriver, the torch and the Head gymbag on the duvet which now, like a cowpat, contained a completely self-sufficient organization of lower life-forms.

He checked the batteries in the torch one more time. It seemed an unnecessary safeguard: he had only nicked them four days ago and they were supposed to last for 5000 hours of continuous use, according to an advert he had seen. They were the best batteries you could nick. Only the best would do.

The day passed slowly. The sun hung heavily at the top of the sky like it would never come down. Rubbish clattered on the street. A man lost his reason at the Goldhawk Road tube station and dived beneath a train thinking the line a cool swimming pool. On the Green an old woman expired in the heat. On the Uxbridge Road the shop front of a chemist's collapsed into the basement.

Finally the sun began to sink in the arid sky, and he sauntered down the road to ensure that No 51 was still unoccupied. It was. He prepared himself in mind and body for the forthcoming job. He dined lightly on two pieces of Arkansas Fried Chicken, a can of Lucozade Isotonic and a packet of strawberry-flavoured Dextro Energy. You need the NRG. Run like a panther, stealthy as the wind. Eye of the tiger, thrill of the chase.

The sun crept down. He inserted the screwdriver into one of the low baggy pockets on the side of his trousers, the torch into the other. Looked at himself in the mirror, legs angled apart for maximum poise, mean scowling face that says Don't you fuck with me, man. The killing machine.

He moved crisply down the stairs. A game show on his mother's television was rising to a crescendo. Someone had hit the dartboard *and* answered successfully the question: Name the Prime Minister of the United Kingdom. There was now a frenetic display of prize-giving. Feet avoiding the creaking floorboards, he paused outside his sister's room. Reverberation of springs, slap of damp flesh, grunt of tired lungs: she and Dog were fucking.

Under the dim orange of the street-lights he moved quickly to the end of the road and surveyed the Yuppies' house. No car; no lights. He loitered by a builder's skip, pretending to examine its contents, the meanwhile scrutinizing the adjacent houses for signs of activity. There was a noisy party in one of them. Thud of bass, screech of laughter. That was good: covered any noise from the window. He stared into the dark shadow of the shrubbery in the Yuppie front garden and realized: now is the moment. Don't bottle out now.

One last look up and down the road, like a diligent child doing his kerb drill, and he was in through the half-open gate, across the bed of flowers and into the shadow. The blood was rushing now, every nerve cell tingling. Clean and decisive. He edged in behind the foliage, dropped the gymbag beside him, pulled out the screwdriver, reached up to the small window and stabbed the blade into the crevice between window and frame. The wood crumpled easily; he felt the pull of the hinges as they resisted his strength. He put both hands to the handle of the screwdriver and pushed hard. Satisfying tearing sound: screws wrenched from wood, like teeth from stubborn jaw. He picked up the bag and pushed it through the window, placed his trainer on the pipe which jutted from the wall, and projected himself up and head first through the small hole.

He was oblivious of the window-catch cutting a gouge across his wriggling stomach.

He came down, grasping at the dark, hands catching the cold rim of the toilet bowl. The soft dump of toilet roll hitting the ground. Got to his feet, turned, pushed the window back into place.

The first thing he noticed, even before he got the torch out of his second pocket, was the smell: a clean laundry smell quite unlike his own house. The smell of alpine glades in spring. He flashed the torch on and saw a row of gleaming white machines: washing machine, tumble-drier, neatly folded stacks of clothes on wooden slats. He located the closed door, moved to it, gently turned the handle, and inched out into a hallway beyond. Here too it smelt different:

like flowers and his perfumed sister after a bath. To his left a kitchen, again like a shop window: wood and rows of glass jars and more white machines with tiny red lights. A gentle humming sound. To his right the softly carpeted hall leading to an expansive sitting room.

The torch beam caressed the room. Video, stereo: the swag. Bright splay of children's toys littered across the carpet. Polished, big-leafed plants casting strange shadows in the window. Neatly framed photographs. Row of books.

He found the stairs and proceeded up them. Five clean white doors. The first he tried was the children's bedroom: more books and toys, the aroma of Milton. Two was what he wanted: the Yuppie master bedchamber. Large pristine bed with floral duvet: rows of fitted cupboards; ornamental table festooned with cosmetics; rich sexy smell of female ointments.

He had never seen a house like this. It was like another world. Like people on his mother's TV.

He was filled with a strange voyeuristic pleasure, and moved slowly about the rooms, like a diver moving through a rich coral kingdom under turquoise water. The torch beam penetrated into deep recesses where the eyes of strange-coloured fish lurked. He felt a keen awareness of his own presence here. The intruder. The figure stepped in from out of the dark. From the bad netherworld out there.

He rifled through the sweet-smelling domain of Mrs Yuppie's drawers – her knickers and a rainbow of soft cashmere. In the deep wardrobes lines of shoes with their gentle leathery smell, and rows of sweet summer blouses and skirts and dresses. His torch grazed over the smooth terrain of the Yuppie bed, and with a tingle of erotic pleasure he felt a compelling desire to piss vigorously on to the immaculate duvet.

Due to the hot weather, and the resultant sweat, he was not able to muster more than a short stream which he targeted dead centre of the mattress. But it was good: a well-matured, dark yellow vintage steeped in fast food chemicals.

A pleasingly acrid pedestrian underpass aroma rose up above the gentle perfumes of the room. He replaced his tackle in his fly with a feeling of profound gratification.

Now it was time to set to work. He could find no jewellery in the bedroom, but did locate an expensive-looking camera. In the bag. Search of the other rooms was fruitless and he returned down the stairs to collect the video and other readily available booty.

It had been one of the biggest benders of his life, a really wild jag. He had done some totally serious drinking, the sort you talk about for years afterwards in tones of reverence and awe. He slept solid for close on twelve hours, then crawled out of the muddy depths with his tongue feeling like a stump of charcoal, and a team of Japanese torturers running round inside his brain.

He staggered into the kitchen and drank off a full bowl of water. It tasted good, unbelievably sweet. He looked at the biscuits he hadn't eaten last night and felt sick: couldn't eat a thing.

He wondered about his erstwhile enemy. What had inspired this sudden, inexplicable outburst of generosity? Two massive Johnnie Walkers – and first thing in the morning as well. He didn't even want to think about it. He went back into the room and flopped down behind the settee. He was just aiming to get some more kip when he heard the creak on the stairs. He listened attentively, ears pronged up. A light patter of feet descending.

He sniffed the air. An unfamiliar odour. Intruder smell. It was always the way – just when you felt like shit. Just when you felt like curling up in your grave. Still, duty called.

Gaz located the video by the gentle pulse of the digital clock. Rested the torch on the arm of the chair and knelt down to unplug it. Wrenched at the confusing tangle of wires which would not come loose. Got down on his belly with the torch to look for the socket in the wall.

Patrick approached in complete silence. He could see the youth clearly in the pale light that filtered from the street. He targeted a good, succulent strip of vulnerable flesh on the side of the youth's face. This necessitated the full deployment of teeth and claws.

It was as though you were running through the dark and suddenly collided with an invisible threshing machine. A hot agony whiplashing into your eyes. He leapt to his feet and wrenched at the small hot thing which was implanted on the side of his head. A vampire bat: these freaks kept a fucking bat! He tore it loose and hurled it across the room, grabbed the Head bag and ran for the front door where he twisted the handle of the Yale. There was something he had not thought of during the weeks of meticulous planning: the mortice lock. Locked from outside.

Patrick regrouped. He was slightly dazed from his collision with the Parker Knoll, but otherwise intact. He listened to the intruder scrabbling at the door. Let him sweat. The ground war would commence soon enough. He inched round the corner into the hall and waited.

He turned and peered into the gloom. He had left the torch behind the television. Where was the bat? He sheltered his face with one hand and crept forward. He was going to have to go back out of the window.

Patrick glimpsed sock, below where the baggy trousers had ridden up. He remained stationary until the youth was within striking distance. Teeth into Achilles tendon. A consummately satisfying sensation of flesh and gristle squelching beneath the raw power of his mandibles. Lush taste of blood mushrooming into the sock. Steak tartare.

His howl of pain echoed through the house. He ran

blindly, not even trying to shake the source of pain from his foot. It was unquestionably a rat: the Yuppies kept bats and rats. Designer pets. He leapt up on to the toilet and hit the window so hard it dropped right out into the garden, threw the bag out and dragged himself after it. He fell face first into the shrubbery, got to his feet, seized the bag and ran out into the road. Round the corner into Wilson, sprinting lopsidedly on the damaged foot until he was a good hundred yards clear. Crawled into a dark alleyway and collapsed against the wall. Lungs going like pistons; heart like a bass drum.

Twenty minutes later he crept silently into his house, intending to avoid everyone. The humiliation. He stashed the bag with the camera in his room, then barricaded himself in the bathroom. What he saw in the mirror over the basin was not at all nice. A flap of flesh hanging from his cheekbone. Blood oozing from the wound, trickling down his neck into his T-shirt. Gash marks right down across his face.

The foot was in an equally parlous state. Coagulated blood sticking trainer to sock and sock to foot. Tearing it off was like ripping a plaster off, only about a thousand times worse. A fresh fount of blood gushed on to the lino. I'm crippled. My foot won't work. I'll spend the rest of my life in a wheelchair.

Post-coital tristesse was not a condition with which Dog was afflicted; rather, he suffered from a post-coital urge for competitive sports – darts, pool, arm-wrestling, fighting. So when he had completed his coupling with Christie and freshened up a bit he said, 'Just popping out for a drink,' and headed off for the Stumbling Block. On the road he saw a light on in his mate Bri's house and knocked. They continued together down the road and, turning the corner, noticed the missing window on No 51.

Dog was a dilettante when it came to thieving. He could take it or leave it. It wasn't like a vocation with him. He had nothing against it, in principle, it was just that it had never really attracted him the way the building trade did. He was a casual, opportunistic burglar, a gentleman amateur rather than a committed pro. Sunday afternoon league stuff. He knew pros, and it'd be an insult to them to claim any kind of pro status: so long as that was understood.

On the other hand, when an obvious opportunity like this presented itself it was folly not to exploit it.

Dog looked at Bri. Bri nodded. Quick squint down the road. Leg-up through window. Into living room. Small altercation with small dog which Bri kicks into the kitchen. Video and CD extricated. Ornamental clock from mantelpiece. Wad of cash from desk drawer. Small haul of silver from sideboard in dining room. Back out of window. To Bri's Viva, drive to Bri's girlfriend's flat, dump gear. In Stumbling Block by five-past-ten.

CHAPTER SIX

ELEVATED ON A SLIGHT hillock at the western edge of Barrett Meadows, Dorian Savage's house afforded a panoramic view over the scrubland beyond the housing development. Acres where litter blew and sparse life eked a living from the dead soil.

In the last month he had watched from the upstairs windows as the scrubland cracked and withered under the assault of the sun. The weather had become news. Every evening he watched *News at Ten* and heard about standpipe queues in Devon, commuters keeling over on Waterloo Bridge, a new cult of sun-worshippers based in Bognor. Every evening there was an in-depth analysis of the greenhouse effect.

He thoroughly enjoyed it all. It confirmed his view of human existence as inherently absurd. He liked to pour a large drink and plonk himself in front of the television to observe the calamity. The great serpents of traffic coiling round the M25; the sullen eruptions of commuter violence against BR employees; the happy scientists bobbing up and down banging on about global warming. He grinned broadly, fixed another drink, and awaited the last article of news, generally some cheery, sentiment-inducing bulletin from the world of kittens and puppies which would affect him with a small lump in the throat and reassure him that, contrary to widespread belief, he was not a completely heartless bastard.

There was, however, one aspect of the hot weather which

had caused him considerable consternation: the ban on the use of hose-pipes which was threatening the pristine beauty of his lawn. The ban was being enforced by helicopter patrols circling the sky over lush and rustic Barrett Meadows, and it was a matter which had roused in him civic feelings quite without precedent. He expressed it this way:

'Fucking water company interfering with my lawn – what do I pay water rates for, so they can tell me what to do with my own fucking water?'

Rebecca, his current girlfriend, said, 'I suppose it's the same for everyone, Dorian,' which seemingly reasonable contention he dismissed with a wave of his hand.

Early on Saturday morning, prior to the expedition down to Bradwell to admire his new boat, he went out on to the parched lawn and marked out upon it a grid with the aid of canes from the greenhouse and two balls of string. He then phoned Stan the gardener, a pensioner who supplemented his meagre income with the Savage shilling, and bullied him into coming straight over to water each square metre of the grid with a full three-gallon watering can. The lawn was some twenty by thirty metres in extent.

He had one of those mini-tractor things, three grand's worth, which he liked to drive round the garden, wearing shorts, salmon-pink Fred Perry, and an I♡NY baseball cap. He was now doing this, the better to intimidate Stan and encourage his industry. There was, of course, no question of Stan being permitted even to touch the tractor.

After a pleasant twenty minutes engaged in this activity he garaged the tractor and stood on the patio inspecting Stan's endeavours. He surveyed his garden, his kingdom. At the far end the row of *Cupressus* disguising the security fence and hiding the existence of his neighbour, some bastard in Import-Export whom he had never actually spoken to in three years of geographic conjunction. The closest approximation to communication had been a hostile glare exchanged between Porsche and Audi one morning when they nearly collided on their way out of their respective remote control gates.

There was another occasion, one of his happier memories, when a bright yellow tennis ball arced over the *Cupressus* bank, its trajectory bringing it to ground feet away from the mini-tractor, from where it bounced across the lawn into a bed of lilies. He retrieved it, took it into the house and placed it carefully into the ferocious jaws of the Widowmaker waste disposal unit. He switched on and listened contentedly for a second or two to the gratifiying action of blade on ball, switched off and attempted to fish out the tattered remnants with a fork. Regrettably the ball had disappeared into the belly of the Widowmaker and he had had to get down on his hands and knees and unscrew the hub under the sink. This way he disengaged the grease-sodden shreds of the ball.

Just on time, the bell alerted him to the caller at the gates. He went to the screen which monitored the road beyond the gates and there was Mrs Import-Export, clad in a pretty little tennis skirt, leaning expectantly into the microphone set in one of the gate's pillars.

'Hello, I think our tennis ball came into your garden. Could I fetch it?'

'Of course.'

Smooth electric whirring of the gates; Mrs Import trotting towards the front door. He waited a few moments, then opened the door delicately holding the mangled wreckage of the ball between finger and thumb, and inspecting it as though it was an exotic cocktail snack composed of uncertain ingredients.

'I'm so sorry. My dog got hold of it.'

'Oh . . . oh dear. I didn't know you had a dog. I've never heard it.'

'No, you wouldn't. He's completely silent. I had to have his vocal cords removed.'

'Oh dear.'

'Yes, it was very sad. Cancer.'

On the drive down to Bradwell Rebecca quizzed him about his Essex childhood. Generally, this was a topic he did not care to expatiate on, but she was persistent, so he amused himself by inventing a fabulous family chronicle peopled with exotic gypsy types, petty criminals and acrimonious gravel prospectors. For some extraordinary reason this little saga inspired her to speak passionately about something called 'community spirit', the loss of which in the modern world she lamented. Clearly his story was not having the desired effect, so he further embellished it, augmenting the cast with a convicted child molester and, for good measure, a professional organizer of dog-fights. Rebecca was especially susceptible to anything furry and four-legged, so was soon disabused of any notion she might have entertained concerning a visit to his relations. Dorian had not seen any members of his family since his younger brother's funeral seven years ago, and could see no reason for renewing the acquaintance.

A few minutes after they had driven past a children's bouncy castle at the edge of a service station, Rebecca gave vent to a vague utterance concerning the desirability of having a child. This was usually the point in any relationship with a woman when he started to consider alternative arrangements.

CHAPTER SEVEN

BOAT-WISE, KATE REMAINED less than wholly enthusiastic. On the way down to Bradwell Colin tried to assure her that buying the boat was not an unaffordable luxury but, rather, a wise investment.

'Ask Dorian when we get down there, love. These boating people are loaded. You're looking at big policies which means I make a lot more commission.'

She was silent but it was obvious she was unconvinced. Being a sensitive kind of husband, he could tell these things, and was anxious to placate her.

Notwithstanding this, her opinions once again confirmed his view that women were very sensible and quite rightly cautious, but overly inclined to the short-term view. What they lacked was the overall perspective, the long-range strategy. They were good on tactics, but weak on strategy. This was because of their traditional role in primitive societies, right? They stayed at home and tended the crops and the sprogs, but the man had to think ahead, had to plan when he went out into the wilderness for weeks on end hunting a bison or a wildebeest or some other large and ferocious prey. So you couldn't blame women for thinking like this – indeed, it was perfectly reasonable for them to do so – it was just that sometimes they couldn't get their heads round the broader vision.

Actually, he'd discussed this very subject with Dorian and Tony Cotterell once in the Dick Turpin and Dorian had made some quite perspicacious points.

Savage: 'The great achievements of civilization were all created by men. Chartres cathedral, the pyramids, Babylon, the plays of Shakespeare, the Doge's palace, Mozart's operas, the Taj Mahal – '

Nutter: 'Oil rigs – '

Cotterell: 'The M25 – '

Savage: 'Well, that's another instance. All the great scientific and technological advances. Name one thing they've ever done.'

Cotterell: 'Edwina Currie.'

Nutter: 'What – you mean like discovering salmonella?'

Cotterell: 'No, you cunt. You know who I'm talking about.'

Savage: 'Marie Curie, Tone. I think that's who you mean.'

Cotterell: 'That's the one. Invented plutonium, right?'

Savage: 'That's right, Tone.'

Nutter: 'But that's about it, isn't it? Doesn't exactly compare with Einstein and Newton and Gary . . . what's-his-name, you know – '

Cotterell: 'Lineker.'

Nutter: 'The guy who said the world was round – '

Cotterell: 'Oh right. I was reading this book – '

(Members of the cast appear deeply shocked)

Cotterell: ' – and that's what it's all about. Like men's er, you know, working out about the universe like. The big bang and that.'

Nutter: 'And that guy's a cripple, right?'

Cotterell: 'Right.'

So that pretty well wrapped it up: men thought big, dreamt dreams, made plans, changed the earth. If women had been in charge of things we'd still be scuttling round on all fours, desperately staving off attacks from gorillas and baboons. Instead, they were all in zoos, and we had built the M25.

So he had gone ahead with the boat, disregarding Kate's protests.

He parked the BMW in the car-park of the marina and released the children from their belts. 'Look at the sea. Can you see it? Nice, isn't it?' There ensued the usual chaos of decarring the children.

Reaching out into the still water of the marina were a series of pontoons to which the boats were moored in tightly packed rows. Small pleasure cruisers, sleek ocean-going yachts, twenty-footers, thirty-footers, and, in one privileged corner, the emperors of the marina, the great gleaming white motor cruisers such as Dorian's new acquisition, the *Hustler*. It didn't take long to locate Dorian proudly at the bridge of his new toy in shorts, Fred Perry and a livid purple baseball cap he had recently taken to wearing.

'Kate! Colin! Good to see you. Come aboard.' Clambering down from his perch.

Colin was struck with momentary awe. He had seen photographs of similar boats in Dorian's boating magazines, but in reality the thing was breathtaking.

'Sly!' Dorian hailed the child, lifting his frail body up on to the deck of the *Hustler*. 'And Jessie! What do you say to your favourite uncle, eh?'

'Hello Uncle Dorian.'

'Right. How about a couple of Cokes? Rebecca!' called down into the bowels of the boat.

'Is this your boat, Daddy?' asked Jessamy.

'Ha ha!' laughed Dorian. 'Not yet, my love. This is Uncle Dorian's boat.'

'Where's Daddy's boat?'

'Daddy's boat is over there.' The direction in which Dorian signalled was, in terms relative to their present location, a run-down tower block where the lifts didn't work and the kids took smack during the morning coffee break.

Rebecca emerged, her usual immaculately manicured self; they undertook a brief tour of the boat's interior, then had drinks on deck while the children ran around in a state of hyperactive excitement.

Colin returned to the business of inculcating the idea of the boat into his wife. 'And the kids,' he said, 'they love it. Just look at them – look at Jess, she's having the time of her life.'

It was true: the child was scuttling round gurgling with joy. Even Sylvester was unusually animated.

'I was brought up by the sea,' Dorian said. 'It's a more natural life for a child. It's where we all come from, after all.'

'Where?' Colin asked, thinking maybe all four of them hailed from Brighton or Bournemouth or somewhere: only he knew this not to be true. He himself, Colin, came from Feltham.

'The sea, Col. Isn't that right, Kate?'

'Oh, well, yes.'

He sensed he was missing out on something here.

'It appeals to primeval instincts in us,' Dorian continued while looking out at the rows of fibreglass hulls and taking another slug from a bottle of Venezuelan lager. 'D'you know that Hemingway story?'

'*The Old Man and the Sea*,' Kate said.

'The one. I always think of that when I come out on the sea.'

Colin picked up Sylvester and pointed him at the sea. 'Like it, son?'

'Yes Daddy.'

'The opening of *Moby Dick*,' Dorian was saying, '"I am in the habit of going to sea whenever I begin to grow hazy about the eyes, and begin to be over conscious of my lungs." That really expresses it for me. It's revitalizing, rejuvenating.'

'Well, I'm hungry,' Colin announced. 'Are we going to get something to eat then?'

'Colin, you're totally preoccupied with your stomach,' Dorian said.

Kate laughed.

'Sometimes I think you lack an appreciation for life's spiritual dimension,' the champion life assurance salesman continued. 'Well we'll take a recce of the *Dealer*, then I know a nice little seafood place in the town where we can get some lunch.'

After the splendour of the *Hustler*, the *Dealer* was a crushing disappointment. This fact was pointed out by four-year-old Jessamy who had an unerring instinct for the value of consumer durables. 'It's not as nice as Dorian's boat,' the child said. 'I want to go back on Dorian's.'

Dorian found this infinitely amusing. 'Children these days, eh? They're well sussed. Did you hear about Tony's kid? His seventh birthday's coming up, right, and Tony wants to inspire good capitalist instincts in him. So he says, "Son, you're not a little boy any more, it's time to start investing." And he promises him 200 BT shares. Only thing is, Tone puts in his application and only gets 200 and decides to keep them for himself and gets the boy a BMX or something instead and the kid's totally cut-up about it. Locks himself in his room, buzzes his eyes out all day and won't come to his own birthday party.'

'That's terrible,' Kate said.

'Well, they start young these days,' Dorian said. 'That's the enterprise culture.'

After a derisory inspection of the *Dealer*, they repaired to Fletcher Christian's Seafood Paradise where Dorian extolled the virtues of the mussels and the lobster. He, Kate and Rebecca were soon engaged in an animated conversation about the *moules de maison* in a Normandy restaurant they had all, as it happened, once frequented. They spent the next half-hour talking about France and its generally higher level of civilization, a subject which invariably riled Colin. Sylvester shunted his uneaten piece of plaice about his plate; Jessamy threw her chips all over the floor. Colin did battle with a lobster and drank considerably more white wine than he had intended.

After lunch, Dorian bade them farewell and Colin and Kate drove south to take the children to the Southend fairground. Colin compelled the reluctant Sylvester to join him on the dodgems, then insisted that he go on the Circle of Death ride. Kate protested.

He said, 'Stop pampering him, will you? The kid's got to grow up. Right, all aboard.'

During the second centrifugal rotation of the ride Sylvester threw up. The vomit arced out into space, hovered a moment, and boomeranged back on to Colin. After this there were no more rides. Jessamy demanded candy floss. The remainder of the day passed in similar fashion, with a three-hour traffic jam its crowning glory. The car pulled into Esterhazy Road shortly after ten o'clock. The moment he parked he noticed the missing window.

It was not long before he was apprised of the stolen video, the absent compact disc player, the missing ornamental clock, the absconded cash, the pool of piss soaking into the duvet, the dead terrier prone in a circle of blood on the kitchen tiles. It was half an hour later, with a couple of bored police inspecting the scene of the crime, when an ashen-faced Kate took him to one side and brought to his attention the absence of the camera from the bedroom.

CHAPTER EIGHT

IT HAD BEEN A WEEK since the break-in and Gaz's wounds were healing. He believed he would now be able to walk again. He drank copious quantities of Lucozade Isotonic: he knew from the adverts it was good for injuries like those sustained by athletes. The shredded Achilles tendon was repairing, the bat-claw rip on his face solidifying into a nice pickable scab.

He was standing outside Vinnie's Sportswear on Goldhawk Road, his mind turning over various methodologies for thieving a new pair of trainers: that pair of Tomahawk Performance, endorsed by no less a man than British and Commonwealth discus silver medallist Wotan Gainsborough, were well wicked, totally well wicked. They were so wicked it was worth doing something outlandishly wicked to get hold of them. Cosh the assistant, maybe. Do a runner and never go back to Vinnie's. Only there was the risk of getting coshed back, a serious risk when you considered the physical dimensions of the guys who worked in Vinnie's emporium. Towering gymnasts who spent all their free time doing weights and gavaging on steak and steroids. It was one scheme that was totally out of order.

He was unsuccessfully searching the remoter corners of his skull for another scheme when two black kids approached him. He knew them from school, that was to say, from the remote period of pre-history when he and they had bothered occasionally to put in a show at school. Two or three years ago. He had seen them on the streets, in the sportswear shops and amusement arcades and McDonald's, loitering with malign intent at junctions and in doorways.

The tall one was Luke: a swaggering frame encased in voluminous trousers and a tan leather jacket slopping a couple of feet off each shoulder. The awesome sartorial sense of these guys! Where did you get trousers *that* baggy? They were unbelievable: the seat of the pants was actually beneath the knees. Was it some special shop they didn't allow whites in? He wore also a colossal pair of trainers, like a space satellite. The other guy was Matthew. He looked about the same, but without the complete sartorial authority. Both wore impenetrable masks of hostility.

He eyed them warily, expecting threat. Adjusted his posture for max defiance, stared into the window. They came up close behind him, silent and stealthy. He could feel their presence, hot breath like lions' on his neck.

'You done 51 then man?' Luke said.

He said nothing.

'I saw you goin in. How d'you get that gear out on your own then?'

They were taking the piss.

'I eard you got the video, CD – everytin. How d'you do that on your own man?'

'Just did diden I?'

'You kilt their dog man.'

'Might have done.'

He turned to face down his inquisitors, found their sour masks of hatred were subtly transformed, the contempt, the murderous intent, laced with a suggestion of *respect*.

'How d'you know then?'

'We was watchin,' Matthew said.

'You dint see me come out?'

'We had to split,' said Luke, the talker. Black guys were like this: one of them was the spokesman, so to speak, the one that did the talking. 'We had tings to do man. I eard you cleaned that place out well good. And kilt that dog.'

He didn't have a clue what they were talking about, but this brief conversation totally altered his conception of his crime. It had not, after all, been a humiliating failure. But what had it been? And how come Matthew and Luke laboured under this delusion? It was profoundly puzzling.

'You need to shift that gear man?' Luke asked.

'Might do. I got rid of most of it.'

'How much you get?'

'Enough. There's a camera I might need to move. Fujitso Delphic – it's good gear.'

'No problem. You give it to me man.'

'Might do. But I'd wanna know what you're gonna get for it, wooden eye?'

'You show it me man, I'll tell you, all right? You know where to find me. Be seen you round.'

'Take care man,' Matthew said.

'Right. Yeah, man,' said Gaz.

Respect. It was unbelievable. These guys were criminals, proper black criminals, and they had just casually talked to him about moving stolen gear. His brain reeled under the impact. I kilt that dog. I fucking blew it away. Man.

To have some understanding of how monumental an event this was, you'd have to know about these guys, especially Luke. He was a legend, man. In his own lifetime.

He had nicked a car when he was *nine* and couldn't even get his feet down on the pedals. At ten he started house-breaking. He was awesomely agile and scaled drainpipes to get in unlocked windows, then let his cohorts in through the front door. It was the family business. His big brother handled the thieving. His uncle handled the distribution side. No one knew what his dad did.

At eleven he attempted – unsuccessfully as it happened – his first sub-Post Office hold-up with a sawn-off Stanley knife; at twelve he did a Paki off licence for, it was rumoured, £400. He had form, awesome form. If the quantity of social workers you amassed was a true indicator of your status crime-wise, Luke was like a general reeling under the weight of his medals. This guy was so wicked he'd nicked his social worker's handbag and tried to go on a credit card spree when he was thirteen.

From where Gaz stood, it was like you'd just worked out where middle C was and the infant Mozart breezed in and took over on the keyboard. There was no competition. This guy completely blew him out. *But* – and this was the key thing – the guy had just talked to him about burglary, casually, as an equal, as a colleague, as a business partner. To be seen to associate with such a guy, to just be around, was massive.

He continued on his way down Goldhawk with the same snarling smirk, the same nonchalant gait. But inside he was on fire. Inside he buzzed and fizzed with new chemicals.

I killed their dog.

He walked past the Bombay Sati, the Chicago Pizza, the Goose Green. Dog was probably in there getting bammeranered. For some reason Dog seemed to have a lot of cash at the moment which meant he spent all day in the pub.

He rammed a cassette in the Walkman, pulled the phones into his ears, listened to FYM telling the world to fuck off. Crossed the arid Green, through a sea of Fried Chicken cartons and Alsatian turds, and reached his destination on the far side: Blitzprint, the photo printing shop which guaranteed to develop your film and print your snaps in seven minutes.

Quite why he had brought the film here was uncertain, in view of the fact that he had no money with which to pay. It had taken four days to rustle up the necessary cash.

The film in question was the one which had come out of the camera he nicked from the Yuppies. Why had he decided to spend three quid getting it developed? Nicking a developed film was, for obvious reasons, pretty hard: it was one of the few things – along with McDonald's and trainers – which it was almost impossible not to hand over cash for.

Short of taking collection and then doing a straightforward runner, there was really no way. And the trouble with that was, it meant you couldn't go back to the same establishment for an age without the risk of being ID-ed and nicked. Anyway, he was about to just chuck the film when an instinct persuaded him to take it down to Blitzprint and wait till he had funds to get it developed.

It was like power: power over the lives of Mr & Mrs Yup. A voodoo charm which possessed their souls. Maybe the idea had been suggested by his rummage through his mother's photos, and the great power trip he got over her from what he now knew about her past.

Without mentioning the rummage and the theft of the pictures of his dad he had been subtly deploying this power ever since:

'Didn't your air used to be blonde?'

'What's it to you?'

'Oh nothing. I just thought I remembered. Didn't you used to ave mini skirts like?'

'What's got into you? You trying to be funny?'

'Like when you was young.'

'Get out of ere! I don't wanna talk to you.'

'You got three quid?'

'No.'

'I'll get you some ciggies.'

'Piss off.'

'Did you ave a lot of boyfriends when you was young?'

'I said fuck off.'

'Didn't you used to go with this bloke who had a missing tooth?'

'Piss off!'

So he shuffled into Blitzprint and handed over the scrumpled receipt. 'Three twenty-five,' the girl said listlessly. He excavated the coins from a deep pocket, paid and left with the envelope of photographs. He returned to his house through the Bush soundscape, the urban mix of police siren and pulsing music, the urban smellscape of kebab and dry pavement. His brain was gnawing away at the weird new developments in his life. The black kids, his dad in the picture, the fact that he'd done it – a proper house-breaking (his mind was already recasting the event, dropping the humiliation quotient, pumping up the respect quotient).

He slunk into the house and listened. The TV was going – revolting Bette and pals blowing the breeze – but there was nothing else. Dog was out; Christie was out doing a *Heave* centrefold.

His sister's career had been going very well recently. She had an agent now somewhere up in Soho, and offers of work arrived once or twice a week. The telephone had been reinstalled after she paid off the bill, and the agent was forever on the phone. He listened to his sister's conversations with him:

'. . . no, Mr Hatcheem, you know I don't do work like that . . . I just don't think it's right, I mean, for me anyway. Anyway, I don't think I could, not with another girl . . . I know it's only pretending, but I just couldn't . . . Cos, Mr Hatcheem, you know the sort of work I want to get into. You know, glamour and advertising and stuff. It's not that I mind doing the sex stuff, but I want to expand my career. I don't want to get sort of typecast. I'm thinking about the future, cos I won't keep my looks for ever, will I? D'you know what I mean . . .?

'I know I've got big boobs, Mr Hatcheem, you don't have to remind me. But a lot of actresses have got big tits, in TV and stuff. I saw this girl in *Dough*, she had really big tits. I know I can't do fashion work, but I really want to get into acting . . .

'The *Joke*? Really, Mr Hatcheem? £500 . . .? Course I'd like to do it, so long as it's not that photographer from before because he – you know . . . Well I'm not working with him again, however much the money is. My boyfriend would kill me . . . No, of course I didn't tell him . . .'

Cognizant of the sudden influx of dosh Christie's career advancement was bringing in (weird new events like Christie getting dolled up and taking Dog to restaurants) he was trying to improve relations with his sister. Sadly, there was a lot of lost ground to be made up, and his grovel-efforts had so far proved disastrous. When he knew Dog was out he went and knocked on her door.

'All right?' he said.

'What d'you want?'

'Nuffing. Just being sociable.'

She said nothing, scowled at him.

'I am. You're my sister like, aren't you?'

'Worse luck. Don't think you're getting any money out of me, dirt-box.'

'You used to be nice to me when we was little. Remember that time we went down to Auntie Frankie, down in Peckham.'

'Yeah, I remember.'

'That was good.'

'Mum had fucked off, hadn't she? I had to look after you.'

'Where'd she go then?'

'Off with one of her fellas, whatchew fink?'

'Which one?'

'How do I know. It was years ago.'

'You was nice to me then.'

'You were only three. You weren't such an obnoxious little toe-rag then.'

'All right, be like that then. I was only trying to be friendly.' Slam door.

So re-establishing sibling harmony wasn't going too well just at the moment, but he was too busy with his other concerns to lose any sleep over it. He climbed the stairs to his lair, whacked a tape in the Toshiba, pumped the vol to max, sat on the bed and opened the envelope of Yuppie snapshots.

The Contents of the Film in Mr Yuppie's Fujitso Delphic

1: Mr Y with son in garden playing football.

2: 〃

3: Mr Y looking prattish holding up daughter.

4: Y sprogs grinning.

5: Y son still grinning, Y daughter throwing a wobbler.

6: A Y sprog party, a birthday he reckoned, though birthday parties weren't exactly something he knew a bundle about being as how he'd never had one. A load of sprogs sitting round a table stuffing food in their faces.

7–13: More of the same.

14: A group of yuppies, including Mr Y, in someone's garden sitting round on a patio boozing and talking.

15–23: Likewise. A big garden. A couple of prats playing some weird game with big hammers and coloured balls. Boring boring boring.

24: Mrs Yuppie naked on the bed, her smooth white arse poking into the air affording an ample view of vaginal lips and just a hint of dark-hued arsehole.

25: A frontal view, Mrs Yuppie rubbing her totally wicked tits.

26: Likewise, but with her hand straying into the pale auburn bush.

27: Mrs Yuppie's fingers delicately parting the pink anemone lips of her cunt.

28: Mrs Yuppie naked except stockings, spread-eagled on the bed, wrists and ankles secured to the four corner posts with scarves. An expression of terror on her face.

29: Likewise.

End of film, the remaining seven shots unused.

It was too much. He laid the six pertinent snaps out on the floor, whipped his cock out and pummelled it for no more than five seconds – eyes whisking back and forth between the pictures – before – *whoosh!* – a splurge of spunk sprayed all over the carpet and two of the photographs. Hasty wipe-up with discarded T-shirt, replace tackle in trousers, rummage round to find Snickers to consume, and return to a more leisurely perusal of the other photographs (meanwhile secreting the Mrs Yuppie shots for reappraisal in the near future – like about ten minutes).

And it was at this point, slowly masticating the toffee and bits of peanut stuck between his teeth, and idly scrutinizing the remainder of the photos, that the greater shock began to percolate into his mind. It began with a disconcerting sense of familiarity, a *déjà vu* which was haunting and slightly unpleasant. Something was amiss, out of kilter, but he couldn't grasp what it was.

It was that dreamland green garden, lawn stretching away into infinity, rich bastards and yuppies laughing and drinking and playing with wood hammers and glowing pink with booze. There was something about it, something which troubled his soul, itched away at the back of his brain like a burrowing insect. Then it just floated up out of the void and something told him what it was he was looking at, what he had been looking at for the last twenty minutes without understanding it. This was epiphanic, religious: like peering at melting snow on the road and seeing Norman Bellwether's face gradually taking shape until the man himself, Norman, was looking back at you. It was a soul-rupturing experience of that order, and yet it was so simple – it had been staring him in the face all along and he just hadn't seen it.

That five o'clock-shadowed guy in the shorts, peach Fred Perry and purple baseball cap: it was him.

My Dad. My Father.

Older – older he reckoned by about fifteen years (that being the duration since his conception), tubbier round the face, but unquestionably him. My Dad. My Father. He got the old photos, the two he'd got from his mother, and compared the two faces: there was just no doubt about it.

It was all too much. He had to lie flat out on the bed to think about it. The tape in the Toshiba came to the end and he hardly noticed, didn't even get up to replace it. His heart was shivering, his spirit soaring up in the stratosphere.

The Yuppie knows My Dad.

The Yuppie will therefore be a conduit, a route to My Dad.

BOOK THE NINTH
Chapter XIV:
The Foundling Learns of the Connexion Between Mr Yuppy and His Father, Lord Dundingley.

Wicked.

Once he had steeped his soul in this knowledge of – or at least means of ascertaining – the paternal whereabouts, and wondered a little longer at the strange coincidence by which the knowledge had been vouchsafed him, more down-to-earth matters once again weighed upon his mind. Specifically, he could no longer hold out from having another wank over the Mrs Yuppie snaps.

He took them from their place of concealment and arranged them upon the putrescent duvet, hitched his trousers down round his ankles and knelt before them. This was going to be a more considered, involved sort of wank – more of a meal than a hasty snack. He began slowly, scrutinizing each nuance of Mrs Yuppie's anatomy, savouring the firm protrusion of nipple, the pink spread of mysterious gynaecology. Inevitably the proceedings did not endure as long as he had purposed, and he was now going at full whack when Dog barged in through the door.

'Ha ha,' said Dog. 'You little wanker. What you got ere then – pictures of your sister you dirty little bastard? That's called insect – d'you know that?'

The humiliation was overpowering.

'*Fuck off*!'

Desperately trying to drag the strides up. But Dog was across the room and had grabbed hold of the photographic material. He inspected the pictures thoughtfully.

'Very nice . . . very nice indeed. Where d'you get these then? I know this bird – who is she?'

'Fuck off – you got no right coming in my room – '

'I thought you was the one doing the coming. Ha ha.'

'Fuck off!'

'No, seriously – who is she?'

'I don't walk in on you – how would you like it eh?'

'Simple. I'd kick your fucking teeth out of your arse, then carry on where I'd got to. Now come on. Who's this bird – where d'you get these pictures? I wanna know.'

'I nicked em, diden I?'

'Nicked em . . .' Dog's brain processed this information for a while. He picked up the envelope containing the other photographs and rifled through them, brow furrowed, tongue working over his lower lip as it always did in times of intense intellectual activity.

'It's that bird that lives up the top of the road, right?'

'Could be.'

'You naughty little bastard. Fancy her then do you?'

'She's all right.'

'More than all right. I wouldn't mind giving her one myself. I'm going to be confiscating these pictures for your own benefit like. To save you from a life of depravity and possible blindness.'

'No! You can't. I need them.'

'You do fancy her then, don't you?' Dog laughed.

'No – the other ones. I need the other ones.'

'These? What d'you want these for?'

'You can have the negatives – I've gotta keep the other ones. Please . . .'

'You're not a very good thief, are you? How come you got in there and only managed to nick this?'

'I got plenty of gear.'

'No you didn't, cos I fucking did. You ran away from that dog, didn't you? You was frightened by that little dog.'

'I didn't know what it was. I got a camera.'

'With this film in, right? Camera in the bedroom where the old man's been taking dirty pictures of his missis.'

'Yeah.'

'All right, you can keep the others, I don't want em. But I'm taking these, these could be very handy. And the camera. Where is it? If you're very good I might even let you have the prints of the bird back when I've made use of the negatives.'

'I ain't got the camera. I sold it.'

'No you didn't, cos it's ere.' By some unerring instinct, Dog had immediately located the camera in its position of concealment beneath a pile of rancid clothing.

'You can't. That's mine.'

But Dog had removed the negatives and now threw the envelope containing the remainder of the photographs at the bed.

He curled up on the bed in a ball of misery and despair and contemplated various means by which he might rid the universe of his sister's boyfriend. Like, for instance, didn't it blow up if you put sugar and something in someone's petrol tank? It was a fragment of information he dimly remembered from a school chemistry lesson. For the first time ever, in a wildly unexpected development, he lamented not attending school more often. Maybe then he would have the means to a sure and safe elimination of Dog.

CHAPTER NINE

COLIN AND DORIAN were in the Crash Landing, near the airport, near Feltham, scene of Colin's conception and childhood and comprehensive education, sitting by the window with a view over the dual carriageway. The heavy sun was setting in the parched peach sky, but its descent heralded no let-up in the throbbing heat.

'My dad used to come in this pub,' said Colin, and lit a Bensons. The remark hung on the air, awaiting further developments. His early life had been so stultifyingly dull there was nothing more to add. A steel twist of smoke spiralled gently into the dome of the pub.

'Then he died,' said Dorian.

'Yeah.'

'Of boredom was that?'

Colin stared into the amber dregs of his lager, a scum of foam clinging on the walls of the glass. He went for two more.

His father had been a customs man at the airport, his greatest moment of achievement some minor role – third spear-carrier, fourth dog-handler – in a big drugs bust. He had spoken of nothing else for years afterwards. 'Months of painstaking tracking across Turkey and Pakistan, son. They were brilliantly disguised, false passports, the lot. But we spotted them. You can always tell when you've been in this game as long as I have. Look at their eyes. Dilated.'

It had been an enormous relief when his dad was fired for some minor piece of corruption involving half a dozen bottles of Johnnie Walker. It had put an end to the endless repetitions of the Big Moment, but that had soon been replaced by new stories from his new job as a supermarket security man, a still more tedious litany of butter-fingered till girls and red-handed shoplifters. 'It's the rich ones you've gotta watch. Fur coats, expensive gear. They do it for the thrill of it, see. Not cos they need the stuff. This woman. The moment I saw her parking this Rolls in the car-park I says to myself . . .'

His mother had endured all this with the stoicism of a sloth. He had responded by spending the first seventeen years of his life being as obnoxious as humanly possible without actually committing genocide. Missing out on the customary intermediary stages, he went straight from bed-wetting and crimson-faced tantrums to immediate full-blown adolescence. He went in for serious vandalism, doing over a bus shelter one week, the school buttery the next. He started fires in wastebins and dustbins and burnt down a neighbour's garden shed. Vividly he could recall the thrill of the moment when the flame reached the fuel tank of the Atco mower and the mossy creosoted panels blew out over the dwarf-festooned rockery.

At seventeen he got out; signed on; took speed in crumbling squats; played bass in a punk band for four months before anyone noticed his total inability even to tune the instrument; worked as a hod-carrier on a building site; drank as much lager as possible every evening in the same Sisyphean circle of pubs (condemned for ever to drinking too much, getting in a fight, getting thrown out, moving to the next pub, repeating the same, until eventually returning to the first pub and repeating the procedure); saved up enough money to go to India with two mates; smoked hash for three months and complained of an endless agony of the bowels; returned to Staines . . . And somehow, one day, one grey morning with the lemon sun hanging low over the Thames, a couple of bedraggled swans drifting on the oily drift, unable to find the money to have the Viva MOT-ed, he ended up in the sales game.

What hadn't he sold over the years? He'd done it all: photocopiers, Amway, time-shares, cleaning services, pub games, cars, video-conferencing, pornography, office equipment, stone-cladding, double glazing . . .

In and out of jobs, a bit of commission here, company Cortina there, a life on the road, on endless grey roads through endless grey suburbs, past newsagents and launderettes and hairdressers and row after row of houses. And another grey morning, quite likely in the same pub or one no different, the same two swans now near death, the same tide of shit drifting back and forth, another pint of lager, another scotch egg, another packet of Rothmans, and he turned idly through the rear pages of the *Middlesex Monitor* or the *Egham Event* or the *Staines Sensation* or the *Feltham Freebee* and read:

Make £1000 a week!

We are looking for motivated and dynamic salespersons to work in the fast-expanding financial services sector. Wasters and freeloaders need not apply. Only aggressively achievement-oriented young people who want out of the rut of the nine-to-five. Ring for details on ----------. Ask for Sally.

It was three days later that he found himself locked in that cupboard with the Carlsberg bottle to piss in and the telephone to talk to. Dorian standing at the door, mouth to the keyhole, shouting: 'Come on then, cunt! You're the big achiever. You're the hungry young man. Get me a fucking prospect! Go on! Get me one fucking punter into this office!'

That baptism of fire.

*

He returned from the bar with his pint and Dorian's bottle – some fancy newly fashionable Peruvian lager with a slice of kiwi in the neck and a pickled rain forest beetle floating round at the bottom.

'Ta,' said Dorian. 'I've never understood why you live there, Col,' he continued. 'Bang in the middle of the urban jungle. Every time I drive round the Shepherd's Bush roundabout I see at least ten loonies.'

'Kate wanted to live there.'

'You ought to move out somewhere like Barrett Meadows. You can't bring kids up somewhere like the Bush. Before you know it they'll be abducted on their way back from school. The crime statistics where I live are like one stolen garden gnome per decade, two kids done for dropping litter, and generally some housewife goes off her rocker and stabs her hubby with the electric carving-knife. But that happens everywhere.'

Colin took a long draught from his Dopplerbrau and lit a Bensons. He was sweating ferociously in the heat.

'We've got a Neighbourhood Watch scheme,' he said.

'Exactly. Neighbourhood Watch. The neighbours watch from behind their curtains while a bunch of coons do your house over. No one wants to get involved, Col. It's the same everywhere. I wouldn't rely on my fucking neighbours – they'd sit there watching through binoculars while my house burnt down. "Oh, sorry, Mr Savage. We didn't like to interfere. We thought perhaps you were having a barbecue." You've got to look after yourself. No one else is going to do it. Good security system is what. You tell your nig-nogs to come and try and nick my fucking stereo. It's like trying to get into Fort Knox.'

Colin thoughtfully masticated a pork scratching. 'There's something else,' he said. 'No, shit, it doesn't matter.'

'What you talking about, Col?'

Every time he felt this confessional urge, he remembered the test tube incident and reconsidered. He hedged around it, approaching cautiously.

'It's Kate. She's been sort of weird since it happened.'

'Quite natural. Consider it this way: it's a violation, isn't it? A rape. Someone's come into your house, rootled around among your private things, pried into your life. Of course she's upset.'

'Yeah . . .'

Dorian swigged the bottled Peruvian lager straight from the neck, spat out the rain forest beetle.

'What did they find then, Col?'

He knew: that sure instinct for the weak spot.

'It was some photographs – a film actually.'

'Bedroom?'

'Yeah. You know, it was just a bit of fun. Nothing nasty or anything.'

'Sure . . .'

'I mean, they probably won't even develop the film, will they? They just wanted the camera.'

'But on the other hand, they *might* develop the film.' Dorian grinned.

'Yeah . . .' A gloomy silence.

'Tell me something, Col,' Dorian enquired. 'What exactly was the point of taking naughty pictures of the missis with an ordinary camera? Aren't you supposed to use a Polaroid for that kind of thing?'

'Well, yeah. I don't know. I was pissed. We were both pissed. Matter of fact, it was after that party out at your place. You remember – I brought the camera. I don't know, it just seemed like a good laugh when we got back. Kate was very pissed. Oh fucking hell . . .'

'Don't worry about it, mate. So there's some burglar somewhere getting his rocks off wanking over your wife. I can't see the problem.'

'And there's her sister's fucking dog as well. They killed it. And she hasn't told Julia yet.'

'Not nice,' said Dorian. 'Julia – she's the actress, right? Good-looking one but mad.'

'Yeah. Piss-artist and off her trolley.'

'Did that advert, right? The turkey slices or whatever it was.'

'Yeah.'

'She's certainly a looker – very attractive woman.'

'Yeah. But mad.'

'Shame that.'

'Yeah.'

'Take my advice, Col. Put that place on the market and find somewhere round here.'

'I can't at the moment. We'd take a loss on it.'

'You bought at the wrong time, Col. Right at the height of the market. You were a prat. I told you so.'

'Yeah.'

Cars came down the street creating fields of ambiguous noise: the hostile pulse of their music, their language of hooting and revving. The mad antics of vehicles were just one aspect of a more thoroughly altered world. Anyone loitering on the street corner was immediately the denuder of her house, come back to savour their destruction. Anyone whose head turned and glanced in at the window was gloating over the scene of their crime, their violation. Anyone who momentarily caught her eye on the road was silently cackling to her. Their bleached eyes fresh from the desecration of her body.

'Look, love. No one's going to go to the trouble of developing the film. They were just pinching the camera,' Colin reasoned. She did not believe him. She knew someone was at this very moment examining the photographs. Her world was transformed by the burglary. The house smelt of it, despite the fact that she had thrown out the polluted duvet. She sensed threat everywhere.

She telephoned Julia the morning after the burglary.

Patrick was in a plastic bag under the sink, a means of disposing of the carcass not yet decided upon.

Colin: 'For Christ's sake, it's dead. I'll put it in the dustbin.'

Kate: 'We can't. We'll have to bury him.'

'All right. I'll go out in the garden now. I just don't want Jess having another fit when she finds it in the morning.'

'We can't just bury him in the garden. She'll see.'

'All right, there's a skip down the road. I'll put it in there.'

'Don't say that, Colin.'

So Patrick was concealed under the sink in a thick shroud of Sainsbury black bin-liners when she spoke to Julia. Fresh from her drying-out Julia was her bubbly, mad usual self. 'How's Patrick? This weather, it's incredible, isn't it? Give Patrick a big kiss from me and tell him I'll come and fetch him in a day or two. You don't mind hanging on to him a bit longer, do you? He's no trouble. Have I told you about Alan? I met him at the health farm actually. I'll tell you all about it when I see you.'

At the best of times it was hard getting a word in edgeways with Julia. Breaking the news of the dog's demise was harder still.

'There's something I've got to tell you, Julia,' said Kate.

'Not now, darling, I'm in an awful hurry. Alan and I are going up to Yorkshire. His family live up there.'

'It's about Patrick – '

'He drinks – I didn't tell you, did I? I completely forgot. I was in such a state before I went away. I can't tell you how much better I am now. Don't worry about it – just put some beer in his water bowl. Anything, he's not fussy. If you've got the dregs of a bottle of wine or something. Otherwise he gets bad-tempered.'

'It's not about that. Something awful's happened – '

'If he shits on the carpet just chuck him out in the garden for a few hours. He'll get the message.'

'He's dead, Julia. I'm sorry.'

'Anyway I must fly. Alan's waiting in the car. I'll speak to you when we get back from Yorkshire. Toodle-oo.'

Three days later there had still been no word from Julia. Kate rang her answering machine a number of times, leaving urgent messages for Julia to call her. The answering machine seemed too cold-blooded a means of informing her of the death. The corpse was now buried in a pet cemetery, for which last resting place she had paid a vet £40. Colin's reaction had been predictable: 'Forty quid? You can hire a skip for forty quid. What kind of place is this? What was it – full requiem mass, was it? Music by Andrew Lloyd Webber?'

Meanwhile, Colin had contacted a local security firm to arrange for the urgent installation of comprehensive security measures, and two men had appeared on the door-step on the Thursday morning.

'Mrs Nutter? David Richardson, Castle Security.'

'Of course. Hello. Do come in.'

'This is my lad, Dave. Huh – two Daves so to speak.'

'Uh,' the lout said.

'Bring the stuff in, Dave.'

Richardson was a tall middle-aged man of slightly sinister aspect, his suit and black shirt suggestive of a gangster movie. His face was mottled as though by childhood small-pox, the eyes sunken, mysterious and shifty. His lad Dave was a colossal lout with a skinhead haircut and Doc Martens who appeared vaguely familiar to her. He now went out to the van double-parked in the road.

Richardson came into the hall, punctiliously wiping his feet on the mat. 'Your husband tells me you've had a burglary, Mrs Nutter. Very unfortunate. But very common nowadays. We live in barbarous times, Mrs Nutter. No respect for property, no respect for other people. You'd be shocked by what I see in my line of work.'

'Yes. Would you like a cup of coffee?'

'Thank you. My belief is, the whole social order is

crumbling. Look at kids these days. No respect for their elders, no patriotism, no religion. It's just a free-for-all, grab what you can and sod everybody else. Excuse my language.'

Richardson had followed her through into the kitchen where she filled the kettle. Sylvester and Jessamy were through in the living room with their Ninja Turtles laid out on the carpet.

'Take that lad of mine out there,' Richardson continued, indicating the simian form out on the road hauling equipment from the back of the van. 'Always in trouble. Spends half his life in the pub drinking and playing pool. Can't hold down a regular job, can't see the point. When I was his age I was in the Army learning a skill. It's as though there's no tomorrow for them. No horizon further than the next pint of beer. Nothing to believe in.'

'Yes, I see what you mean.'

'It's very sad, very sad. Mrs Nutter, would you mind if I smoked?'

'No, of course not. I don't but my husband does. There's an ashtray here.' She poured the water into the coffee-maker, which gurgled murmurously.

'Filthy habit. I picked it up in Malaysia, never been able to shake it off.'

'Would erm, your – Dave. Would he like coffee?'

'Don't mind about him.' Richardson lit a strange cheroot-like thing which fizzed and gave off an aroma of bonfires. He shuffled about the kitchen, his eyes darting back and forth like a lizard's tongue. 'Nice place you've got here, Mrs Nutter, if I might say so.'

'Thank you. Do you take sugar?'

'Not for me. Black, no sugar.'

'Well, perhaps I can leave you to it. I'll take the children out for a while, get them out from under your feet.'

'My theory is, it's the bomb. Ever since Hiroshima and Nagasaki, we've all had a little bit of it in our bones. Radioactive. And it gets worse every time there's a leak or something like Chernobyl. It sort of poisons everybody. The young are more susceptible to it, whereas older people have more immunity.'

'Well, I – I hadn't looked at it that way.'

'It's just a thought. Might not be that at all. Could be this ozone thing, couldn't it? More rays getting at the brain.'

'Yes.'

'Course, you read about the Middle Ages or something and it all seemed just as bad then. The extinction of the dinosaurs, things like that. Maybe things have always been bad and we just didn't notice.'

'Yes, perhaps it has. Anyway, I must be getting on.' And she backed towards the door, calling for the children.

Sorties into Shepherd's Bush now filled her with strange terrors. Everywhere people seemed to be degenerating, disintegrating. She walked down the Goldhawk Road, past lunatics and listless huddles of youth who peered suspiciously at her. She cut through the market, past a butcher advertising **Whole Donkey: £15** and a record stall with booming speakers and a stall laden with second-hand pornography, great serried ranks of flesh under the banners of *Heave*, *Hump*, *Shag*, *Grunt* and *Quarter-to-Three*.

She could not prevent her eye glancing at the magazines: they now possessed a terrible new significance.

She circumnavigated the Green and ventured into the underpass beneath the roundabout. Notorious scene of muggings, rich with a redolence of acrid urine. From here she walked towards the more genteel purlieus of Holland Park, past embassies and BMW showrooms towards the park.

She sat under the canopy of trees while Jessamy chased the squirrels and Sylvester checked his digital watch to see what time it was in Bangkok. Doing this seemed to be his favourite activity. It was one of the many disturbing aspects of the child's behaviour which she worried about. She spent a great deal of time worrying about the children.

CHAPTER TEN

DOG SOUGHT HIS girlfriend's professional advice on the saleability of the photographs.

'But you can't – it's not right,' said Christie.

'Why? What you talkin about?'

'Cos they're private, aren't they? It'd be like exploitation.'

Dog sipped at a can of Wobbler Brew and peered distrustfully at his bird. 'What? You turning into a feminist or something?'

'No. I just don't think it's right.'

'It wasn't right knocking their house off, was it? You didn't say nuffin about that,' he shouted.

'Well that's diffrent, innit?'

Dog thoughtfully sifted through the photographs. Will you take a shufty at those tits? Smallish, but beautifully porportioned: this was class gear, sophisticated. 'But these are all right, aren't they? How much d'you reckon I could get from *Grunt* or one of them?'

This subtly but profoundly wounded Christie's sense of her vocation.

'Not much,' she said, casting a derisory glance at the pictures which he had laid out for inspection on the kitchen table between the margarine and the peanut butter. Actually, she was vastly, tragically jealous of those neatly formed boobs: they were what you needed to get into modelling and TV and fashion work. 'They're amateur, see. No lighting, bad angles – '

'What's wrong with the angles? You can see everything can't you?'

'It's not that simple, you know,' said the artiste. 'A lot of technique goes into taking good pictures.'

'Don't talk fucking crap. I could fucking do it. Get a camera and some bird with her legs open.'

'Well that's where you're wrong. There's a lot of artistry in it actually.'

'Fuck off.'

'You don't have to listen. I don't care.'

'I'm not.'

Following this exchange of views, he fished another Wobbler out of the fridge and went up the stairs to the lair of Gaz. He edged the door open and could see the boy sitting on the bed with his back to the door twitching strangely with the *tss tss tss* on his headphones. He took a moment to scrutinize the room. Tatters of magazine on the wall in a weird iconography – giant poster of Norman Bellwether in the centre.

Gaz was deep in the stereophonic soundscape of N-V-Scratch – bass equalized up to max so it resonated in his stomach, a primordial throbbing. In this peaceful environment he was thinking deeply about the major problems of his life at the moment: how to parlay the photographs of My Dad My Father into knowledge of the name and whereabouts of MDMF. He had nicked a magnifying glass from the Paki shop to inspect the details of the photos, but it was a fruitless exercise. So instead he used it to subject his spots to minute investigation in the mirror and to examine the mountain ridge of miniature hillocks running down the shaft of his cock.

This is what he now knew about MDMF:

He was a mate of Mr Yuppie; he lived in a large house, whereabouts unknown; he was rich, *seriously fucking rich* – the photos shouted it out: *Dosh!*

But how to go further?

He put in some viewing-time on 51 in the hope that MD would put in an appearance, but there was no show. He copped Mrs Yuppie walking down the road with her sprogs and tried to think up an excuse to talk to her and wheedle out the ID of MD. But how – without revealing his burglary? He had, of course, considered the blackmail possibilities of the Mrs Y open furburger shots ('Tell me his name or I mail these to your granny'), but that option had been swiftly curtailed by Dog's appropriation of the items. He returned to the garden snaps for further in-depth analysis but still there was no enlightenment.

Melancholically he was turning all this over in his mind when he felt a sharp stab in the middle of his back. He sprang up on the bed, ripping the headphones off. It was Dog's stinking fucking revolting size 12 Doc Marten.

'What d'you fucking want?'

'I wanna talk to you.'

This was a first: things were really looking up communications-wise round here.

'Why?'

'Why you so interested in those photos, eh? Ones of those cunts sitting round in that garden.'

'Just am – what's it to you?'

'You wanna be careful, see. 1) Cos I might be able to tell you something you don't know, and 2) Cos I might decide to kick your teeth in if you don't cooperate.'

'What d'you know?'

'I'm not gonna tell you if you don't ask nicely, am I?'

'What please.'

'Not good enough. Now you tell me what you want with those photos then I might tell you what I know. Guess what I did last week.'

'I don't know do I. Played pool?'

'No. I was workin, wasn't I? Where d'you think I was workin?'

He thought about this. A connection gradually took shape in his synapses while Dog grinned at him and took swigs out of the Wobbler can.

'51.'

'Clever. So I know things, don't I? Cos I ad a good shufty. Now you tell me why you want them photos.'

This was a monumental moral dilemma: did he trade his innermost intimate secret for Dog's supposed knowledge? He wrestled with the implications, the ramifications, like Karpov and Kasparov.

'I know what,' said Dog. 'I'll make it easier for you. You tell me or I break your arm. Fair?'

He beheld the powerful musculature of Dog's simian forearms and made a snap decision.

'All right. You gotta promise one thing though.'

Promise was a word in Dog's personal thesaurus which was located immediately adjacent to *broken*.

'What's that then?'

'You won't tell mum.'

'All right. Promise.'

A shiver went down his spine as he spoke the words, realizing it was the first time he had said it to anyone: 'My dad's in those photos.'

'Which one?'

'Bloke in the pink shirt like.'

'Wooftah, is he, your dad? Queer-boy?'

'Don't you fuckin say that!'

'Sausage-jockey? Mattress-muncher? Bum-bandit? Shirt-lifter? Ginger beer? Shit-shagger? Pillow-chewer? Uphill-gardener?'

'I'll fucking kill you,' said Gaz, doing something he would never before have contemplated in a billion years – namely, attempting to hit Dog. Dog easily parried the blow and threw his assailant down on the bed. He was finding all this terribly amusing.

'So how d'you know he's your old man then?'

'I just do. Now you've gotta tell me what you know. You said you would.'

'Hah. I think I've changed my mind.' His fat red face grinned disgustingly.

'You got to. You said you would.'

'Changed my mind.'

'What's his name – bloke in 51?'

'Why d'you want to know that?'

'Go on, you bastard, if you worked there you must know his name.'

'So you can go and ask him who the woof is – that it?'

'No. I just wanna know.'

'All right. He's called Colin Nutter.'

'How d'you spell that?'

'I don't know, do I?'

'Colin Nutter?'

'That's right.'

When Dog had left, he faithfully recorded the information on a copy of *Boot!* COLIN NUTTER (No 51). Armed with this knowledge he swaggered down Esterhazy further to eyeball the house on the corner, as though it might now offer up some secret it had formerly withheld. It did not, but an idea which had previously managed to elude him now crept on to the frontiers of consciousness. If he followed the yuppiemobile – might it not lead him to MDMF? This would require a mode of transportation, such as one of the mopeds the black guys drove round on. He retraced his steps up the road and hung around outside Alabama Fried Chicken, Cortex Discs, Byzantium Kebabs, Vinnie's, Meisterburger. He put in hanging-about overtime, five hours of it, until he saw their strange forms loping down the sidewalk through a sea of parting pedestrians.

'How ya doin man?' said Luke.

'Awright.'

'You got that Delphic?'

'Nah, I shifted that. I need a bike, don't I?'

'Wha chew want man? Overture? Suite? Concerto?'

'Don't mind.'

'You come round this evening, eleven. Cost you 200.'

'Nah, I just need one for a day like.'

'Nick one, man. You know how to start it without keys?'

Well, natch.

'Er, not exactly – '

'I'll show you man. Ts'easy.'

They proceeded down Schenectady Road, past the Stumbling Block and into a tree-lined street. Matthew espied an unattended red Sonata concealed behind a hedge in a front garden. They rang on the door-bell; no reply. Swift surveillance of road, loud cracking of wheel-lock, and calmly wheel bike out on to road. Gaz and Luke followed as he rushed it round the corner into the thin path by the side of the Block.

Luke's space station trainer swung up and kicked the panel away from beneath the speedo. Expertly his hand ripped two wires from the exposed cluster and snapped them out. He climbed on to the bike and separated the wires.

'Now you jus put the two together and pump on the pedal man. Snow problem.'

This he did and the bike revved into action. He jerked it forwards, ten yards down the path, stopped and pulled the machine back on to its stand, the motor still purring. He kicked the lock off the luggage container at the rear of the bike and removed a helmet.

'Helmet – ' throwing it at him. 'The bike's yours man.'

'What – like – '

'Take it. Remember who your friends are man.'

And with that the two disciples loped away down the path, leaving him the proud possessor of a freshly stolen Sonata. It was awesome – the ease and assurance with which these guys knocked stuff off. Totally awesome. Righteous.

In an adrenalin rush he wheeled the Sonata back up the path and roared off down the road. He wove the bike up and down Schenectady, Esterhazy and Belgrade, trying to figure an overnight stash-point where he could collect it tomorrow morning. He fixed upon the car-park at the rear of the

Drunken Goat and secreted the Sonata there after the brisk drive down Goldhawk. He repaired the visible damage to the bike, then retreated home with his helmet concealed in a carrier bag.

On the morrow he rose early and donned his baggiest pair of strides, which still seemed like drainpipes in comparison with Luke's parachutes. All was quiet on Esterhazy as he set forth, having breakfasted on a Snickers and a Bovril-flavoured Cuppasoup. He swaggered down to the car-park of the Goat and retrieved the Sonata, drove it back and parked it on Esterhazy about fifty yards from the BMW. It was just on 7.50. He now had to appear inconspicuous while waiting for his target to emerge from 51. This he did by solemnly reading the copy of *Boot!* he had especially brought along for the purpose. It was the copy with the Norman Bellwether interview in it. He had v-e-r-y s-l-o-w-l-y reread the interview seven times when his target emerged from 51 in a blue suit, swinging his keys like he always did, chaining through two ciggies in the time it took to get from the door to the motor.

A car chase! The journey down Goldhawk Road and Chiswick High Road and along the M4 was not the invigorating cinema-style affair he had spent much of the night anticipating. Instead it was a painfully sluggish journey, the chief problem being trying to drive the Sonata slowly enough to stop it stalling. Two times the congestion cleared for a few minutes and he was left behind, but there was no problem in relocating Nutter in the next concertina of vehicles.

When Mr Yups pulled into a car-park at 9.15, he was thirty yards behind, toddling along at a sedate twenty mph. He pulled the Sonata into the side of the road and watched CN enter the office, parked the bike and took up a position of low concealment in a clump of purple-flowered rhododendrons adjacent to the car-park, from where he was able to monitor developments.

He doned headphones, switched on FYM, and waited,

waited more, waited still more, while carefully masticating the peanut residue left in his mouth by the breakfast Snickers.

Dog had a leisurely few pints in the Goose Green, during the consumption of which he endeavoured to copy out the address of *Grunt* on to a large buff manila envelope. Sadly, this task was beyond him and he was eventually forced to ask his friend Nige to perform the operation for him.

'What – you sending off for a prescription?'

'No, I got some gear to sell them.'

'Yeah? Let's see.'

When Nige had completed this operation, Dog offered to buy him a pint if he would serve as amanuensis in the composition of the accompanying letter. Nige agreed.

> Dear Selena, *wrote Nige*,
> I would like to offer these photos of a model I know for publication in Grunt. The negatives are available if you offer a satisfactory sum. I understand £250 is the normal rate for material of this kaliber.
> Yours Sincerly
> Dave Barber

After a further four pints it was agreed that this missive was a succinct expression of what needed to be said. Over a few games of pool and a pork pie he did some more rumination, then returned to the house to interrogate Christie. She was lying on the bed listening to music and painting her nails.

'Who was your dad then?' he asked.

She looked at him suspiciously.

'I'm just asking.'

'He was called Bill. I fink he's doing time.'

'You don't see him then.'

'No. Bastard . . .'

'Is he toe-rag's dad as well?'

'Fuck, I ope not. I don't think mum was sure who his dad was.'

'So she don't know?'

'She never said if she did.'

'Right.' He produced one of the photographs he had yesterday had developed and asked, 'D'you recognize this bloke? One in the pink shirt.'

'No. Who is he?'

'Dunno. You sure? Like from when you was a kid maybe.'

'No – I said I don't.'

'All right.'

He replaced the photograph in its envelope, and then insisted upon the immediate consummation of his conjugal rights. Thereafter he repaired to the Stumbling Block for a further thirteen pints of lager.

The metronomic pulse of the music had lulled him into a pleasantly somnolent frame of mind during the four hours he waited in the rhododendron bush. His mind had cast far and wide over such diverse matters as Mrs Nutter's oyster-pink beaver, the infamous Bellwether tackling technique, his desire to murder Dog, the consumption of another Snickers, and the radical pair of trainers endorsed by Wotan Gainsborough, the Commonwealth Games discus silver medal-winner.

Then, on the dot of 13.15, it happened:

BOOK THE SEVENTH
Chapter IV:
Our Hero Sees His Father, Lord Dundingley, For the First Time.

It was a jolt: like seeing a TV celeb in the flesh, transmuted from one medium into another. A collision between two previously discrete worlds.

He leapt to his feet and stuck his face out between the waxy leaves. MD, clad in an elegant dark suit, a bit fatter than he seemed in the pictures, was striding across the car-park wiggling a chain of keys between his fingers. At his side a woman, awesomely tasty, long blonde hair ruffled by the breeze blowing over the car-park.

He ripped the headphones off his head in time to hear a smattering of dialogue, the briefest byte of the paternal vocals:

MD: 'Tash, I was thinking maybe you and me could go down to the boat at the weekend. Have a dirty weekend by the sea.'

Girl: 'Dorian, you say the sweetest things. A born romantic.'

MD: 'How about it then?'

Girl: 'How would Rebecca feel about this?'

MD: 'Rebecca need not know. Rebecca is away at the weekend.'

The girl giggled and said something incomprehensible.

The remote locking system on the red Porsche clicked smoothly, the security system made its friendly little disarming beep, and the two figures slunk down into low bucket seats. One swift ejaculation of exhaust and the vehicle roared out of the car-park. He was already macheteing his way through the foliage of the rhododendron, but by the time he made it back to the Sonata MF's motor had disappeared over the brow of the hill.

Dorian. My Dad's name is Dorian.

DOOR – EE – ANN.

Dorian.

He sampled the word in his mouth, saying it different ways, savouring its every nuance, weighing it up, allowing it to permeate his being.

DORIAN.

CHAPTER ELEVEN

THE GALE ROLLED across southern England, uprooting trees and small children, throwing lorries off the motorway, laying waste gazebos. Interest rates went up again. Colin got drunk in the Drunken Goat. Kate told Julia about the demise of the Yorkshire terrier, and Julia had a pill-taking relapse. Now she would not talk to Kate. Maybe she couldn't talk. Maybe her speech centre was obliterated.

At the Savage ranch, Dorian watched the storm damage on TV and supervised the vacuuming of leaves from the pristine lawn. On Saturday he played a new version of polo with the mini-tractor and the croquet set. Approach ball at about ten mph, swing back hammer – *whack!* – ball scuds over silky grass towards hoop. So much more entertaining than traipsing round on foot.

The Saturday morning post. Catalogue from his Compact Disc Club which he ruminated on whilst dispatching a firmly rounded stool.

'The three greatest tenors of the day joined forces: Domingo sang Chas 'n' Dave's "We're on Our Way to Wembley (Come On You Spurs)"; Pavarotti replied with Andrew Lloyd Webber's "Memories"; Carreras gave a show-stopping rendition of a haunting Phil Collins ballad.

'But it was the finale – a stupendous medley of songs including "Rockin' All Over the World", "Honky Tonk Women", "House of the Rising Sun", "Hey Joe", "Route 66" and "Whole Lotta Love" which really set the house on fire that unforgettable night in the Milton Keynes Bowl.'

He turned the page.

'Anyone who has discovered Vivaldi's superb musicianship via the unique talents of Nigel Benn will relish this excellent collection by the charismatic Steve Davis. The one-time snooker champion now turns his talents to the violin with the same devastating results he brought to the green baize. The backing by the Matchroom Players is of the first rate quality we have come to expect from Barry Herne's superbly drilled team of musicians. Listen out for that superb break by Tony Meo in the second movement!

'Kiri and Gazza! Together for the first time on tape and CD! Gazza's superbly melancholic tenor blends perfectly with Kiri's soaring soprano in this unique collection of the Pet Shop Boys' Greatest Hits. Not to be missed!

'Dame Janet Baker and Willie Nelson – together at last! One of opera's best loved sopranos joins up with the red-headed stranger in a romantic selection. Includes the NWA chart-topper "Fuck the Police".

'Tracy from TV's hit soap *Partners* gives a superb account of Dvorak's Piano Trio in E Minor with other members of the cast.'

Dorian felt that the CD club had gone rather down-market since he first joined it. He thought it might even be necessary to cancel his subscription if future catalogues showed no signs of improvement.

He turned his attention to a wad of junk mail, then to a strangely scruffy envelope upon which his name was daubed in thick, ill-formed felt-pen capitals. The document inside the envelope was daubed in a similar fashion, and read as follows:

Dear Mr Savage,

I hav found out U R my dad. I found a photo of U my mum had from wen U + her were bonkin. U lokes jus like mee + the dates is rihgt 1976 in fact. If U dont belive me theyres a test U can do I saw on TV. U test the jeans in yor

> Sperm + its a 1000000000 to 1 chance yor not my dad if the cromo [this word deleted] khemicals R the same. I hav all ways wonted to no my dad + Im reely pleazed to hav found out who U R. Honest I dont wont nuthin from U jus to no my dad. I dont think yule wanna see mum + she dont wont me to see you so I will cum to yor hous on sonday at 12 (lunch-time).
>
> Yors
> Gary (Gaz) Hoskins
>
> PS I wood like to change my name by deep hole so its Savage if U agre.

Gaz had worked out his father's name from the registration plate on the car (DS 69) and the brass plaque at the front of the office (Savage Life Assurance) and had put in an afternoon with the phone book ringing all D Savages and asking for Dorian. A woman's voice informed him that Dorian wasn't in at the moment and he had the address he needed. He carefully engraved it on to the back of a *Boot!* and stared at it.

He wanted to look his best for the first meeting with his father. It was an important occasion for which he should dress in the very height of sartorial splendour. He rose early on the Sunday morning while everyone else was still asleep, showered and scraped at the thin layer of down which had accrued on his face. Shaving was a rite of passage he hadn't fully got his head round yet. There was a blood loss of transfusion proportions and his face ending up looking like a letter bomb had just gone off. After using up half a roll of Andrex to staunch the haemorrhage he deliberated about the appropriate choice of wardrobe.

Since making the acquaintance of Matthew and Luke and being accorded their criminal respect, he had been doing some more thieving. He had seen that his former cautious approach was not only unnecessary but also deeply uncool. You want something – you take it. He wanted some new trousers, big parachute strides like theirs. Easy: locate them, check they're the right size, steal them. He had ventured to Hammersmith, checked out a couple of stores in the mall, found a momentous pair of totally critical leggings costing £49.99, dropped them in his plastic bag, and eased nonchalantly towards the door. When he was a few feet from the electronic security device on the door he did a runner. *Whoosh!* Straight out into the crowded mall, round the corner past Vinyl Virus, out on to the Broadway. That easy.

He couldn't think why everyone didn't do it.

There had been other sorties too: a crucial pink shirt (like Dorian's; he had been inspired in his choice by the paternal photograph – it seemed to him his dad, unlike most dads, had a well wicked dress sense), a very awesome baseball cap likewise modelled on the paternal sartorial sensibility, a devastating haul of Marlboros from the back of a delivery van outside the Paki on Uxbridge. Six cartons: 1200 cigs. Value about £100. Sadly, they were not his mother's favoured brand so it had not proved possible to sell them to her on a pack-by-pack basis, but he had managed to squeeze a fiver a carton out of Dog – £30.

Also there had been house-breaking with Matthew and Luke. He hadn't actually seen any gains from this just yet, but they assured him they were fencing the gear and would give him his cut when they got the money. In any case, it had been a useful learning experience. This is what had happened:

One afternoon he went to Vinnie's to see what he could spend the £30 he got from Dog on, which turned out not to be a whole lot. It would have taken a van-load of Marlboro to secure the Gainsborough-endorsed Tomahawk Performance. Luke – who had a pair, natch – approached down an aisle of ski-suits. 'You wanna do a job man?'

'Yeah. Awright.'

Outside Meisterburger Luke explained the plan. There was a house four doors down from him which they knew to contain a stash of stereo equipment. Frontal access was problematic: they had tried some time back kicking the front door in but it had proved too sturdy. The windows were large and liable to make a racket when broken. Rear entry was what was required, via the gardens at the back of the houses.

'So when d'you want to do it like?' he enquired, thinking probably the schedule would involve maybe a fortnight's surveillance of the site, a dress rehearsal possibly, a cooling-off period during which you could iron any glitches out of the system.

'Now man. When it's dark.'

'What like – '

'We go up there later. He snot in man, we checked it out. Holiday.'

'The people in the downstairs flat like,' he said. 'We'd have to get through there.'

'We handle that. You jus let us in your house man.'

They hung around the rest of the day, patrolling the streets, circling the Green, playing the electronic games in the amusement arcade next to Blitzprint. When darkness fell they rolled down Esterhazy and he opened the door of his house. Luke produced a chisel from one of the deep pockets on that awesome jacket and pried open the door of the downstairs flat. No one was in. Out the back door into the small garden which was more of a sort of mini-tip than a garden: mouldering nappies thrown out of the window, a few bin-bags, a covering of nettles and weeds. Over the fence and through the next couple of gardens until reaching 28. Chisel into lock of back door; kick; door collapses. Inside.

All of this happened in a dizzying flurry. They proceeded directly to the front room where an impressive bank of equipment was lined up – CD, turntable, amp, equalizer, keyboard, tape, speakers – and immediately set to work dismantling it and placing the articles in black bin-liners. The whole operation took about ninety seconds. Matthew opened the sash window and climbed out; Luke passed the equipment out; the trio proceeded to the end of Esterhazy brazenly carrying the loot, turned right into Wilson, and along Schenectady to a flat he had never been to before. As they pushed open the door the wail of police sirens was clearly audible from two streets away.

That simple.

Matthew and Luke took the equipment inside and Luke said, 'Be seen ya man,' and closed the door.

(There was one minor complication ensuing from this incident: the police wanted to know how come the door had been kicked off the downstairs flat. Dog – this was a source of deep delight to him – had been taken in for questioning. A search of the premises had failed to turn up anything and things seemed to have died down now.)

He settled finally upon the new purple and green trousers, the pink shirt, the new orange baseball cap and his favourite black jacket, a trusty old friend. The only blight on the whole impact was his trainers, which were scuffed and showing signs of age. He cleaned them as best he could with his toothbrush, then remembered he hadn't cleaned his teeth yet. Now his mouth tasted of leather and mud.

After breakfasting on a doughnut and some cold oven-ready chips, he headed down the quiet Sunday morning street. He proceeded down Uxbridge to the Green and waited for the bus which travelled out to the airport. It would stop, he calculated, not more than about a mile from Barrett Meadows. Winds gusted through the bare branches of the trees. A flotilla of McDonald's packaging whirled in spiralling patterns. A madman conducted a conversation with an advertising hoarding on the bus shelter.

Routine stuff.

After a half-hour journey he disembarked on the outskirts of the airport, gazed across the flat horizon at radar dishes and hangars and car-parks, consulted the map and began the walk to Barrett Meadows. The hulk of a 747 lifted itself into the sky. He walked some way along the dual carriageway and came to the point where it forded a stagnant stream. Consulted the map again and clambered down the bank – shit! got shit on my trainers man! – cut through a thicket of nettles into the scrubland. He proceeded over the marshy ground, delicately negotiating the unseen hazards of broken glass and surprise puddle. Out here was the great dumping ground. Bin-bags, tyres, old furniture, gutted TVs, mashed-up motors, mutilated dolls.

He tramped through it all and emerged on the thick ochre clay of the road building. Lines of yellow earth-moving equipment, bulldozers, JCBs, trucks. Over the trunk road beyond, down into the lane which burrowed into the foliage. Stepping over the first of the sleeping policemen, he walked a way down the curving lane and came to the first of the gardens. He checked its name at the gateway: The Cedars. It was weird – why didn't these people live in houses with numbers? How were you supposed to know where you were going? He walked on to a second beamed mansion which was called Shangrila. Over a small hillock and round a curve in the lane to a ranch-style bungalow called Montezuma where a gaggle of kids were running round the garden in little green wellington boots with a spaniel called Elton.

Walking on, he thought for the first time: what if My Dad has other kids? What if I've got like brothers and sisters? He tried to picture himself in little green wellington boots running round a great big lawn with a dog and talking in a weird voice like that. Gaz sitting in the back of the Mercedes as the chauffeur drives him to Lord Wensleydale's Academy for Young Gentlemen . . . Gaz standing to address the school debating society in a languid Wildean drawl . . . Gaz punting on the Cherwell, girls called Clarissa and Persephone sipping champagne in the prow of the boat . . . young Gaz allowing his name to go forward . . . entering Parliament in the

Conservative interest . . . his dazzling and witty maiden speech drawing the attention of the Prime Minister . . . promotion to PPS . . . Meanwhile, his business interests prosper, he marries Persephone and they live in a large house in Knightsbridge . . .

Perhaps it would have been better if he'd never watched the first episode of that Jeffrey Archer mini-series on his mother's TV.

He came to a crossroads and wondered which way to go. A couple walking a dog approached.

'Where's Souffork?' he asked.

'Sorry . . .?'

The dog, a low-slung dachshund, snarled sullenly at him. He eyed it closely: he now knew from hard-won experience that these small dogs could be a lot nastier than big ones.

'Where's Souf-ork like? Please,' keeping eagle eyes on the hound.

'Suffolk?'

'No. Sow fork like.'

'Southfork?'

'Yeah. Mr Savage lives there.'

'I'm afraid I can't help you.'

'Dorian Savage.'

'I'm sorry. Come along, Poldark.'

The couple and Poldark the dachshund proceeded hurriedly on their way.

He waited until a bicycle came past and tried to hail it, but it veered past him. Cars came by every few minutes, purring quietly through the leafy lanes. Presently another pedestrian rounded the corner, jogging in a tracksuit, and he repeated the question.

'Where's sowf hawk please?'

'Southfork?'

'Yeah. That's my – that's what is ouse is called.'

'Very droll . . .'

'Er . . .'

Why were these people so weird man? Like they were all on drugs or something.

'What did you say his name was?'

'Dorian Savage.'

'Chap with the red Porsche?'

'Yeah! That's him.'

'It's on the left up there. About half a mile. You can't miss it.'

'Fanx. Fanx a lot . . .'

He hurried down the lane, his heart now aflame with expectation. The odyssey comes to its end, the boat approaches the harbour. He broke into a gentle trot, trainers thudding on the tarmac and wet leaves. Rounding a bend he beheld two houses, a thick bank of greenery cutting a swathe between them. Two gateways set some twenty yards apart. The first was called The Bowery, the second – he had glimpsed the vivid red of the Porsche already – Southfork.

He paused to collect his thoughts. Smoothed his hair down. Stood at the bars of the gate and peered in. A purple drive curved through a clump of bushes to the car, and then the large house. Fucking palace: he remembered a line from an N-V-S song: 'Now I'm livin in a fuckin big palace!' His hand tried the gate but it was firm. Then he saw the camera peering down at him from beyond the bars, and the entry-phone set in the pillar of the gate. He cleared his throat and pushed the button.

Dorian and Rebecca were making love in the Jacuzzi when the bell rang. 'Ignore it,' Dorian said. 'It'll be a Jehovah's Witness or something.' They ignored it. It was a particularly delicious sensation, the way the spout of warm water bubbled up between your thighs, tickling your bottom, while you were in the act of congress.

The bell rang again a minute or so later.

'Oh Jesus.'

'We didn't invite anyone for drinks, did we?'

'I didn't.'

'Nor did I.'

They resumed hostilities.

The bell rang a third time.

'Maybe it's something important,' Rebecca said.

Hauling himself out of the Jacuzzi, Dorian said, 'Stay here, I'll get rid of them.'

He wrapped a towel round his waist and trotted down the stairs to the monitor screen. He flicked the switch and the screen sizzled into action. A gangling, ugly youth scratching his nose and staring up at the camera with an expression of moronic enquiry. Probably wanted to wash the car or recover his football from the garden.

'What is it?' he shouted into the mike.

'Er – is that like – like – Mr Savage?'

'Yes. What do you want?'

'I'm – I'm – my letter – you know . . .'

'What are you talking about? Look, I don't want my car cleaned, I don't want my lawn mowed, I don't want to buy anything. It's Sunday morning. I admire your enterprise but not now. Goodbye.'

'No! You doughn unnerstand. I'm Gaz like – you know. My letter. You're my dad.'

Dorian paused. He looked at the youth craning towards the entryphone, face staring up with horrible imploring eyes.

'Very fucking funny. Did Colin put you up to this?'

'I don't know what you're talkin about. My letter – '

'Yes, I got the letter. Tell Colin the joke's over – I rattled him straightaway. Now piss off.'

'But you doughn unnerstand! You're my dad. I found out. My mum – '

'Look, you've been warned. Tell Colin what you like if he's paying you. I don't give a shit. In fact, you do that. Tell him I totally believed you and committed suicide on the spot. Now piss off. If you ring that bell once more I'm calling the police.'

'But – '

He replaced the phone and returned upstairs. He jumped back in the Jacuzzi and ravaged Rebecca with new-found energy.

CHAPTER TWELVE

GAZ SAT ON THE DUVET with a strip of old lead he had nicked from the back of Dog's van when helping unload some gear. With the chisel and a hammer he was carefully winding the heavy metal round a sawn-off length of broom-handle, fashioning a new implement:

The dog-disabler.

The hound-hitter.

The pooch-pounder.

He worked all afternoon, N-V-Scratch throbbing on the Tosh, until the lead was tightly coiled on the wood and smoothed free of sharp edges and abrasions which might threaten the pocket-lining on his combat fatigues. Now he was burnishing the metal with a piece of old rag, spitting on the cloth and polishing away the dull patina, munching on a Snickers.

The canine-cobbler.

The rover-reaper.

The mongrel-mangler.

The mutt-muter.

He went now to the Head bag and laid the new tool with his stash of equipment. Chisel. Five-inch retractable blade knife, bought off Luke with the £50 proceeds from the stereo heist. New torch. Roll of gaffer tape for window noise-suppression. There weren't going to be any more foul-ups. No more humiliation.

At half-eight he left the house and proceeded west through back roads, under sodium light, to Armitage Road. He moved swiftly into position in the shadows on the derelict land opposite the target house, settled on his haunches, let his fingers run once more over the outlines of knife, torch, tape and cosh neatly filed in the thigh-pockets.

No 12 Armitage Road was a two-storey detached dwelling he had first eyeballed ten days ago with a view to burglarization. From the adjacent scrubland he had clocked up 32 hours' surveillance during which he had ascertained:

1. Two occupants, both male 25–35, probably shirt-lifters.
2. Shirt-lifters out most evenings, probably at a shirt-lifter club, rarely returning before one in the morning.
3. Excellent rear access to premises through back garden and no signs of security system.
4. No evidence of a dog, but don't rely on it. Hound-gyp must be avoided at all costs.

The shirt-lifters' car, a beaten-up old Renault, was still on the road; lights on in the front room, movement behind the blinds. At nine, as anticipated, the two mattress-munchers came out of the front door and one turned to lock the mortice (he wouldn't be caught out by that one again). They sashayed to the crap motor and pulled off down the street.

He counted to ten, grid-searched the street, monitoring only a mangy cat rousting its fleas under a car bonnet. Stood up, crossed directly over and hit the thin alley intersecting the houses, head swivelling gardens and rear windows. Good ground-level fence protection, no sign of movement in first-floor window. He goose-stepped the fence, his trainer impacting on gravel beneath. Assumed a low crouch and spider-crawled to below the kitchen window. The smell of the drain hit his nostrils, rotting odour of the shit-shaggers' supper. Ears registered the distant report of TV – the *Nine O'Clock News* theme tune.

His head periscoped up to recce the kitchen which was bathed in the light from the hall. (He had anticipated this: the bum-bandits always left a couple of lights on.) Nothing. Spider-crawl to french windows, the scrunch of gravel replaced by suction of trainer soles on patio. Careful manoeuvre around half-barrel planted with dead herbs. Eyeball through crack in curtains into room: nothing. Last scan of vicinity: all clear.

He slid the chisel from his left-side thigh pocket and teased it into the cleavage in the soft wood, feeling for the lock. The wood crumbled; paint flakes curled on the brushed steel blade. He pumped the chisel, splintering wood until he felt metal on metal and gouged round the lock. Knee to door, he felt it give as the lock loosened; one big wrench cracked wood and the door imploded inward, buffeting the curtain. Cold, calm, military, he scanned the gardens one more time: nothing.

Two seconds later he was in the room, the door eased shut behind him, the curtain pulled back into place.

The room smelt musty and fishy, like the sausage-jockeys had recently been chewing the pillow in here. Everything about the room instantly confirmed his suspicions: a hunky male model calendar on the wall, a copy of *Gay News* – there could be little doubt. Feeling for the pooch-pounder in his thigh pocket, fingers ready to draw at a split second's notice, he examined the room. The little green clock on the video winked 21:04 at him. Plenty of time.

Since the occasion when he had stood in the Yuppies' bedchamber, inhaling its aromas, thrilled by its otherness, Gaz had become obsessed with his glimpses of other people's lives. He now planned his solo missions so as to allow for a lengthy scrutiny of the premises during which he could absorb himself in the minutiae of the victims' existence. He settled into their lifestyle, tried it on for size, discovered whether he liked it. He would pour himself a drink, light one of their cigarettes, watch their TV, rootle through their photograph albums, eat food from their fridge, inspect the mysterious contents of their cupboards and drawers for the sorts of things which made solid their lives. It was a buzz, a total buzz.

In bedrooms and bathrooms he sought out soiled panties and sniffed the crotch. He pulled back bedcovers to examine the site of the victims' bonking. Sometimes he whipped his trousers down and climbed into the bed for a wank, leaving a globule of spunk as a visiting-card. He went through bottom drawers and hidden corners, the sort of places he knew secret things would be stashed. One time he found a giant pink vibrator which he took, thrilled with the idea of what it had done. He found wank mags and sex accessories, stashes of drugs, hidden letters (which he would take home for in-depth analysis), secret, mysterious mementoes. He stole now not for fiscal gain but for the pleasure of appropriating part of the victims' life. Sharing in their lives.

The hoard in his room now contained: bottles of pills and perfumes; graduation photographs (he did not understand what these people were doing in square hats and Batman capes); children's bears and dolls; assorted articles of underwear; a small archive of letters and postcards he would while away the hours scrutinizing; watches, cufflinks, ear-rings and birth control devices; diaries. Anything which was intimate, which brought him closer to the victim. One time he nicked someone's pet hamster, but he changed his mind on the way home and set it free outside McDonald's.

He went upstairs now and found two bedrooms, each belonging to one of the bum-bandits. He rifled through drawers and found a photo album full of pictures of turd-burglars on holidays and at parties, a wallet with forty quid which he pocketed. He found a tube of KY, sniffed at it, squeezed it out all over the wall and into the innards of the radio-cassette. He picked up a half-drunk mug of coffee by the bedside and dumped it on to the duvet.

In the bathroom he poured Domestos into the laundry basket, jetted Sanilav over a poster of a bronze-muscled beach bumboy, squirted the rest round the other bedroom, at discarded clothes and into the pages of books. He gouged the lid off a can of talcum powder and sprayed it over the room.

Downstairs he laid waste the kitchen with a bottle of sunflower oil, a tub of muesli and a dozen eggs. He put an unopened pint of semi-skimmed milk in the microwave and watched it explode. He pissed in the earthenware breadbin, drenching the wholemeal loaf, then popped the lid back on. He squirted scouring cream into marmalade pots and cereal packets, sprinkled Flash in the sugar, opened a can of Whiskas rabbit and liver, took it into the back room, pushed the jellyish offal into the back of the TV, daubed it on the settee.

He rifled through the drawers on the desk, pocketing calculator, ring and Filofax, then hit the back door, scanned the alleyway, grid-searched the street, sauntered out and down the road, turned the corner. He felt righteous, powerful, awesome.

Next morning he strolled past the house and saw the distraught bum-bandits piling the harvest of his destruction into the dustbin. It was a total buzz.

He feared Dog. Since Dog had quizzed him on his interest in the photos of Dorian he had grown suspicious of Dog's attentions. Dog was planning some sinister manipulation of his knowledge. He sensed his room was subtly rearranged when he returned to it and concluded Dog was rummaging through his gear. He plucked a hair from under his baseball cap, licked it and secured it between door and frame like he'd seen done on TV. His suspicions were confirmed: someone was entering his room during his absence.

He needed a stash-place for his growing loot pile, and he knew where it was going to be. He filled the Head bag and headed up Wood Lane, past the BBC, under the M40, to the Scrubs. Lines of soccer and rugger goalposts stretched across the grass. This sacred turf where Norman Bellwether the young boy had come with his dad and developed his early skills. This hallowed ground where the legend had been born. He gazed reverently at one set of goalposts and thought, maybe this one. Maybe this was where he stood waiting for his dad to run at goal. This was where he performed that tragic terminal tackle that did his dad in. They ought to put a plaque up or something:

To the Memory of Billy Bellwether
First Coach and Trainer
He Dwells Among the Dribbling Greats

A lump lodged itself in his throat each time he thought of that awesome day, that epic event, that massive moment.

He headed across the grass up towards the north-western corner where there was a patch of trees and bushes. As he walked the prison came into view, its four massive blocks like four ocean liners. He reached his destination and swivel-searched the area. Only a couple walking a dog two, three hundred yards away. His eyes ran over the vista – the prison and the remote vision of Telecom Tower; the railway running out from Paddington, the tower blocks and gasworks. He went into the bushes and found a suitable stash-point, flicked the knife out from his thigh pocket and started gouging a hole. He worked for two minutes then swivel-searched the area; two minutes, swivel-scan; two minutes, swivel-scan. After twenty minutes he had a deep enough hole and carefully secreted the carrier bag of proceeds: jewellery, passports, perfumes, photos, credit cards, knickers, watches.

He replaced the lump of turf, patting it down, and marked the spot with a crumpled Tango can. At the edge of the bushes he sat and practised smoking a cigarette while looking at the prison. Since deciding to take up smoking he had endeavoured to get through ten a day but it was proving hard work. The smoke kept getting in his eyes or going down the wrong way so it made him choke. He practised taking deep draughts and drawing the hot smoke slowly into his lungs. Then he felt dizzy and wanted to chunder.

He fell to thinking about Dorian and the failure of his first approach. Clearly there had been a misunderstanding. Dorian had said he had received the letter, but he didn't believe it. He thought it was a wind-up to do with Colin Nutter. The question was, how to go from here. Slowly the strategy took form in his mind: he would have a copy of one of the old photographs of Dorian made and would send this to Southfork with another covering letter. The one where Dorian was shoving his hands up to Adeline's tits, cos that would remind him who she was. He returned to the Bush down Loftus Road and found a shop which would copy the photograph. He nicked a new Pentel and notepad and returned home. With a supply of Snickers and Isotonic, he hunkered down to his literary labours.

Dear Mr Savage,

Pleez find inclosed a photo off U from wen U + my mum were bonkin about 15 years ago like I sed befor. This is to prove i wasent joking wen I cum to yor house last week. U R my dad i nos. Like I sed I dont want nothin just to no U cos I never had a dad. Mum dont no i am riting to U honest. I nicked [he deleted this word and replaced it] borered the photo from her room and recognized U from a nuver photo I saw of this guy U no round hear.

This part was difficult to phrase without implicating himself in the Yuppie burglary, but he would now be able to explain his knowledge of the photograph by claiming to have seen it while Dog was installing the security system at No 51. Things had worked out quite neatly really.

That is how I fond out U were my dad. i never arsked mum cos i dont talk 2 her no mor. She jus whatces tv alday. Pleez phone me my no is [number

supplied] so i can tork 2 U. Jus hang up if sum 1 els ansers. If i dont her from U i will cum 2 yor house agan pleez let me jus tork 2 U I dont wont money or nothin.
Yors Sinserly
Gary Hoskins

He posted the letter that evening on his way out to another job.

No 17 Babbage Street. A basement flat and a maisonette occupying the first and second floors affording easy rear access via back path, garden and wooden staircase. Low visibility from adjoining properties. One female occupant, 30–35, quite tasty, out at work all day (double-check for presence of silver-grey Fiat Uno on street). Basement flat similarly occupied by working woman (check for blue Metro) but with bars on windows suggesting security-conscious occupant. (Anyway, she was considerably less tasty.) Entry to be achieved either through kitchen window (concealed behind trellis of wistaria) or through conservatory/balcony into living room.

The street searched for the two vehicles, both of which were absent, he strolled with nonchalant demeanour down the path, rubbernecking, eyeballing the adjoining gardens. Nothing. He proceeded into the garden, hopped the steps two-at-a-time, secured himself behind the trellis. Swivel-scanned the area: zilch. He tried the conservatory door. It was open. As he stepped in among the yuccas and the tomato plants he reflected: the government was right – people made no effort at safeguarding themselves against the tide of criminality sweeping the country. They only had themselves to blame.

He tried the door leading from the conservatory into the house and it too was unlocked. He stepped into the house, denied the pleasure of breaking in. It was almost a downer.

He wandered into the kitchen, opened the fridge and helped himself to a glass of orange juice. The food looked suspect, the kind of weird crap people like this ate. He dumped it on the floor. Back in the open-plan living room he added a tot of Smirnoff to the orange and took a good whack at it. It hit the back of his throat with a firm satisfying kick. He inspected a neat cluster of photographs arranged on the sideboard – old brown photos of these codgers from back in the twelfth century or whenever. They were a total blast: this guy in a Navy hat grinning, and his wife in a totally OTT frilly dress. Flowers and archways and crap in the background. It was irresistible. He flipped the photo out of its frame, took the Pentel out, drew tits and a cunt on the woman. He took another blast at the vodka-and-orange, well pleased with his wit. Then he drew a massive cock and balls coming out of the Navy bloke's mouth.

He fixed another vodka.

Another photo was of this wedding back in the Iron Age. The couple coming out of the church, loads of grinning guys in Army get-up. He drew in huge cocks on the blokes so they were all wanking off, spunk spurting all over the bridge. There was this young chick posed against more flowers and trees. He drew a Hitler moustache on her and then wrote FUCK OF on her forehead like it was a tattoo. He put all the photos neatly back into their frames and recapped the Pentel.

Through in the front part of the house there was an old TV with no video, a *Radio Times*, some knitting on a table, and a little desk. He rootled through the desk drawers, finding old letters, pressed flowers, neat bundles of bills and bank accounts. Boring. He inspected a letter from Australia:

> Darling Moppet,
>
> I am in hospital in Melbourne with rheumatoid arthritis and mania. I don't think I can have known what I was doing because I was found in the neighbour's garden in the middle of the night in my nightie sprinkling rat poison in the bird-bath. I shall have to make amends when I get home though

> Joey says Mr and Mrs Casavetes have been understanding. He's half-caste you know, but he always seems a very nice man. Some of the aborigines are quite civilized these days. Your Uncle Neil has been ill too having trouble with his prostate and they think he might have cancer as well. I know God will look after him.

Ding-bats.

He pocketed the bundle of letters for further leisurely perusal.

He returned to the kitchen and fixed another drink, rifled dresser drawers. Nothing. Went into the hall and headed up the stairs. First room before him was the bathroom. He searched the cabinet above the basin which housed a massive selection of drugs. He pocketed a few of the more interesting-looking bottles for later experimentation.

Proceeded to the first bedroom, instantly recognizable as belonging to the tasty woman. A dressing table offered a wide selection of sexy-smelling unguents and defoliators. Bingo! Top left-hand drawer full of knickers. He pulled them out for examination, sorting through the different colours and textures. More drawers disgorged a giant economy pack of Tampax and an interesting array of tights and bras. He took a pull on the vodka and picked out one of the raunchier brassières. He wrapped it round his head, sticking his nose into the generous cup. Then he heard the creak of the floorboard, turned and saw the old woman standing in the doorway.

She was old, well old; ancient, ninetysomething. Her face was a carapace of wrinkles, her hair a straggling bleached white. She was dressed in a house-coat.

She just gawped at him. Her weird milky blue eyes totally freaked him, completely horrorshow.

Wrenching the bra off his face, he reached for the mongrel-mangler, brandished it at her.

'Freeze granny!'

She didn't look like she was in a hurry to go anywhere.

His hand ran down his left thigh, looking for the gaffer tape. He kicked a chair towards the old bird.

'Sit in the chair you don't get hurt. One squeak you die. Sit!'

Her mouth hung open, a dribble of drool hanging on the lip; her turkey-neck wobbled. Totally fucking disgusting – old people always made him want to puke.

'Sit now!'

He pushed the chair under her legs and she collapsed into it. He pulled the knife out. Terror in her milky eyes.

'No,' he said. 'It's to cut the tape right. I'm not gonna hurt you less you try anything.'

He had to drop the hound-repeller to unwind the gaffer tape. It didn't look like the old lady was going to make a sudden dash for it. He stuck the end of the tape on her shoulder and started wrapping, circling the chair. She didn't move.

'This is just so you don't move. I'm not gonna hurt you.'

When he'd wound a good twenty yards of tape down as far as her legs he reckoned she was pretty secure. She kept making this totally revolting whimpering noise. He cut through the tape and inspected his handiwork. There was no way she was planning a quick escape. He scanned the room, found what he wanted – a pair of tights. Shoved them in the crone's wet mouth which canned the whimpering. Perhaps she'd be able to work the tights free with her tongue and shout. He slashed another strip of gaffer and plastered it over her mouth. He grabbed the pooch-puncher, hesitated, picked up the bra and shoved it in his pocket with the letters.

'Don't move!'

He took the stairs in twos, grid-searched the downstairs, stepped into the conservatory. He swivelled the garden, the path – nothing. Walked out, dead casual. Closed the garden gate behind him. Two minutes later he was strolling down Goldhawk window-shopping.

CHAPTER THIRTEEN

THE DOORBELL RANG. Kate was in the kitchen. Sylvester and Jessamy were at school. She went through into the front room and stood behind the net curtain in the bay window.

Two figures lurked on the door-step. Twice before she had seen them: the enormous black woman and the minuscule white woman. What did they want? Why did they keep returning? On the previous occasions she had not answered, but now she was curious. She could not see that they posed any threat. The big black woman looked kind and friendly. Surely she could not be casing the joint for a car-load of murderous thieves. One had to have some trust in human nature.

She went to the door and spent some time disarming the security system and disentangling the locks and chains. The two women were smiling. There was a ponderous silence, then the black woman said:

'Hello, dear.'

Oh God what if they're just lunatics who go round knocking on people's doors for no reason at all then just stand there and grin like idiots?

'Hello,' she said nervously. The black woman had huge glowing white teeth.

'My name is Gloria and this is my colleague Susan.'

Susan nodded and smirked.

Gloria continued: 'We're going round this area today asking people if they see any hope for the future.'

'I'm not sure – I'm sorry. I don't quite understand – '

'Many people have lost all hope for the future, dear. They have made no provision – '

She understood immediately and took evasive action. 'Thank you but we're completely covered. My husband works in assurance himself. We're very well taken care of. Thank you so much for calling – '

Susan was now smiling ecstatically. Gloria said, 'No, my dear. I am not talkin about money. I am not talkin about the temporal world. Have you thought about the future of the earth? Everywhere there's the wars on the television and the environment fallin apart and the hole in the ozone. Do you have time to think about these things, dear?'

'Well, yes. It's terrible, but – '

'And you can make sense of these terrible things, or does it just seem like the whole world's goin crazy?'

'Well . . .' She smiled but this was wrong: Gloria and Susan weren't smiling any more. They were looking very serious. She stopped smiling too. 'I suppose it does, yes.'

'And crime everywhere you go – people being mugged and killed and raped and families breakin down, no one able to talk to each other no more, the children runnin wild, in trouble with the police.'

'Well, yes.'

Susan was smiling again. Gloria paused.

'But God has told us all about these things a long time ago, dear.'

Susan nodded and continued to grin broadly.

'And he's told us how it's all goin to come right at the end. How these things will be just a memory and the earth will be a beautiful place again where people live in peace without disease and crime and the ozone and the killings.'

Gloria stopped; Susan continued to nod for a few moments afterwards, like one of those dogs in the back of cars.

'Are you Jehovah's Witnesses . . .?' she asked.

'That's right, dear.'

'Well, I'm not sure if – '

'What I want to do, dear, is just leave you some literature to read about these things we've been talking about – like why young people is turnin to drugs and all the cities choked up with smoke from the cars and the factories and the greenhouse.'

She found the leaflets being pushed into her hands.

'And if you could manage it, dear, a small contribution towards the cost of printing the books. Just twenty pence maybe.'

'Yes – I'll – could you just wait a moment.' Leaving the door ajar she went to the kitchen. This was how they did it, of course: the mama and the grinning anorexic got the door open, by the time you returned the burglars were in with the door shut behind them.

'God bless you, dear,' Gloria said when she returned with the twenty pence. 'We'll come again when you've had time to read those tings and we can talk about them.'

'Well, perhaps. Thank you.'

'What's your name, dear?'

'It's, er, Catherine.'

'It's very nice to meet you, Catherine. And goodbye for now.'

The grinning anorexic sort of nodded and mumbled something.

'Goodbye.'

And she shut the door.

Colin was driving home from Savage Life for the last time.

I'M GOBSMACKED!

Cross boss headbutt outrage

Insurance salesman Colin Nutter, 34,

> couldn't believe it when he went into work on Monday morning and his boss pushed him out of the front door and called him a 'c***!'

This was the only way he could think about the incident which had occurred this morning. In order to comprehend the event he automatically translated it into *Joke* language and then it seemed to make some kind of sense. It was the sort of random, irrational occurrence which happened on every page of the *Daily Joke*.

It was a perfectly ordinary Monday morning so far as Colin was concerned. Nothing was amiss. His equanimity had been ruffled only by the discovery of the fresh envy-scratches on the flank of the BMW. In all other regards it was a perfectly ordinary Monday morning. Then he went in through the door of the office, was just saying Hello to Petra on reception, and Dorian comes running at him like a bullock and pushes him into the wall.

> Colin had worked for insurance boss Dorian Savage, 36, for nearly five years when the attack took place.
>
> 'I'm totally gobsmacked,' he said last night. 'Dorian wasn't only my boss he was a good friend too. I just can't believe this has happened.'
>
> According to friends, the insurance salesman has always had a fiery temper, but they've never known him to sack someone for no reason at all.
>
> Colin said last night: 'I don't know what the problem was. I honestly think he's gone mad or something. He's sick. But I can't feel sorry for him, not after the way he's treated me. I've got a wife and family to bring up.'

He pulled the BMW up in the car-park of the Merry Yeoman. It was 11.05.

The newly refurbished Sherwood bar was open and empty and he went straight to the bar.

'Large g-and-t, thanks.'

Over on the wall the *Beer Wolf* machine was making spontaneous gurgling noises.

The barman put the drink in front of him. 'Two-fifty.'

He had a couple more in quick succession and nibbled at a packet of peanuts. Before long, nine half-smoked Benson stubs were heaped up in the ashtray before him. Now anxiety and puzzlement were turning into anger. He had one more and got back on the motorway.

He stopped in Chiswick and bought a packet of extra-strong mints to disguise the smell of drink, then went into the building society where he withdrew £1000 in fifties. This was a secret contingency fund which Kate knew nothing about; he had maintained it throughout their marriage for articles of expenditure he preferred she remain in the dark about. He was withdrawing the money because he knew the moment the salary cheques stopped coming in and the mortgage and bills and direct debits kept on going out the bank and various credit companies were liable to cause problems. In times such as these he liked to have a buffer of cash. He carefully packed the notes inside his wallet, secured the wallet in his back trouser pocket, and returned to the car. Cutting down the Goldhawk Road he knew that he could not face Kate yet, not until he'd had a couple more drinks.

'But why, Colin? I don't understand why,' she would say, and he would be unable to reply because he didn't know why either. Then she would start talking about the mortgage and the boat and money in general and he would become angry and storm out of the house and go to the pub. So the logical thing to do was to go straight to the pub, cutting out that stage of the proceedings.

He found a parking space in Purblind Avenue and walked past a chemist advertising discount perfumes – **Odium** £14.99 **Obession** £13.99 **Poisson** £13.99. He bought a *Joke* from the newsagent on the corner, checked the wallet was still safe, and went into the Stumbling Block. It was fairly empty: half a dozen Irish congregated at one table, unshaven and peering mournfully into their Guinness. A group of lads clattered balls round the pool table, a few other miserable morning drinkers were spread across the pub. A television in one corner showed the sodden view of Newmarket; a juke-box played a heavy metal song called 'Semtex Jockstrap'; two fruit machines beeped and burbled. He ordered a pint of Dopplerbrau and a morbid beef sandwich and got change for the cigarette machine. It was 12.42.

He sipped quickly at the pint; read bits of the *Joke*; festered on Dorian's maltreatment of him. He was a way down a third pint when someone sat on the stool opposite.

'Mr Nutter.'

He looked up from the paper. Recognized the face, but couldn't immediately put a name to it.

'Richardson. David Richardson – Castle.'

'Of course. Yeah.'

'Get you another pint?'

'Thanks.'

He lit another Bensons, thought, I've smoked thirty and it's not yet two o'clock. Richardson returned with a lager and a Guinness.

'Job was satisfactory I hope, Mr Nutter?'

'Oh, yeah, fine.'

'Can't be too careful these days is what I say.'

He felt his head going slightly wobbly and wished he'd eaten some breakfast this morning. It was now nigh-on impossible to get a proper breakfast out of Kate who was currently indoctrinating the children with a new diet which involved eating two pounds of dried fruit every morning. A little fragment of music rose above the mêlée of pool, TV and fruit machine. It was Crystal Knight and the Munich Sound Machine performing their new hit 'Broken Windows'.

'No. I didn't used to think about it. Shakes you up when you get burgled like that.'

'Course it does. I'm always trying to tell people – you know, get security now before it happens. You can't be too careful these days.'

The two men sipped philosophically at their beers.

'Don't normally see you round here,' Richardson said. 'Thought you worked out near the airport somewhere.'

'I do,' he said. 'I did. Just lost my job.'

'Happening to a lot of people. Recession. Doesn't make it any easier though, does it?'

'No.'

'Company went down then? These interest rates, bloody scandalous.'

He siphoned half an inch off the top of the pint. 'I was fired.'

'Yeah?'

'Yeah. This morning. No reason given – just chucked out. I've been there five years. I can't believe it.'

'You can go to the European Court about that. Bosses can't just go round firing people for no reason. Not these days.'

'Mine can. Could.'

'Isn't right.'

Now he felt the floodgates of his grievance opening. Here was a neutral third party, an indifferent bystander, to whom he could pour out his anger and misery.

'I thought he was a fucking friend, that's the worst of it. We used to go drinking together, have dinner, go down to Essex at the weekends. It's unbelievable.' He shook his head ruefully.

'First mistake,' Richardson said with enormous authority. 'Never hobnob with the bosses. It's like when I was in the

Army. Officers and men don't mix – ever. That way you know where you stand.'

He found himself warming to the topic of conversation and went for two more pints. When he returned Richardson was lighting one of his ferocious, fizzing cheroots.

'Cheers,' the former soldier said. 'You'd never find me getting friendly with Castle, see. Sure, I have the odd beer with him on a Friday evening, but that's strictly business. He's just an ordinary bloke like you or me, done well for himself, but I don't want to get involved. You want to keep your distance.'

'You're fucking right,' he concurred, thinking about Dorian and his trout and white wine and Brahms.

'This the same bloke you bought the boat off then?' Richardson said.

'Yeah.' He was surprised for a moment, then recalled blagging off to Richardson about his new possession.

'Boat going well, is it? Must be a nice pastime. I've often thought about taking it up myself. Cost a lot, did it, this boat?'

'Eighteen grand.'

Richardson exhaled deeply and shook his head. 'Bit beyond my price range, that. Still, I might be in the market for something smaller one of these days. You can pick up a little twenty-foot job for three or four grand, do it up yourself.' He sipped at his Guinness. 'I've often thought, you know, be nice to just piss off for a few weeks. Put a sleeping-bag and a box of food in the boat, few cans of beer, and just sugar off, moor the boat wherever you end up. Just go with the current, so to speak. Very nice. All on your own, nothing but the sea. Time to think things through, that sort of thing. Freedom, that's what it's about.'

'Yeah,' he said morosely. 'I'll probably have to sell it now unless I can get another job soon.'

'That's a shame. A real shame. Wish I could help you out there.'

And then a couple of hours passed and they drank three

or four more pints and Colin was nodding solemnly, his head slightly askew, glad of this new camaraderie, while Richardson talked about his time as a mercenary in Angola or was it Nicaragua with Major 'Mad Max' Muller.

They were coming through a clearing in the jungle and this bunch of rebel wogs ambushed them. Richardson got into cover and grenaded their dugout but he was too late to save his mates. When it was all over there was only him and Major Max left and one bloke shot up so badly the Major put his revolver to the side of the bloke's head and finished him off. It was that or let the giant ants strip his dying body bare. They were down to one canister of water between them, the rest having been destroyed by the rebel attack. It was 120 in the shade. They walked for a week. Richardson was bitten by a snake (at this point he whipped his leg up on to an adjacent stool and rolled up his trouser-leg to expose the scar on his ankle) and Major Max flung him on the ground, slashed his knife up his calf and sucked the venom out. He would have died otherwise. They got to a village loyal to the government and the loyal wogs looked after them. He lay in a hut made out of dung for a week, the village girls coming every hour to minister to his needs. A week later they were on a plane out of Luanda or was it Managua, and he was sitting in the pub back in Shepherd's Bush forty-eight hours later.

'That's incredible,' Colin said and took a fistful of peanuts.

'And I'll tell you, I was totally loyal to that man. I would have died for him, no second thoughts.'

'What happened to him then?' he asked.

'They got him. They got him in the end. Lived up in Acton when he wasn't on a job. Fine man.'

And a further, indeterminate period of drinking time passed by, ranging over the football, women, the breakdown of contemporary civilization, drinking bouts, and at some point Colin blurted out: 'I could kill that cunt. I really could.'

'Savage . . .?' Richardson said quietly. His face puckered into a scrunched expression of enquiry. His eyes narrowed.

'Course fucking Savage,' he replied, slurped at his drink and ground a half-smoked stub into the ashtray. 'He thinks he can just treat me like this. No reason. Cos he feels like it. Cos he's pissed off about something. I could do that bastard.'

Richardson looked solemn. 'But that's the whole point,' he said. '*You* couldn't do him, could you? Cos it would be very obvious who'd done him.'

'Still . . .'

Richardson drew slowly on his Guinness and looked distrustfully about the pub. It was now eight-thirty and the place was filling up.

'Fancy a game of snooker?' he said. 'Get out of this place. My club's just down the road.'

'Yeah. Why not? I've just got to piss.'

When he returned they proceeded up Goldhawk Road in the direction of the Athenaeum Snooker Club. 'One guest,' Richardson said, and gave his overcoat in at the door. They walked down the steps into a long basement room with half a dozen tables and a bar at which they sat. Lights illuminated a couple of the tables where players cued intently. The remainder were unoccupied. 'Same again?' Richardson said. 'Beer's piss here, you're probably better on a short.'

'Yeah,' he said. 'Scotch.'

Richardson ordered two large scotches. 'We'll get a table in a minute, no hurry. It's always quiet in here on a Monday.'

'Fine.' He sipped at the scotch and it sort of dimly dawned on him that he was now catastrophically pissed and that he'd better get an Indian or something before he went home. Home. Kate. The interrogation.

'Course, I know people,' Richardson said.

He was just lighting a Bensons and had to think about this a bit. Everybody knew people, didn't they?

'My former line of work like. People who take care of the business.'

Then he thought he knew what Richardson was talking about. 'I see . . .' he said very deliberately. 'I s'pose you would do. These people . . .'

'Pros. No fuck-ups.'

'Right,' he said, and punctuated the statement by downing the rest of the whisky in one hard jolt. 'Two more large ones,' wiggling a note at the barman.

He paid for the drinks and Richardson said, 'Let's get a table.' Richardson switched a light on over the table at the far end of the room and went round the pockets pulling the balls from their sacks. Colin stood watching very solemnly, noticed that the green baize seemed to be wobbling a bit. Richardson plonked the reds into the triangle, shook it and rolled it into position. 'Pick yourself a cue,' he said, and Colin found one in the rack and very intently massaged chalk on to the tip. He thought he'd be quite happy just standing here very carefully rolling the chalk round the end of the cue for rather a long time. It was a nice, simple activity which calmed the mind no end.

'How much per frame? Quid say?' Richardson said.

'Fine. Yeah.'

'You want to break?'

'Okay.'

'I'd take your jacket off. Inhibits the cue action.'

'Good thinking.'

He neatly hung his jacket on the back of the seat where their drinks were. Picked up his cue. Stood at the table. Rolled the white on to the line. Tried to remember just where it was on the side of the pack you wanted to get the white so it would return smoothly into safety at the baulk-end. He slid the cue gently over his arched hand to sense his action. Focussed both eyes on the reds and struck.

'Unlucky,' Richardson said.

The reds had broken apart much as they are supposed to but the white had collided with the blue on its return up the table.

'Haven't played for a while,' he said.

'Soon get your hand in again,' said Richardson.

Richardson potted a red; the pink; another red; leant down to squint but seemed to have gone out of position, and played off the green into safety tight on the baulk cushion. 'Eight.'

Colin sized up the table. 'House rules,' Richardson said. 'No cigarettes at the table.'

He put the cigarette in the ashtray and returned to survey the baize. The white was on the cushion neatly wedged behind the yellow. Just one red seemed pottable in the right side pocket. It would require a fine slice which would then take the white off the top cushion back for the blue. He concentrated his entire intellectual apparatus upon the red; envisaged the flight-path of the white, the sweet sound of ivory clinking, of ivory on leather as the target ball clonked into the pocket. He remembered a Snooker Masterclass with Jim 'Apocalypse' Stephens or Dave 'Maelstrom' Jameson or Steve 'Earthquake' Black he'd watched one night on television: *Visualize your desired shot: Make It Happen!* It was the same as that book he had by John Harvey-Jones, part of his small but responsibly chosen library of the world's classics.

He cued. It was a rare moment when all seems right with the world. The cut on the red perfect; the red rolling slowly, majestically into the pocket like a model of the Newtonian universe; the white bumping off the cushion and returning down the table. Not perfect position, but not at all bad.

'Good shot,' Richardson said.

Now he was on fire. The blue was pottable but he had to hold the white for a difficult red. Again he focussed everything. The blue flew clean and straight into the side pocket and the white dribbled slightly down-pocket on the left of the table. This was the gear. He should never have gone into the insurance game; he should have put in ten hours a day on the baize, he'd be world fucking champion by now. There was a possible red top-left. He looked up and Richardson seemed to have summoned more drinks out of nowhere. Went round and returned the blue to its spot. Looked at the white and realized he needed the rest. Started grappling round under the table to find it.

'Hate the rest myself,' said Richardson.

Sliding the cue back and forth on the rest it occurred to him that his action resembled the masturbating of a four-foot long penis. *Put all superfluous thoughts out of mind. Concentrate on the shot.* The shot was a disaster. The red went four inches wide and the white careered into the cluster of reds, opening them out for Richardson and freeing up the black.

'Unlucky. Six.' Richardson said, marking up the score.

He settled into his chair, sipped the whisky, drew on the Bensons. Richardson started potting with depressing regularity, counting off the break as he went: one, eight, nine, sixteen, seventeen, twenty-two, twenty-three. When he next got back to the table he had not even played his shot when Richardson said, 'Foul.' He looked down and saw his arm had brushed against a stray red. When next he returned there was nothing to pot and he played a miserable safety. Then he was aware of Richardson triumphantly spearing the black into a pocket and saying, 'Eighty-seven – six. Another . . .? Double or quits?'

He supposed he must have agreed to both. When he awoke at eleven the next morning he remembered very little. He remembered going to the bar once more during the second frame. Dimly recollected a red that might have gone in, but he had a niggling suspicion the white had followed straight in after it. Remembered for some reason being in the car-park at the back of the club later: the darkness, the cold air, the smell of the adjacent dustbins and of Richardson's bonfire cheroots. And then . . . Then nothing; he had no idea how he had got home.

He was fully clothed and on the settee in the living room. He could sense Kate through in the kitchen. She would say nothing when she saw him, a favoured tactic. Then she would say imperiously, 'Aren't you rather late for work?' Within the hour they would be engaged in a long and futile argument.

CHAPTER FOURTEEN

RICHARDSON AWOKE before dawn. He needed only three hours sleep a night and never took more. He believed that excessive sleep weakened the muscles and the brain. He shaved in the harsh strip light over the kitchen sink in the two-room flat while the kettle boiled on the draining-board. He poured the boiling water on to the five heaped spoons of Red Label in the tin teapot, then walked down the corridor to the communal bathroom where he pissed, showered and defecated. He liked to get all of these morning arrangements out of the way long before any of the drug addicts and students and boozehounds were up and about.

He remembered the previous day with vivid clarity. He always did. He had trained his memory as a young man in accordance with the Pelman System and had kept it in superior condition ever since. For practice he memorized technical specifications from *Jane's Defence Weekly*, or articles from the *Encyclopaedia Britannica* which he studied in the library on the Uxbridge Road. He was a mine of information on a great variety of subjects, primarily of a military or technical nature.

Yesterday he had had only the one job in the morning, a simple burglar alarm installation down in Hammersmith. He had started the job at eight and been through by twelve. He had had lunch in the Inter-Continental Grill: roast pork, roast potatoes, peas and carrots, a cup of unsweetened black tea. He had fancied a pint and gone into the Stumbling Block. To his surprise he had immediately recognized Colin

Nutter of No 51 Esterhazy Road where he had installed a system three weeks ago. He was pleased to see someone he knew. He did not seem to have many friends he could talk to in pubs. It was rare that he did not sit alone nursing a pint and reading the court reports in the *Daily Telegraph*.

'Mr Nutter?' he had said.

He had offered to buy a pint and been accepted which was a less rare occurrence. He found people nearly always accepted the offer of a drink. They had talked, a really very interesting conversation. They had drunk quite a lot and it had seemed to affect Nutter somewhat. It had not affected him: alcohol never did. That was the way his constitution was. He could drink a bottle of whisky and it was just the same as if he'd drunk a pot of tea. It didn't make any difference.

Nutter had just lost his job and was despondent on this count. He had advised Nutter on his legal rights, but the grudge against his erstwhile employer had seemed to go deeper, a more personal kind of thing. Every time the subject of Dorian Savage came up – which it did with great regularity – Nutter got more and more worked up about it. Maybe Savage had screwed his wife or his mistress or his sister, or maybe he'd screwed someone he shouldn't have and Savage knew about it. Maybe they were a couple of secret queer-boys having a lovers' tiff. You could never tell with people, especially when it came to the business of sex. Anyway, he didn't need to concern himself with that stuff. What was obvious to Richardson was that the bloke wanted something done about Savage.

When Nutter said, 'I could kill that cunt,' he paid careful attention. It was clear Nutter was angling, testing the water. The question was, how serious was he? How far was he prepared to go? You met a lot of bullshitters in pubs. You had to be careful.

He didn't like the way the Stumbling Block was filling up. They could easily be overheard. He suggested they go up to the Athenaeum and play a few frames. The atmosphere would be more conducive if Nutter was serious, if he wanted to talk about serious business. He left it to Nutter to make the first move.

They played a frame. He won 87–6. It was obvious Nutter wasn't much of a player so he deliberately missed a couple of balls to give the man a chance to get back into the game. He didn't want to humiliate the guy. He was 37–0 up in the second and purposely missed a red to give Nutter a go on the table. There was no point in wiping him out. It was something that tended to upset people, particularly when they'd had a few. Nutter was about to cue when he stopped and said, 'I could wrap this fucking cue round his head for starters.'

Savage. He wanted to talk about Savage.

Nutter missed the red, an easy one, and slumped back in his chair. Richardson took a long red, screwing back for the black. He chalked his cue and said quietly, 'You want to get rid of this guy?'

Nutter said, 'Yeah. Fucking right.'

He said, 'Tell me about him. Where does he live?' and cleanly cut the black in stunning on to the next red.

'Barrett Meadows. Up Chertsey way. Chertsey – Staines, round there. New estate. House is called Southfork.'

'Expensive?'

'Fucking millions. I don't know. Cunt.'

'Where's he work?'

'Savage Life. Just outside Stanwell, industrial estate.'

'I know it.'

He potted the red, came off the cushion on to the pink. Pink ran a couple of inches forward for the open red. Perfect. Nutter took a belt at his whisky and said, 'Blow the cunt away. Fucking blow him out. Bang bang. You're dead, pal.'

He said, 'Keep your voice down. There's people on that table. D'you want to talk about money?'

'Yesh. Money.'

He slammed the red down, screwing back for the black.

'Two grand. No questions asked.'

'Done,' Nutter said. 'Two gran.'

Black rolled in gently, white ran on to the red on the cushion.

'Half up front.'

'Okay,' Nutter said, and started reaching for his wallet.

'Not in here,' he said. 'Outside.'

'Outside,' Nutter said. 'I've got the cash. All ready. One grand. Spondulicks. Doberries. One gwan folding.'

'Like I said,' Richardson said, 'can it. Keep your mouth shut or the deal's off.'

'Yesh shir,' Nutter said.

He pondered the matter: Was the guy serious? Did he carry that sort of cash? Had he come prepared for this? They'd see later in the car-park. Red. Black. Yellow. Green. Brown. Blue. Pink. Black.

'One more?' he said. 'Or let's pack it in. You owe me two quid and it's your round.'

He smoked a cheroot while Nutter went to the bar and tottered back with the drinks, dropped the two quid on the table, said, 'Pish,' and went through the door to the toilet.

When they had finished their drinks he said, 'Let's go.' Nutter followed him through the door and into the car-park at the side of the building. He stood in the thin gauze of sodium light. He liked this light, liked the way it lent him a sinister pallor.

'You've got the cash then,' he said.

Nutter reached into his wallet. 'A gwan. Count it,' he said.

He took the bundle of fifties and counted them. Twenty notes. One grand. The guy was serious, and he knew the score. There was no mistaking it. He looked like a booze-hound, but he knew what he was doing. He'd come prepared and found his man.

'The other half when the job's done,' he said, targeting Nutter's eyes in the orange light. 'You'll know when it's been done. I'll contact you to arrange the rest of the payment. Don't try and contact me. No phone calls. No other form of contact. If I need to talk to you, you'll know. Is that all straight?'

'Is stwaight,' Nutter said.

'Any fuck-ups and the job's off. Understand?'

'Undershtood.' Nutter nodded.

'It's been nice doing business with you, Mr Nutter.'

They shook hands, and parted outside on the Goldhawk Road. Richardson reflected: it was quite sad that he wouldn't be able to renew the acquaintance with Nutter. He seemed like a decent enough bloke, and he didn't really know many of them. Come to think of it, he didn't really know anyone much. Still, business was business.

He had two jobs on today – finishing up some wiring out in Ealing, and an alarm to install in Holland Park. He didn't get through till four. He placed the thousand in his Nationwide Anglia Extra Interest Account. On the way to the Inter-Continental he purchased a new Ordnance Survey map of the Staines area. Over braised beef, mash, cabbage and tea he marked the locations of Barrett Meadows and the industrial estate. He flung his binoculars on the back seat of the Avenger and drove out to Barrett Meadows.

He found the house after a ten-minute patrol of the quiet suburban streets. Kids were playing football on a green lawn; women were gardening; husbands were just getting home from work. It was a nice, decent, orderly kind of place: he approved of it. These were honest, hard-working people: they deserved their good fortune. He did not begrudge it them.

Savage's ranch-style house was well back off the road, the entire third of an acre rimmed with a nine-foot wall which he could tell instantly was wired up. He needed a surveillance point and located one in a tall oak on the scrubland beyond the houses. He parked four hundred yards away in the shelter of rhododendrons and tramped through the undergrowth. It was necessary to crawl through the long grass at the bottom of a garden adjacent to a tennis court. He threw a length of rope around the lowest branch of the tree and pulled himself up into the cover of the foliage. From a high spot he trained the binoculars on Savage's house.

The view was good, a clean angle right through french windows into a large living room. Later he would ascertain whether the glass was bullet-proof: it might be necessary to know. He thought it probably was not, however.

He waited, assimilating detail, committing it to memory.

He maintained his vigil throughout the evening; got a good look at Savage and a wife/girlfriend. Savage drove round the garden on a miniature tractor: this was worth knowing about. You could stage all sorts of unpleasantness with those things. The woman cooked some food and they ate in the living room sprawled on a couch. He was unable from this distance to identify what they were eating. They watched something on television and talked. Savage drank white wine.

At eleven he came down from the tree and returned to the Avenger. He checked on the two cars, a red Porsche and a green Polo, as he drove by the gates of the house. Took the numbers then returned into town. It had been a useful evening's work. He did a hundred press-ups on the kitchen linoleum, drank a pot of tea, and had an early night.

CHAPTER FIFTEEN

THE TWO MISSIVES now exerted a hideous power of fascination over Dorian. Regularly he returned to inspect them. The ghastly sub-literate scrawl. The hideous phraseology. The smears of chocolate on the cheap notepaper. All conspired to nauseate and terrify him.

Certain key phrases were now imprinted on his mind. He would wake up in the morning with the words echoing in his head. They would lurch up out of the darkness and scream at him during a meeting or a meal.

I hav found out U R my dad. I found a photo of U my mum had from wen U + her wer bonkin.

U lokes jus like mee + the dates is rihgt 1976 in fact.

U test the jeans in yor Sperm.

PS I wood like to change my name by deep hole so its Savage if U agre.

Pleez find inclosed a photo off U from wen U + my mum wer bonkin about 15 years ago like I sed befor.

U R my dad i nos.

recognized U from a nuver photo I saw of this guy U no round hear. That is how I fond out U were my dad.

This guy U no round hear.

Colin.

At first he had thought it was a practical joke, then he had received the second letter with the nightmare photograph of himself back in the mid-seventies, twenty or twenty-one years old, hands sliding up round the breasts of Adeline Hoskins of the White City Estate. 'Addie' as she was called;

'Addled Addie' to her friends. It was strange how he had not recognized her surname from the boy's first missive. He supposed he had been so certain it was Colin's idea of a good wind-up – Colin's long-gestated revenge for the test tube and countless other practical jokes – that he had simply not noticed. Anyway, that was now history. There could now be no doubt about the reality of the situation: here was the photograph, stark documentary proof.

In his entire life that surely had been the lowest he ever sunk. Those sordid liaisons up on the White City. Her rank sheets; the stench of perfume failing to conceal the locker-room smell of other men – of other gangsters and hoodlums and conmen. The baby girl squalling in the next-door room. The stench of nappy-change and tinned baby food.

Were they all conspiring? Was this an elaborate blackmail scheme? Colin, Addie, the boy recruited to play the part of long-lost son?

How had Colin found her and found this out?

Or, how had she found Colin? Not so hard, he supposed. That was more likely the way it was.

He did not believe the boy could be his. Aside from the fact that it was inconceivable that he, Dorian Savage, could have spawned something as vile as the creature he had seen by the gates, there was also one overwhelming reason for believing this: even back then in the 1970s, long before AIDS and herpes, he had always worn a condom. Not always, no; but absolutely always with Addled Addie. There was no way he was going to bury the salami in that without a good layer of protective plastic.

The reason was simple: he was terrified of sexually transmitted diseases, and had been since the occasion when the school doctor gave them a slide-show in the Science Block lecture hall which graphically illustrated the multiplicity of venereal perils. He acquired a medical dictionary and learnt that Casanova had used a shield of sheep's intestines tied with a neat bow – the forerunner of the modern Durex. The next Saturday he walked into a chemist and demanded a packet of three Black Knights. He was thirteen. Having no immediate use to put them to he carried them round at all times in his trouser pocket. They seemed a kind of talisman against the rampaging venereal terror.

Other than with the cleanest, nicest possible sort of girls (virgins with rich daddies preferably) he had used them ever since.

He would just get comfortable with the thought that the boy could not possibly be the fruit of his loins, and then the alternative scenario would lurch up from the abyss: the ripped condom, the manufacturing error, the malicious shop-girl sticking a pin through the packet-of-three, the fucking thing simply dropping off when he was too pissed to notice.

His mind ranged back over those drunken evenings fifteen years ago, trying to locate a possible occasion, one night when he removed the Black Panther and was not reassured by the feel of the squidgy sac of seed. It could easily have happened: back in those days he was so pissed so much of the time anything might have happened. God knows, he might have sired half of the North Stand.

So it was possible. It was very possible. It was possible that there had been an inadvertent addition to the illustrious clan of the Savages. And that was what most terrorized him – that was why he so detested the very idea of paternity.

He was haunted by dreams, vivid sweaty nightmares of his father and his mother and the boy on seaside outings. 'A grandson – you've made your mother a happy woman. You know she always wanted to see a grandchild before she died.' (From the last communication he had had with his parents, some eighteen months ago, he understood his mother to be afflicted with the ravage of some kind of life-threatening cancer.) He imagined ghastly scenes of familial reconciliation, weddings and christenings and Christmas get-togethers – Uncle Norm jack-knifed over the bog with Party Seven dribbling down his shirt, Auntie Sue pissed and stripping down to her purple knickers on the dinner table.

He could not help himself. Having ensured that Rebecca was occupied in another part of the house, he went through into the study, closed the door, took the key from its hiding-place behind the clock, and unlocked the drawer in the desk. He shoved the letters to one side and removed the photograph. It was like looking at another person. It was hard to imagine that this had once been him. The gauche, permanently randy trainee hoodlum groping the tart's tits. He wished he could remember the occasion. Who had taken the photograph? One of the crowd of petty thieves, pimps, bouncers, car salesmen and piss-artists he had hung around with back then.

He couldn't remember which pub or club or gambling den he had met Addie in. It hardly mattered. She liked them young, someone had told him, but wasn't too particular. He bought her drinks all evening, then cabbed back to her flat. The sex was very good. It was so good he kept on coming back for more. Addie's game was not precisely prostitution – cash never changed hands, not immediately after the act at any rate. You just picked up the tab the whole time – for drinks, drugs, overdue rent, everything. Then, in August of that hot summer, he stopped. He cleaned up his act.

He remembered the all-night sessions in clubs, the preposterous, doomed gambling, the time they all decided to drive to a pub in Aylesbury at two in the morning. Seven or eight drunks loaded in the one motor. Half of them didn't even notice when he mowed down the pedestrian. '**HE'LL NEVER WALK AGAIN**! Scandal of Hit-and-Run Driver. Hanging's too good for them says cripple's mother.' It was after this that he stopped, completely, stone dead. He moved away; never saw any of that crowd ever again.

He replaced the photograph in the drawer and picked out the two letters once again. The telephone number on the second caught his attention. He reached over to the phone and tapped the digits out, held the receiver to the side of his head and fumbled for a cigar from the J·R Presidente Selección Suprema box. He had taken to smoking a number of these in recent days.

The phone rang seven times.

'Ello?'

A girl's voice. He was silent.

'Ello? Is that you, Dog? Where the fuck are you – I waited in all last night, I fought you was coming back. Ello . . .? Look, oo is this . . .? If you're on some heavy-breathing kick you can fuck off. D'you hear? Piss off!'

And the line went dead.

The girl; the little baby girl who had slept and cried and gurgled in the next-door room while he rutted with the mother.

Dog found himself in something of a moral quandary. Selena, Editor-in-Chief of *Grunt*, had responded to his letter enthusiastically, but it seemed they were not prepared to pay the £250 he had thought a reasonable market-rate for the Mrs Nutter snaps. He had this nasty feeling they might be trying to cheat him here, but it was difficult to tell, this being a trade he wasn't very up on, and Christie being wholly uncooperative in the matter of proffering her professional advice. *Grunt* were prepared to pay £50 and make Mrs Nutter 'Reader's Wife of the Month' in a special and tasteful two-page spread, so long as he returned a signed 'consent form' with the negatives. So the question was, did he take the fifty or tell them to fuck off and try and flog the pictures to a rival publication such as *Heave* or *Slag*? Or indeed something classier, such as *Belgravia* or *Plaza*.

He took the letter and the consent form down to the Goose Green to consult with Nige on this delicate matter. He got some lagers in.

'So what do I do then?' he asked Nige.

'Take it. But d'you reckon she'll sign the form?'

'No. But I can get any bird to sign it, right? They're not gonna know.'

'Good point. In fact, why don't you just sign it? With her name.'

'Oh. Yeah. I hadn't thought of that.'

Over a week had passed and Gaz had received no word from his dad, despite eschewing volume on the Toshiba and keeping a close vigil on the phone. Dorian was holding out on him. He resolved to redouble his efforts at communicating with his progenitor. He thought: He's my fucking dad – he's got to see me. I've got a right.

He went through into the kitchen and picked at the cold tray of last night's oven-readies. His mother came in.

'I've got a letter about you,' she said.

His heart sprang into his mouth. 'Where? What's it say?' He'd communicated with Adeline! He was going to see him! To acknowledge his long-lost son!

'It's from the edjacation people – they wanna know why you aven't been to school for six mumphs.'

His heart sank back into his chest. He pushed another oven-ready in the slot. 'Cos I fucking ate it,' he said, and tried to push past her out of the kitchen.

'You'll get me in trouble. They're gonna come round.'

'I don't care. Tell em to piss off.'

'Maybe they'll take you into care.'

'Couldn't be any worse than this dump, could it?'

'I don't know why I bother wiv you.'

He took a handful of oven-readies and went back to his room. He slotted N-V-Scratch in the Tosh. 'I wan your car!' the singer yelled. 'I wan your wo-man!' He rootled under the mattress for the fruits of his most recent forage which he purposed this morning taking up to the stash-point on the Scrubs. The gear came out: wallet, little bottle of Odium, packet of low-dose contraceptives, necklace.

Dog barged in, big grey sacs round his pink eyes, clad only in his blue briefs and his 'I Fought the Law' T-shirt. 'Turn that fucking crap down,' he said and punched the Eject button with his fat finger.

'Piss off,' he responded. 'It's my ouse. I live ere – you don't.'

Dog slurped at the mug of coffee in his hand.

'Your mummy wants you to go to school.'

'Piss off.'

'So I said I'd drag you down there for er.'

'Fuck off.'

Dog picked up a packet of Marlboro and a lighter and lit a cigarette.

'They're my fags,' he said. Dog took a deep draught on the cigarette which fizzed down into a long red ember. The smoke started back out of his mouth and he coughed, spilling coffee on the carpet. He took another blast at the coffee, returned the cigarette to his mouth, rubbed his fingers over the grizzled layer of stubble covering his fat face, scratched his balls. His big pink eyes looked thoughtful.

'I wanna talk to you.'

'I don't wanna talk to you.'

Dog used his foot to heave a pile of clothes on to the floor and sat himself on the chair. He rested his vast stinking foot over his other leg so that a gigantic pink testicle dangled out from the blue briefs. This was unfamiliar: Dog sitting down in his room. He was not accustomed to entertaining at home.

'What jew want?' he said.

'Nice chips?' Dog enquired. 'I made those. I'm getting quite a dab hand at cooking.' This was new: Dog as house-husband; Dog as New Man.

'They're all right.'

'You found out who that bloke is then?'

'What bloke?'

'Queer one – in the pink shirt.'

'Fuck off!'

'All right – your dad. That nice bloke in the photo.'

He was on alert. He scanned Dog's enormous ugly face. 'What's it to you?'

'Just taking an interest. Must be important to you, finding out who your dad is. I'd want to know if I was you – it's only natural. Jew find out his name then?'

'Might have done.'

'What you gonna do then? Go and see im – say, "Hello, Dad. Give me a load of dosh."'

'Piss off.'

'I'm just asking. Looked like he was rich, didn't it?'

He didn't reply. Whatever it was Dog was digging for, he wasn't going to give anything away.

'Course,' Dog said, 'if I was to go back to number 51 maybe I could find out who he is.'

'How you gonna do that then?'

'I could say there was a fault with their alarm, couldn't I? Then I could get chatting to the bird, say somefing like, "Aven I see you with this bloke that wears a baseball cap and a pink shirt? I'm sure I recognized im – what's his name again?" See what I mean?'

Gaz saw exactly what he meant and didn't like it one bit: he didn't want Dog having anything to do with this. He bitterly lamented that he had told Dog about his father, especially in view of the fact that Dog's information concerning Nutter had proved of no value whatsoever. He knew, furthermore, that Dog was only interested in one thing: money.

'Maybe I'm not interested any more. Maybe he's not my dad – I just fought he was.'

'Why don't we go and talk to your mum about that then?'

'She don't know.'

'Jew wanna know somefing?' Dog said. He stubbed the Marlboro out in the coffee mug and lit another one.

'What? And don't nick all my fags.'

'I eard Richardson talking to Nutter, right. Nutter was saying how he's got this boat out in Essex and how he just bought it off this mate of his who's got another boat. How they both go down there and go out on these boats. So maybe that's your dad he was talking about.'

This piece of information whizzed through his brain – made all his synapses tingle. The boat – the boat Dorian had mentioned to the bird. He thought maybe it showed on his face; tried to make out like he wasn't interested. 'Where's this boat then?' he said, dead casual like.

'Why jew wanna know? I fought you said he wasn't your dad no more.'

'I didn't say that. I jus said I wasn't sure.'

Dog blew smoke and grinned and readjusted his wayward bollocks. 'Might not be the same bloke, though, right? Could be someone totally different.'

'Could be,' he said. 'Where is it then?'

'Sounded like it was a very pricey boat this one. Which suggests your daddy's loaded, don't it?'

'If it's him . . .'

'See, I've been thinking. You get a woman in the club right, you scarper and don't hear nuffin about it, then like fifteen years later this ugly little bastard – no offence intended – shows up and says, "You're my dad." You see what I'm driving at? He's not gonna want to know, is he? So what's he gonna do? Eh?'

'How jew know any of that?'

'Simple. Cos if I lived in a big ouse like he's got and ad a nice big yacht and a nice sexy little wife and a couple of nice little kids and you turned up on my fucking door-step and said you was my kid I'd cut my fucking throat.'

'Well, you're not im.'

'Any bloke'd be the same. It's male instincts, right? Blokes don't want kids like women do. Specially not if they're like you.'

'Fuck off.'

Dog lit a third Marlboro off the stub of the previous one.

'Get off my fucking fags – I've only got two left now.'

'No you haven't – you've got four hundred under your stinking fucking bed.'

'You've been looking frough my stuff!'

'Your thievings.'

'You can talk!'

Dog puffed on the Marlboro. 'My line of thinking goes like this: we find your daddy – we say, "This is your kid. You give us money or we tell your wife about you and the kid's muvver. We tell all your posh friends how you deserted that poor pregnant woman who loved you so much. We tell your boss how you liked being spanked and having a dildo shoved up your arse when she was gobbling you off – "'

'You don't know all that!'

'Doesn't matter. Cos we've got you as leverage, right. He's gonna do what we say or we're gonna blow is nice cosy little world to bits.'

The hideous malignity of Dog's grin was the worst he had ever seen. Like a cross between a pit-bull and a cobra.

'What's all this "we"? What's it got to do with you?'

'Cos I know about is boat and where it is.'

'So? You don't know it's him anyway.'

'Which is why you're so interested in it.'

'No I'm not.'

'I can see right through you. Your fucking tongue's hanging out.'

'All right then – where is it?'

Dog leant back in the chair and sucked the smoke up from his fat mouth into his nostrils. 'What – so you can go and see daddy all on your own then? And leave me out of the deal.'

'He's my dad!' he protested. 'Why don't you jus tell me? Maybe I don't want no money from im.'

'I do though.' Dog grinned.

'That's not fair. What's it got to do wiv you? Why can't you leave me alone? How would you like it if it was your dad?'

'So he is your dad again now then?'

He said nothing. Dog's debating technique seemed once more to have outwitted him. More than ever he wished to obliterate his sister's boyfriend from the face of the planet.

'You ave a think about what I've said,' Dog said, rose from the chair, and lit another Marlboro.

'Get off my fucking fags, you cunt,' he said.

Dog went out of the door.

CHAPTER SIXTEEN

'I'M NOT IN AT THE moment. Leave a message after the opening bars of the "Eroica".'

'Er, Mr Savage, it's me – Gaz – Gary – Hoskins, you know, your son. I've got to talk to you – it's really important. Please. I don't want nuffing, honest. This bloke – he's found out, like about you being my dad. I didn't wanna tell im, but he made me. He's gonna try and blackmail you like. Honest, I told him to fu – to not do it like, but he won't listen. He's a fu – he's a total headcase. I'll come up to your place this evening like – you've got to talk to me. This isn't a wind-up. I'm really serious. Honest. He's fucking crazy – he beats people up like just for a laugh. I'm not joking.'

Dorian sat at his desk, the answering machine, a stiff gin and the Presidentes spread before him on the embossed leather surface. He wondered which of the conspirators had penned this little fiction, with its ill-disguised sub-text of violence. It would be Colin. It had all the unsubtle hallmarks of Nutter's stupid and crude brain. He was very impressed by idiots who savaged foreigners at international football matches and punched people in public houses; thought people like this – 'total headcases'; he could just see Colin savouring that particular *bon mot* – were intimidating, whereas he, Dorian, knew that they were losers, no-hopers, trash.

He had, fifteen minutes earlier, explained the situation to Rebecca. It had been she who first listened to the message with an expression of dumb incomprehension on her pretty face, so there had really been no option. She was now watching television in the sitting room and drinking one of her hideous cocktails.

He walked through into the hall and inspected the screen of the video monitor on the gate. No one. He walked through into the sitting room and poured another g-and-t.

'Perhaps he won't come,' Rebecca said.

'I don't know what they're up to,' he replied. 'I'm going to sort this out though. Today.'

'It seems really strange,' said Rebecca. 'I just can't imagine you with a son – particularly that old. You must have been very young when – '

'Can it, will you? I've already told you. There's no way he's mine. You know how careful I am.'

'Accidents do happen.'

'I said shut up.'

Despite the rain he opened the french windows and marched out on to the patio. He surveyed his beautiful garden in the greyish light. At the far end there was a speck of yellow on the wet lawn, another of Import-Export's tennis balls. He walked the length of the garden and bent to pick it up. He returned to the kitchen and inserted it in the Widowmaker. Ground it for a couple of seconds, extricated it from under the sink, returned into the garden via the utility room and hurled the tattered remnants back over the wall. Teach you to knock your fucking balls in my garden.

Rebecca came out on to the patio. 'He's here. He's by the gate. The boy.'

The bell rang again. He looked at the screen. The gangling youth stood in the rain, bent down with his ear to the microphone. Drops of rain dribbled from the peak of his baseball cap. Dorian pressed Speak and said, 'Yes?'

'Dorian – Mr Savage like?' He was peering up at the camera now. 'It's me.'

'That much is painfully obvious.'

'You've gotta talk to me. Please . . .'

'You'd better come in then.' He activated the electric gates. Slowly they slid open and the boy pushed his way through the thin gap and started lolloping up the drive. He really was the most unprepossessing creature – awkward and ugly and uncouth. If this nightmare had to be visited upon him, could not the Creator have come up with something a little higher on the evolutionary scale?

Gaz felt his trainers scrunching on the wet gravel. They were a brand new pair of Yakasotos – totally serious Japanese gear. They'd cost nearly two hundred quid but were worth every penny. They were so good he kept them on when he went to bed.

His heart was palpitating fast. He ran his hand down his right thigh checking the pocket was undisturbed. It contained the photo of Dorian and Adeline and he didn't want the rain getting at it. It also contained the knife, but not the pooch-pounder: it hadn't seemed like a cool idea, going to your dad's gaff with the muncher.

He had been scrupulous in his preparations for this evening. He'd had a shower and a shave, though the advantages of the latter were doubtful: his face was now the customary post-shaving Somme of scars and scabs. He had left plenty of time for the journey and had taken elaborate precautions to ensure against Dog trying to follow him.

Dog had stopped him on the landing. 'Where you going then?'

'None of your fucking business.'

'Thieving again?'

'Fuck off.'

He had taken a circuitous route to the bus-stop on the Green, grid-scanning the streets behind him as he turned each corner. Waiting for the bus he stayed well-hidden in the shelter. He sat upstairs at the back and scanned the receding road for any sign of Dog's van or Bri's Viva or Nige's Dolomite. It was all clear. He disembarked at the usual place and walked the now-familiar route through the big yellow machines on the road construction site and the squishy marsh of the littered scrubland.

Now he was passing between the Porsche and the Polo and felt no urge to whip out the knife and envy-scratch their flanks. He stood under the portico at the front door and shook his head to clear the rain. This was it. The massive moment. The epic eventuality. He was actually gonna talk to My Dad. A little shiver passed down his spine.

He looked up and saw another video camera peering down at him. Thought: that must be worth a couple of hundred on its own. And the whole place was probably wired up with them. There was no doubt about it. Dorian was seriously fucking loaded. Livin in a fuckin big palace.

The door opened. Dorian was standing there in a dark grey suit – really well-cut, Italian smutter. It was really good having a dad who dressed so sharp – some blokes had dads who looked like lumps of shit.

'Come in.'

'Er – right. Hi – '

'Shut the door behind you, wipe your feet on the mat, and follow me.'

He hauled the soles of the Yaks over the mat. He was going to have to be careful about this sort of thing: one glance and it was obvious the whole place was full of expensive gear. This place was way ahead of any gaff he'd ever burgled.

He followed Dorian along the hall and through a wide pair of doors into a massive room with chairs and sofas and old-style lamps and pictures. There was news on a big TV, and then he saw an incredibly tasty chick – not the same one he'd seen from the bushes outside Savage Life.

'Rebecca, this is Gary Hoskins – that is what you're called, isn't it?'

'Yeah, like. I mean most people call me Gaz but I don't mind.'

'Rebecca, this is *Gaz*.' He spat the word out.

'Hello Gaz,' the chick said and smiled at him. She was totally magazine. Like a bird in a fashion show or a make-up ad.

'Right. Hi,' he mumbled.

'Sit,' Dorian said and pointed at a chair.

The bird spoke again. 'Can I get you something to drink, Gaz? A Coca-Cola or something? Or are you old enough to drink beer?'

Etiquette: it was not a strong point in the Hoskins household. He was rather stranded for the proper response here.

'Yeah, er, like I don't mind beer like.'

'Get him a beer from the fridge,' Dorian said.

This was great: drinking beer with your dad, shooting the breeze, and in an awesome gaff like this. He thought he could get accustomed to this standard of living without too much trouble.

The bird was sashaying out into the kitchen. He tried not to look at her arse too obviously like. Dorian was over at a big table with swirling gold legs, fixing himself a drink.

'It's really great to see you like. I've been really looking forward to it,' he said. This was a line he had rehearsed many times over the last few weeks.

Dorian said nothing.

He plonked some ice from a silver bucket into his glass and came and stood on a rug in the middle of the expanse of cream carpet. He looked at him. 'Who put you up to this?' he said.

'What – like – '

'Who told you I was your father?'

'No one like. Honest. I saw this photo of you – like you and my mum – '

'Yes. I know, thank you. The photograph doesn't mean that I am your father. Do you understand that?'

'No, but – I could tell. And like it was nine mumphs before I was born. Know what I mean?'

'I know exactly what you mean. Let's get a couple of things straight.'

The chick returned from the kitchen with a glass of beer. 'Here you are, Gaz,' she said, and smiled again at him. This was awesome. He thought she was probably the tastiest chick he'd ever actually spoken to. Tastier even than Mrs Nutter. Well tastier. Totally airline hostess. And the way she smiled at him – no one ever did that.

'Fanx. Fanx a lot,' he said.

Dorian circled the room, moving round behind a long yellow settee. 'Firstly,' he said. 'Yes, I did know your mother and I did sleep with her as she has doubtless told you in graphic detail.'

'No, I never talk to er. She's totally spaced out the whole time. I mean she just vegs out in front of the TV all day.'

'Be that as it may. Secondly, I took elaborate precautions against impregnation.'

'What?'

'I always wore a condom. You know what a condom is?'

'Yeah, course I do.'

'Of course he does,' Rebecca said. 'He's not a little boy, Dorian.'

'I didn't ask for your opinion,' Dorian snapped. 'Thirdly, your mother slept with a great deal of men besides me.'

'Yeah I know but – '

'Your mother, not to put too fine a point on it, was a whore. D'you know what that is? A hooker – a prostitute.'

'Dorian, don't talk like that about her,' Rebecca said. 'You're talking about Gaz's mother.'

He looked icily at her.

'Yeah, I know,' Gaz said. 'I seen these pictures.' This was not going the way he had planned it at all. 'But the dates, and like I said, you know, there's this test – kromothings – what're they called?'

'Chromosomes,' Rebecca said. 'Genetic finger-printing. That's a very astute point, Gaz. Did you learn about that in a biology lesson at school?'

Dorian looked at her. His disbelieving expression said: Whose fucking side are you on all of a sudden?

'No, I saw this thing on TV. Like about how these scientists can look at a bloke's spunk – I mean, er, his – '

'Sperm, I think you mean,' Rebecca said. 'Spermatozoa. Yes, I think I saw that programme too. It was very interesting.'

'Yeah?' This was totally blowing him out: talking about this kind of stuff with a chick like Rebecca. He felt his cock hardening down in the parachute trousers.

'Yes, it was fascinating. Apparently it's just like a finger-print. Completely individual. They can tell with absolute certainty if someone is someone else's father, for instance.'

Dorian made a snap decision: when he had got rid of the brat he was going to beat Rebecca senseless: if this was her idea of a joke she was going to have to have her sense of humour radically overhauled.

'Have you finished the science lesson?' he asked.

Gaz glugged at the cold beer which was still grasped in his hand. He really liked the chick: imagine like if she was your mum.

'Well, it would settle the matter, wouldn't it, Dorian?' said Rebecca.

'I don't believe this. If you think I'm sticking my dick in the end of a test tube on the say-so of this – this . . . Will you shut up for a moment?' Dorian turned back to him. 'There is absolutely no way you could be mine – get that into your head once and for all. Now, I want to know – I want a straight answer: did Colin put you up to this?'

'Colin?'

'Colin Nutter. He lives in the same street as you.'

He had to think carefully about this: had Dorian sussed the burglary? Was he about to get dumped in the shit? 'No,' he said. 'Honest. I've never talked to im. But I saw this picture – my sister's boyfriend, right, I was helping him move some stuff – he works for Mr Richardson, right – '

'I'm not following you.'

'Like doing burglar alarms, you know – '

'Colin was having a burglar alarm installed?'

'Yeah. And I was helping Dog move this – '

'Dog?'

'Yeah, he's the bloke I was trying to tell you about. Like he made me tell im. I ad to. He was gonna beat me up. But, you see, I was moving some gear for him in Mr Nutter's house, right? And I sees this photo of you and im together and I recognized you from the uver photo – the one of you and my mum.'

'Yes,' Dorian said ruefully.

'So that was how I found you like.'

'You asked Colin who I was?'

'No – I – I followed im to work, and then I sees your name on the sign and I sees you getting in the car wiv – wiv this girl, see.'

'That sounds like good detective work, Gaz,' said Rebecca, whose interest-level had just gone up a number of notches. 'How's your beer going? Shall I get you another one?'

'Oh, right, yeah, fanx – '

'Sod the fucking beer,' Dorian said. 'Your brilliant bit of investigation does not make you my son.'

'No, but – '

'You're telling me Colin Nutter doesn't know you're here?'

'Yeah, like I said – '

'And how about your mother?'

'No, like I said – '

'Stop saying *like I said*!'

'Sorry like.'

Rebecca had returned from the kitchen with another can

of cold beer. 'Here you are, Gaz,' she said. 'Tell me about when you saw Dorian getting into the car with a girl.' She smiled radiantly at him – it was like an angel. An angel giving you a cold can of Stella. Totally TV ad. 'What did this girl look like?'

'Shut up, will you, Rebecca! I'm trying to tell the brat that I'm not his fucking father.'

'I don't think you're setting a very good example with your language. Don't mind him, Gaz. He's got a filthy temper.'

What if she fancied him? Didn't older chicks sometimes fancy younger blokes? It was unthinkable. It was unthinkable but that didn't stop him thinking about it. He was starting to feel a bit pissed from the beer on an empty stomach. He'd only had one Snickers all day cos he was so steamed up about coming out here. Now his brain was on fire: full of these crazy fucking thoughts.

'Shut up, Rebecca.' Dorian came round and sat on the yellow sofa opposite him. 'Gaz,' he said. 'It's not that I'm unsympathetic to your situation. You've had a very unfortunate upbringing. It can't be nice not having a father, not even knowing who your father is. I understand that. But I want you to understand that *I* am *not* your father, that I couldn't possibly be your father.'

'But if you did this test – '

'Will you listen to me? I'm sorry for you, and I'm prepared to help in any way I can. What I'm going to do is go through into my study and get £200 which I'm going to give to you to do what you like with. Then you're going to go, and we're going to say Sayonara, Ciao, Goodbye. Have you got that?'

'But like I said, I don't want no money. Honest.'

'All right then. We're going to say Goodbye now then. Finish your beer and then you're going to skedaddle. I'm sorry, but that's how it is.'

'But you can't know you're not my dad – you can't!'

'I can, and I do. Now get that into your head and stop pestering me. Drink the beer and then you're going.'

He glugged at the Stella. It was cold on his teeth and bubbles came down his nose. He had to think fast: this couldn't be it. Dorian couldn't just chuck him out now, not after all he'd done to find him and get here. He felt a great wave of emotions coming over him – mangled, weird, confused emotions all jumbled together. He wanted to cry like his near-namesake Gazza because his father wouldn't acknowledge him – he wanted to get angry and smash his father's face in – he wanted to look at Rebecca's face because it was so beautiful and she was so nice to him – he wanted to look at Rebecca with no clothes on and stick his cock in every orifice on her body till gallons of spunk poured out into her – he wanted – he wanted – he didn't know what he wanted any more.

He was sitting forward in the chair now, grasping the beer glass. 'But if you just did this test,' he blurted. 'That's all I'm asking. What if I am your son? You can't know I'm not! You can't! If I'm not I'll go away – I'll go away and you'll never ave to see me again. I promise. But you can't just chuck me out – you've gotta do this test. Why won't you if you're so sure? It's cos you aren't! You don't know!'

He realized there were tears coming out of his eyes but he didn't care any more.

'Out,' Dorian said. 'Out now.' He pointed towards the door. His face was bright red, his eyes staring murderously.

'All right, I'm going, but I'm not gonna stop. *I'm not.*'

He started towards the door.

'Shouldn't I give him a lift to the station or something?' Rebecca said. 'How did you get here, Gaz? Do you need a lift anywhere?'

'You're not giving him a lift,' Dorian said firmly.

'I'll give him a lift if I want to.'

'You've drunk too much. You'll get stopped.'

'I've only had two. I'm going to give him a lift. It's raining. Come on, Gaz, I'm giving you a lift.'

'All right, give him a fucking lift then. Just get him out of this fucking house.'

Dorian stomped through to his study, slamming the door behind him. It was obvious he was pretty pissed off.

He thought fast: even in this maelstrom of emotions he retained one rational objective. He said, 'Like can I go to the bo – the toilet?'

'Of course, Gaz. There's a downstairs one, through there on the left.'

He went down the hall, eyes swivel-searching the walls and the open doorways for any clue. Nothing. He locked himself in the bog and pointed his dick at the white bowl. There wasn't much time left. He must find out. Maybe Rebecca would tell him. Then he eyeballed the huge framed photograph on the wall above the cistern. Dorian and Rebecca and some other people standing on this boat. The boat was called the *Hustler*. It was unbelievable.

Sitting in the passenger seat of the Polo, right next to Rebecca, whose sexy expensive perfume he could smell, he thought: What if people could see me now? Driving along with this chick like this? What'd they think then? He said, 'Why won't he have the test? That's all I want. I didn't want is money, did I?'

'I know, Gaz. That was very noble of you. Dorian thinks money's all anyone's interested in. People like Dorian think money solves every problem.'

Yeah, he thought. There's a few problems I could sort if I had his kind of bread.

She backed the car up; the security gates whirred open. The car wove quickly through the green lanes of Barrett Meadows, through the rain and the sodium light and the fallen leaves, bumping over the sleeping policemen. He thought Rebecca had probably lied: it seemed like she was quite pissed. But he was quite pissed too so he couldn't really tell. The car rose up on to the slip-road and whizzed under a canopy of trees. The wipers swished back and forth in front of his eyes.

'If I were you, Gaz, I'd forget all about Dorian. He isn't a nice man. You wouldn't want him for a father. I should get on with your own life.'

'But . . . I don't know . . .'

'Who was the girl he was getting into the car with when you saw him, Gaz?'

So that was her game: now he understood. But fuck it – he didn't owe Dorian any favours now. Anyway, if she wanted info from him she was gonna have to cough up herself. 'I don't know, but I reckon they was – you know, like – '

'I know, Gaz. Was she tall, with blonde hair?'

'Yeah, yeah, that's right.'

'Thank you, Gaz.'

The car looped round a roundabout: he recognized it and knew they were near the bus-stop. He was going to have to do it now.

He sounded well casual, totally laid-back. 'I saw this photo of a boat in the bo – in the toilet like.'

'That's Dorian's little hobby, Gaz. Boating. I find the whole thing terribly tedious.'

'Yeah?' He paused ruminatively. 'Where's that then? The boat.'

'Bradwell, in Essex. It's a horrible place.'

'Right.' A total result: the full spec.

They approached the bus-stop, the desolate shelter at the side of the dark road. The wind was blowing through the trees.

'You'll be all right here? Do you need some money for the bus?'

'No, I got some.'

She pulled the car into the lay-by and reached round to the back seat for her handbag. He smelt the leather and the perfume. She switched the overhead light on and took her purse from the handbag. She was so beautiful he couldn't look at her this close. She was so beautiful it made him want to buzz his eyes out.

A car rolled past them on the road. In the light he glimpsed the edges of a gold Amex card and other serious plastic. And a great wad of notes, twenties and fifties. The thought flashed up: mug her. He instantly crushed it back into his brain. Mug this awesome chick who was being so nice to him? What was wrong with his fucking brain to make it come up with ideas like that? He must be fucking sick. He needed a psychiatrist if he could go round thinking stuff like that.

Rebecca pulled a handful of notes out.

'Take this. Buy yourself some clothes or something. Please take it.'

'Fanx, but I don't want money like. Like I said.'

'I know you don't, but take it all the same. For me. I want you to have it. As a present.' And she was pressing it into his hands. He felt her hands on his.

'Like, are you sure?'

'Please take it. Goodbye, Gaz. I'm sorry your day's been so disappointing. Believe me though, it's for the best. You'll understand that one day.'

He looked at her face; her eyes were damp like she was nearly crying. And then he found he had got out of the car without knowing he'd done it, and Rebecca waved briefly, and the car pulled away into the darkness.

He thought he must be in love with her. He'd never felt this way about anyone, not even Norman Bellwether.

He rifled through the notes – fifty, seventy, ninety – nearly £200. He couldn't believe it: it was nearly better than nicking. Rebecca just *gave* it to him. He hadn't even asked.

He wished he was rich. If he was rich maybe he'd just go round giving money to people. It was unbelievable. No one would believe it, would they? This really beautiful chick just gave me £200. They'd think he nicked it. It was weird.

Totally weird. God, he felt a bit pissed. Actually he felt very pissed. All these thoughts were sort of zooming round his head like flies.

He vandalized the wastebin by the bus shelter and then felt a bit better.

CHAPTER SEVENTEEN

RICHARDSON HAD observed the foregoing with the binoculars from his tree. This is what he had seen:

An agitated Savage, drinking more than usual, pacing the rooms, coming out into the garden, finding a tennis ball, mutilating it inside the house (method unknown) and then throwing it back over the boundary wall into the tennis court.

A scruffy youth arriving at the gates and being admitted. Savage and the girl (Rebecca Christina Stansfeld – he had ascertained her name by getting an acquaintance in the Met to run a check on the Polo's registration) talking to the boy and plying him with beer in the living room. An argument ensuing; Savage storming out; Stansfeld taking the youth out to her car –

This was the moment when he had decided to tail them. He abseiled down the trunk, crouch-ran through the scrub, vaulted the fence, snake-crawled the bottom of the tennis court, hacked through the undergrowth and was back in the Avenger in a total journey-time of seventy-three seconds. This was the best he had done yet. The girl's car had already disappeared, but there were only two directions it could have taken. He gambled on the London road and gear-changed through the sleeping policemen. He took the feeder towards the motorway, hit the roundabout, and was proved correct. The Polo was just rounding the corner into the old London road.

He slowed, leaving a good fifty yards between the two

vehicles, and tailed the Polo. After a quarter of a mile it pulled up at a bus-stop; he passed, turned the corner, killed the lights, shut down the engine and rolled on to the bank. He took the binoculars and crawled to a surveillance position in the scrub. The light was on in the car – either it had been switched on or the door on the girl's side was partially open. The girl looked upset. She was taking something from her handbag. He fine-tuned the focus on the binos. She gave the youth a wad of money. Drugs – it was an obvious deduction. The youth got out of the car and it pulled away. He decided to watch the youth for a moment, it being a safe deduction that the girl would return to the house.

The youth demolished a litter-bin in a frenzy of mindless destruction. He kicked it off its moorings and crushed the metal under his enormous trainer-style footwear. A splay of litter was vomited out on to the road and drifted away under the sodium light. Lilt cans rattled over the tarmac like a modern, more raucous version of the Aeolian harp. The scene confirmed his views on the violent instability of contemporary youth. Was it the drugs that did this – or Chernobyl, as he suspected? He had no time further to speculate on these theories because a bus had pulled in and the youth was boarding it. He waited until it had gone and walked to the Avenger.

He drove back to Barrett Meadows where it was now dark. With a torch he took the familiar route through the foliage and the tennis court, where he pocketed the multilated ball in case it should prove significant. He gained his position in the tree and confirmed the girl's presence in the living room. She was standing and speaking in a heated manner. Savage came into view. They were arguing. Savage struck the girl, a hard slap on the side of her face which nearly knocked her over.

He puzzled over what this might mean.

For a moment the two figures moved out of view. When they reappeared Savage was angrily wiping liquid from the front of his suit. The girl was berating him. He flew at her once more, swinging wildly with an open palm. The girl went down on to the floor behind the settee. Savage stood above her, pointing his finger and shouting. He reflected that it was a good double-glazing installation: he could detect no sound.

He reflected too on the extraordinary quantity of violence he had witnessed this evening, far more than ever seemed to occur in Shepherd's Bush. The girl got to her feet and ran out of the room.

He discounted the drugs. He now had a new theory to account for the events he had witnessed: the youth was the girl's indigent younger brother who had come round to scrounge money. Savage sensibly did not wish to encourage his decadent lifestyle and had thrown him out; the girl, harbouring sentimental feelings for her sibling, had driven him to the bus and given him cash.

He waited five minutes: a light went on in the bedroom upstairs; he caught a glimpse of the girl hurriedly tugging garments out of a fitted wardrobe. Ten minutes later she bundled two suitcases into the back of the Polo and drove off into the night. She was leaving Savage.

This, he reflected, was useful: murdering Savage at home with the girl about had always presented something of a problem. The task would now be considerably simplified.

Gaz debussed at the Green and went straight into McDonald's for food. He walked up the Uxbridge Road masticating a double portion of Chicken McNuggets. He was still feeling pretty weird. Back in the house he walked straight into Christie outside the kitchen. 'Mum wants to talk to you,' she said.

His tongue excavated a piece of McNugget from the back of his teeth. 'Why?' he said monosyllabically.

'I dunno – probly about school.'

He felt sordid: he looked about him and contrasted all this with the grandeur and opulence of Dorian's house where he had been no more than an hour ago. It wasn't fair. It wasn't fucking fair.

The sound of the TV increased as his mother's door opened. 'Where ave you been?' she said.

'Mars,' he said.

'Ha ha – comic now are we?'

He said nothing.

'Come in ere – I wanna talk to you.'

If only she knew, he thought. About Dorian's house and Rebecca and the money and the weird scene in the Polo. That would totally freak her. It was good having secrets. Then, for the first time, he thought: Why did Dorian use to fuck her when he could have beautiful, lovely chicks like Rebecca? Maybe Dorian didn't have so much cash in those days – that must be it.

He went into his mother's room. 'You've been going frew my photographs,' she said. 'You don't touch nuffing of mine unless I say it's all right.'

How could she know? It had been weeks ago and he'd only taken two and put everything back exactly as he'd found it. She couldn't know. He decided to front it out.

'I avēn't touched nuffin,' he said.

'I come back from the chemists and find my drawers turned upside down, it's pretty fucking obvious,' she said.

Dog: it had to be Dog. Dog digging for evidence. Dog leaving his customary trail of ruin. He was about to incriminate his sister's boyfriend when the possible ramifications of this occurred to him. If he blabbed on Dog, Dog would blab on him (and probably hurt him too).

'I dunno what you're talkin about,' he said.

'You know fuckin well what I'm talkin about,' his mother shouted.

He could feel the photographs in his thigh pocket, next to the £200, burning a hole.

'It wasn't me,' he said.

'Who was it then?'

'How should I know?'

'What d'you want?' she said.

'I don't know what you're talkin about.'

'Yes you do. You still tryin to find out oo your dad is, is that it?'

'No,' he replied, with what seemed to him awesome insouciance.

'Dog's been asking questions.'

'I don't know nuffin about it.' This was great: like taking the fifth amenity.

She looked at him strangely. 'It won't do you no good – don't you understand that?'

'I don't know what you're talkin about.'

'Are you gonna go to school tomorrow? I don't want you getting in trouble. Can't you just go sometimes? When the lessons are all right.'

'What's it to you?'

'I'm your mother, aren't I? They'll take you away, you know. They'll take you to one of them pin down places.'

'They won't get near me. I'm too slippery,' he said. He walked out feeling totally righteous.

He went into his room and barricaded the door with the chair so no one would barge in on him. He stashed the photos and the cash under the mattress, put 2 Ded Krew on the headphones and curled up on the bed in a tight ball with his hands around his head. So much had happened today that he had to think about. It all went round in circles in his head. There was so much he couldn't figure which bit to begin with. Dorian, Rebecca, Dog, his mother – it was all totally weird.

Richardson tested the strength of the cheese-wire by placing it over a branch of the tree and applying the full force of his rock-like musculature. Pecs and biceps went taut like steel, the veins stood up on his vice-like hands, his face contorted into a savage grimace. He pulled the wire away, took the torch from his pocket and examined the indentation in the mossy bark. It had cut cleanly two or three millimetres into the wood. It was strong enough. He hoped, however, that it would not be necessary to use the wire. His preferred implement of dispatch was a Sabatier knife of the sort he was confident of locating in Savage's kitchen.

It was now raining heavily. He had sat deliberating in the tree for over an hour before persuading himself that this moment presented the perfect opportunity for eliminating Savage. This was not how he had planned the killing, but it was unlikely a better chance would ever present itself. Savage was alone in the house. The girl had left after a violent argument with marks on her face from Savage's blows, thereby clearly indicating that a fight had taken place. In the heat of the moment, what could be more natural? The girl impulsively grabs the nearest weapon – one wild stabbing gesture which proves to be fatal – the slow-dawning horror as she stares at the goggle-eyed carcass slumped on the kitchen floor, gore pumping on to the Kingfisher floor-tiles – the chilling panic – the frantic, irrational drive into the night with the hastily loaded suitcases.

The law would not linger long in their assessment of the situation, especially when they found the Sabatier thrown into the bushes at the side of the road a quarter of a mile or so from the house (precisely the kind of bungled effort at murder-weapon-disposal which would fit perfectly with their reconstruction of the evening's events). The knife would be identified as belonging to the set from Savage's no doubt well-equipped kitchen. The sequence of events would be all too obvious. A spur of the moment crime of passion. He doubted she would get more than a couple of years – if that.

Blame it on PMT or one of those women's diseases. He checked his watch: it was 23.13.

The truth was, he now found himself on the horns of something of a dilemma. He now admitted to himself for the first time that he had never been sure whether or not he would actually go through with the killing. He sat in the rain-beaten tree on the edge of Barrett Meadows, Barbour pulled close about him and binoculars trained on the distant light from Savage's windows, and thought that, frankly, he might not be the killing sort after all. It was certainly true to say that he had never actually killed anybody before, had never been nearer to it than a couple of punch-ups in pubs. Nor had he been in Angola or Nicaragua with anyone called Major 'Mad Max' Muller. He had never been a mercenary of any description. Nor had he ever been in the Army. He had never actually seen a firearm, other than old ones in museums.

In actual fact, he thought he might be a bit funny in the head. It was this awful compulsion he had to invent stories when he was with people. He wanted to talk, and there didn't seem much to say in the ordinary run of things, once you'd exhausted sport, women, the general vagaries of fortune, the collapse of civilization. It was then, in the uneasy silence, in the throat-clearing hiatus, that he found himself making a mysterious allusion to something like his time with 'Mad Max'. It sort of brightened up the conversation for a bit.

It normally was this kind of thing – his imagination seemed positively to teem with gun-fights, throat-slashings, and all manner of bizarre unarmed combat. And once he had started, he felt compelled to elaborate, to justify what it was he had said to start the ball rolling. It was also a fact that he found it terribly exciting to say things of this kind, even if he sometimes regretted it afterwards. It was thrilling to summon up these scenes from his imagination, so thrilling he would often be carried away with his own invention and quite believe in it all himself.

Now that he thought about it, he supposed that he had gone around for a long time now believing rather a lot of it. A lot of it seemed to have become a kind of second nature to him. There were times when, even in the cold light of morning, he wasn't totally sure which things really had happened and which things he had made up. Not all the time, of course – he was positive, for example, that there never had been anyone called 'Mad Max'. He wasn't sure what had suggested it to him. Perhaps he had simply made it up.

If he was honest, he supposed he was what people called a bullshitter. It was a terrible thing, but there it was. It all seemed to go back rather a long time. As a boy he was always telling whoppers. Later he was always alluding to deep dark secrets to do with criminals and international conspirators. It was one of the reasons he'd been fired from his job as a Clerical Officer for the Inland Revenue – some indiscreet remark overheard by a superior in a pub near the office. He had borne no grudge – he could see the man's point of view. He had signed the Official Secrets Act, for Christ's sake. You had to take official stuff like that seriously or it meant nothing. He enjoyed signing pieces of paper, important-looking pieces of paper like that. It was like joining the SAS or something. But sometimes he just didn't seem to be able to keep his mouth shut. That was the problem.

He now thought – it was a distressing realization – that all of this might not be wholly unrelated to the fact that he did not seem to have any friends to speak of. Not *real* friends, the way other people had real friends. People who were always touching him for drinks, certainly; but it was pretty obvious to him that they did not constitute proper friends. Anyone would talk to you if you were buying them drinks, especially some of the wasters and paddies he ended up talking to in pubs. This had never actually occurred to him before this evening, but now that he did think of it it made sense. Even the people he bought drinks for never remained long after they had had their fill. Of course they didn't: they were bound to be put off after a while. If you were always telling lies, making things up. It was hardly to be wondered at.

It was extraordinary that he had never thought of any of this before. The strange brush-offs, the phone calls that were never returned, the indistinct laughter that stopped the moment he came back into the room. Now it all fitted into a pattern. Of course! People were laughing at him behind his back.

His mind returned now to the evening he had spent with Nutter. Nutter had come with the money. Nutter clearly believed what he had said – or else he had been calling his bluff. But that did not seem very likely. That seemed highly improbable. Why would he wish to do such a thing? So the question was this: was he going to go back to Nutter with the grand (plus interest) and say, 'Sorry, mate. I can't take the job after all. Circumstances beyond my control.' This would not look very impressive, would it? They had a deal – a contract. Christ knows what Nutter might do if he reneged on it. Nutter might even send someone after him, Richardson. Anything was possible, he supposed: the man was clearly mad enough to do it. No, he could not see a way out of it now. He was going to have to go through with the killing.

He looked at his watch: 23.47. Nearly midnight. Savage was still abroad.

Fortunately there was one thing he had not deluded himself about: he did know about burglar alarm systems and did not think there was any kind he could not safely penetrate. He had subjected Savage's security precautions to his professional appraisal – it was a kind of system he had himself installed a dozen times – and knew there would be no problem getting into the house.

He did a last-minute mental check on everything: his gloves, the Barbour (which would be burnt in case of any blood traces), the cheese-wire in one pocket, the pliers, torch, chisel and other equipment in the other. Everything was in order. He pulled the mask over his face, abseiled down the tree and secreted the binoculars in the scrub for collecting upon his return. He moved to a position where the wall was invisible from the house, concealed behind the bank of *Cupressus*.

The grapple secured itself atop Savage's wall on the first throw. He scaled the wall, masked the torchlight and located the electronic sensors concealed in the ridge of the wall. These were easily rendered impotent with a generous squirt of shaving-foam. Avoiding the splodges of white dimly visible in the moonlight, he climbed on to the top of the wall and pulled the rope up behind him. He lowered it into the garden and clambered down into the abrasive foliage of the wet *Cupressus* trees.

From the edge of the trees he could see the lights still on in the living room. He moved cautiously through a bed of shrubbery, the torch scanning the soil for security devices. From where he stood there was now an exposed twenty-metre stretch leading to the patio. There was a small element of risk involved in crawling to a position of concealment behind the barbecue. He watched the window for one minute; there was no movement. On knees and forearms he scuttled over the moist grass and crouched behind the barbecue. He could smell the wet charcoal ashes. He realized he was dying for a cheroot. It would have to wait now. Again he waited for any indication that Savage had seen him. None came.

Skirting the light cast from the window he moved stealthily to the wall beside the french windows and nestled silently against the dying honeysuckle. He squatted down and surveyed the window. Now he heard water running down the drain from the upstairs bathroom. Savage was upstairs. He had come prepared with wire-cutters and the other equipment, should it prove necessary. But, in his professional experience, there was nearly always a simple fault in security systems of this kind: human error. He was ninety per cent certain that Savage would not have locked the door of the small room beyond the kitchen when he returned from throwing the tennis ball over the wall.

To test this hypothesis he now moved quickly round the outside wall. He stopped outside the luminescent kitchen windows and looked in. He was well versed in the matter of the kitchen equipment belonging to people of Savage's socio-economic group, and was here proved correct: the first thing his eye lit upon was a magnetic rack bearing half a dozen black-handled knives. French equipment, he was certain of it. It was the sort of sophistication he expected of people like Savage. He admired it: he admired people who had standards.

He crouched and moved under the window. Outside the door he listened for a moment. He tried the handle and the door swung open. He stepped quickly into a utility/laundry room. He had been right. He shut the door silently behind him and listened once more. The faint hum of kitchen machines, the distant strains of a symphony wafting down the hall from the living room. Schubert, he believed. This was good: it indicated that Savage had not yet retired to bed. He did not want the messy business of killing him in the bed and then removing the corpse to the kitchen (where it was that the girl would have impulsively seized the knife from its rack and done the deed).

He carefully wiped his feet on the mat and tiptoed to the half-open kitchen door. He listened. He stepped into the kitchen. Tacked to the front of the fridge-freezer unit was a diet-plan brightly illustrated with pictures of apples and cucumbers. He walked to the knife-rack. His gloved hand slipped the longest of the knives from its magnetic band. He moved to the kitchen door and listened again. The slow movement. Andante.

He walked into the hallway. By the front door he could

see the video monitor, a desolate view of the spotlit tarmac beyond the gate, streaks of rain catching the cold light. He looked up the stairway then moved down the hall to the living room. On the cream carpet the damp patch where the girl had thrown her drink at Savage. Savage's drink unfinished on the long glass table next to a plant. He reflected that Savage would never now finish that drink.

He stepped back into the hall and heard the distant hooting of a car horn, then the sound of a door closing upstairs. He moved quickly back to the kitchen. On the monitor screen he saw headlights dazzling the camera. He heard Savage's feet thumping down the stairs and stood behind the door with the knife clasped firmly in his hand. Through the crack he saw Savage's back, clad now in a clean shirt. Savage pressed a button on the monitor. He was admitting the car through the gates.

He knew that something had gone awry with his plan. Had the girl returned so soon? There was no accounting for the mess produced by human passions. He waited. Outside he heard the tyres on the gravel. Savage opened the front door. He felt the gust of cold air waft into the hall.

'Don't honk your fucking horn at this time of night,' Savage shouted. 'This is a respectable fucking neighbourhood.'

A woman's voice replied: 'It's raining, Dorian. I'd have got wet. I couldn't reach your bell-thing.'

He could not see her as she entered.

'Well don't do it again, you're not in Knightsbridge now.'

'If you're going to be like that I'm going to go straight home.'

The door shut behind her. There was a muzzled sound – kissing. He was now certain this was not the same girl who had departed earlier. One girl had gone so Savage had telephoned another one. There were men like this, he had heard: couldn't last a night without it, got a headache if they didn't have a woman. Kennedy had been that way. It was a dependence – like a drug.

'Are you going to get me a drink, darling?'

Drink: that would mean ice: that would mean Savage coming into the kitchen. He clasped the knife tight.

'What d'you want?'

'Brandy'd be nice.'

Brandy: people did not generally drink brandy with ice.

Savage and the girl were moving down the hall. She parked her coat on a chair. She was blonde, a tall, leggy blonde like that tart who was shacked up with Mick Jagger – she was not Rebecca Stansfeld. They disappeared into the living room.

He reappraised his plans for the evening. There were two choices: kill both Savage and the girl (make it look like the work of the jealous Rebecca), or abandon the whole thing until another occasion. He tried to envisage himself plunging the Sabatier into the woman's guts and could not. He did not think he could kill a woman. It was too messy and complicated. There were too many pitfalls. The girl would start screaming while he dispatched Savage. She might run away. He didn't like it. He decided to leave.

CHAPTER EIGHTEEN

GAZ WOKE EARLY the next morning. It was Saturday. He had been dreaming about Rebecca, Rebecca in a vista his imagination had gleaned from a shampoo commercial. He lay under the mangled duvet and had a quick wank, but his heart wasn't in it: his brain flicked back and forth desultorily, thinking about all the things it had to plan.

He came into a discarded sock, got up, went to the bathroom. He dressed, loading the thigh pockets with knife, mutt-cruncher etc., went out and was about to nick a map when he suddenly thought he couldn't be bothered – he had £200 in his pocket, he might as well buy the map, save himself the hassle. It could actually get quite onerous, this nicking business. He took the map into Alabama Fried Chicken and studied it while consuming a breakfast chicken-chilli burger and draining off two cans of Fanta. He figured a route out to Bradwell, through Barking, Brentwood and Billericay. First thing on the agenda was to nick a bike.

He knew which one he was going to take. It was a Concerto in the garden outside a house he had previously scrutinized with a view to burglary. Most times the occupants went away at weekends, leaving the Concerto unattended and an easy target. Breakfast finished, he proceeded up Uxbridge in the direction of Prendergast Avenue where the object vehicle was located.

Curtains were still drawn, only a few people were abroad. A cat scowled at him from by a Montego: the Yakasoto flailed out at the animal, missing it by millimetres as it scuttled under the motor. He strolled past No 37 looking well nonchalant, like he didn't give a fuck. The house looked empty but he wanted to avoid any fuck-up possibility. He rang on the bell preparing his charmingly waif-like 'Excuse me, Mister. D'you want your car washed?' routine. No one answered. No ruffling of curtains.

He swivel-scanned the street, felt the blood-rush that always came before serious thieving. He chiselled off the lock on the back compartment with one clean blow and there was no helmet: the cunts took the helmet inside the house with them. This meant a change of plan. Either break into the house for the helmet, or go back to Esterhazy for his own (which he'd nicked another time). Someone was coming down the pavement. He went and rang on the bell again, innocent-looking.

'Can I help?' It was the owner, a fat bastard coming up the path with a bag full of milk and croissants and orange juice and newspapers and crap.

He did the car-wash routine.

'Yes, why not? You don't seem to have any things with you though.'

He did the 'I come down the street first then collect my stuff' routine. It was a fucking bore and a waste of time and all he wanted to do was wipe out the bloke for inconveniencing him this way. Carve his face up with the chisel; mash his skull in with the pooch-pounder.

'Well, how much do you charge?'

'Fiver,' he said flatly.

'That's a bit steep – do you wax it for that as well?'

'No,' a blank monosyllable.

'Well, I'm not sure if – '

'All right then.' He started to move away. He had sensed Fathead's squidgy pink eyes examining the rear of the Concerto.

Fats started to give utterance: 'Hang on a moment . . .'

He thought about it for a millisecond, decided to do a runner. It was a pain: it meant he'd have to avoid Prendergast for a while. He set off at max speed, the Yaks pummelling the pavement, the hound-hunter beating against his thigh. After a couple of minutes he came out on Goldhawk and stopped for a rethink. Lit a Marlboro and coughed up half a lung. Made a mental note to return one night to Prendergast and envy-scratch the guy's motor with 500,000 deep gouges for the way he had incommoded him this morning.

The morning was not proceeding with the smooth precision he had anticipated. He considered the possibility of utilizing public transport for the journey to Bradwell. Then discounted it. If only he had a motor. If only he was old enough to have a motor. If only he knew how to drive a motor. A motor. He considered hitch-hiking, and instantly dismissed it. He decided to get off the main road because Chubby would have called the police by now. He crossed over and cut down south towards Hammersmith.

At Hammersmith he went into Smith's and bought a couple of Snickers, a can of Isotonic and a boating magazine he eyeballed on the racks beneath the porn. He grazed the mall for a bit, remembering to give Vinyl Virus a good berth on account of having nicked some tapes there last week. Then he had a brilliant idea: he consulted the map and discovered he could get halfway to Bradwell if he took the tube out to Ongar, changing on to the Central Line at Holborn. An hour and a half later he emerged into the alien hinterland of east London and figured a way of catching a bus to Bradwell. He had a bargain bucket of Pork McRibs while waiting for the bus. The bus drove under pylons, past the General Lee pub and the Rebel Burger Bar and the Fortunes of War pool rooms. He felt a bit weird looking at the fields and the cows and the trees. Couldn't handle that kind of shit. He closed his eyes and thought about Rebecca. Tried to imagine doing it with Rebecca, but his imagination just wasn't up to it. It simply didn't have enough to go on.

Dorian came down the stairs in his silk kimono and made a cafetière of coffee with a new Panamanian bean he had recently come across. He plonked three mangoes, two guavas, a pineapple and two pink grapefruit in the Maelstrom Norwegian-designed centrifugal juicer and set it into action. He switched on the radio: the weather was better today, bright patches expected this afternoon, a bunch of paddies had blown up another bunch of paddies, soap stars were inaugurating a new anti-smoking campaign with accompanying song 'Stub It Out', base rates were up again, and there was a war on in some distant clime.

He switched on to the third programme (as he liked to call it) and stopped the juicer. Tipped the pulp down the Widowmaker and poured the juice into an icy pitcher. On the way out he noticed a muddy mark on the kitchen floor near the fridge. It was obvious that Stan had taken to letting himself in again, making cups of tea and purloining biscuits. He would have words with the gardener, tell him to bring a Thermos if he must guzzle tea during his gardening activities.

He returned upstairs where he woke Natasha, plied her with juice and coffee and outlined his plans for the weekend:

'We tootle down to Bradwell, get some lunch – there's a very presentable seafood place on the way – then take the boat out this afternoon. Be in Boulogne in time for a quick pastis round about six, then toodle down the coast a bit, find some dinner, whatever . . .'

'I've never seen this boat of yours,' sleepy Natasha said. 'It sounds like fun. We don't have to sleep on it though, do we? I can't stand camping and sweaty sleeping-bags and boiling up kettles on those little blue things – '

'Tash,' he said, his voice touched with moral outrage, 'I'm

not talking about some piss-arsed dinghy here. I'm talking two double bedrooms, fully equipped galley, lounge with telly and video and all the works, beautiful bathroom with the Jacuzzi – '

'You've got a Jacuzzi on the yacht?'

'Yeah. I keep trying to tell you.'

'You never tell me anything.'

'Well I am now.'

'Well, if it's got a Jacuzzi I'm going to get straight in it the minute we get there.'

After breakfast the Porsche whizzed through autumnal Barrett Meadows, narrowly avoiding a child playing on a skateboard. North on the M25, past airport, gravel pits, World of Leather, Toys Я Us and the Mega-10,000 Car Boot Sale, a World's Fair of Cavaliers and Maestros. He popped the Fauré Requiem into the in-car CD. Natasha looked pensive.

'So you've completely finished with Rebecca?' she asked.

'Totally. Kaput. Over. It's been going that way for a while, last night just sort of brought it to a head.'

'Why was that?'

'Dunno. Nothing in particular. Tell me something, Tash. What is it with you and Rebecca?'

'What d'you mean?'

'Why d'you hate each other so much?'

'I don't want to talk about it.'

'Was it that pony she did in? Your pony. Is that it – that why you hate her?'

'Yes. I can't forgive her for killing Brutus. Bitch.'

'It was an awful long time ago, darling.'

'Still . . .'

'And that's why you go chasing after her men? That's why you like nicking her boyfriends?'

'That's not true! There's only you.'

'And that Sebastian bloke.'

'She told you about that? Bitch . . .'

The motorway whizzed by at ninety mph.

Families, Dorian reflected. What a fuck-up. Brothers, sisters, parents, kids. That Larkin bloke was right. Natasha spends her entire life hating her sister's guts on account of some pony that got deep-sixed when they were kids. Spends her entire life trying to bed sis's boyfriends because of some dumb pony that ran into a barbed wire fence.

He thought about his own fuck-up of a family, his dying mum, his stupid dad, his dead kid brother (motorcycle accident when he was nineteen and already had a wife and two kids). What a fucking mess.

Then he thought about *it* – the problem, the boy. The throwback. There was something about the whole situation: he knew now. He knew the boy was his.

He exited the motorway near Brentwood.

Monday morning, he resolved. Ring the doctor, arrange a vasectomy. He wasn't going to get caught out again. He imagined getting mad Natasha pregnant, all the terrible consequences that would ensue from that. The poor fucked-up kids.

This procreation business. It was about time humanity stopped doing it, there'd be far fewer problems. In fact, after about eighty years or so there wouldn't be any problems at all and the chimps and baboons could take over the planet.

Gaz had walked about a mile from where the bus deposited him in the middle of this totally backward village. No shops like. The whole place was like out of the old-time TV shows his mother watched all day. He had thought they made it all up, that no one could possibly live in such barbaric circs. Now he knew better: the day was proving a real education.

He surveyed the Blackwater estuary, and felt the weird fishy ozone tang in his nostrils. It was the first time he had looked at a stretch of water bigger than the Serpentine. He took the road to the right and could soon see the distant outline of the marina, the pontoons stretching into the still, glassy water, the sunlight glinting on the white hulls. Up ahead he saw a roadside seafood stand and thought: Awesome, I can get some Fish McNuggets. For some reason he had been unnaturally hungry all day.

He approached the stand and caught the whiff off it, like spunk and bleach. A man was taking a carton from the girl and shovelling these totally horrific pink animals into his mouth, like sucking their bodies out and chucking their heads away. It was disgusting. Then he put the carton down and reached for this black shell and slurped a lump of grey jelly stuff out of it – completely raw like. Then he said, 'Excellent. Just what the doctor ordered.' Gaz wanted to boke. It was unbelievable.

The girl said, 'Can I help?'

He looked at the rows of containers full of these weird fucking stinking creatures out of sci-fi. What – people just ate this stuff like that? It was like eating a cow's eyeballs or something, just sucking them straight out of its head while it stood there.

'No – no, like,' he said, and walked on. There'd be a McDonald's somewhere in the town, something civilized. There had to be: there was a McDonald's in every known corner of the planet.

He took a gravel road down towards the marina. Cars were gathering in a field by the side of the road: kids pouring out of the backs of the cars and demanding ice-creams, fat old bastards with walking-sticks levering themselves out of rear seats with tartan blankets and Thermoses. The gravel turned to concrete and he walked down a gangway leading to the boats. No one stopped him. Maybe it wasn't private or anything. Four long platforms ran out into the water, the boats tied up along them. He grid-scanned for the *Hustler*.

Most of the boats to the right looked pretty tacky, but far over on the left he could make out the big white hulls and the radical electronics. That was where the *Hustler* would be. He walked down the row of boats taking in the specifications: a thunderous Thunderhawk, a totally tyrannical Turborosso, a terrible Tropicana, a wicked Watereagle, a critical Fairline Turbo Carrera, a radical Sea Ray Pachanga Express.

A cap-wearing yuppie swilling some gin gave him the eyeball as he eyeballed the boats. He eyeballed the cunt back like to say, 'I've got as much right to be here as you. My dad's got a more crucial boat than yours.' The guy backed off. He wondered if you could envy-scratch the side of a yacht.

He proceeded down the pontoon, dead insouciant, pimp-rolling on the heavy soles of the Yaks. Then he saw it. He saw Dorian's boat and it totally wiped him out. This was the most critical piece of machinery he had seen. Of course: he would have: My Dad would have the most awesome boat in the whole marina.

The Wolfe Turbo Nemesis. Uncompromisingly individual. The pinnacle of the leisure principle. Fifty-six feet of white streamlined fury.
⋆DeGroat Plotter and Navigator.
⋆TV & Video.
⋆Fjord SeaGod Radar.
⋆Parabolic Viking Autopilot.
⋆Flybridge.
⋆Air-conditioning.
⋆Superb luxurious lounge area.
⋆Two luxury double cabins.
⋆Separate fully-equipped galley.
⋆Two 800hp MAN diesel engines.

He knew all this because he had looked for something like the *Hustler* in the boating magazine while sitting on the tube and had scrutinized the specs. He had no idea what most of it meant, but it sounded extremely serious.

He did not hang about. He scanned the adjacent boats, stepped up on to the side of the *Hustler* and jumped over on to the rear deck. There was a small motorized inflatable hanging from some kind of pulley mechanism at the back of the boat. He remembered it from the spec: it was called a davit. Above his head various aerials, a radar device like a satellite dish, a floppy flag lying limp against the short mast. A ladder leading up to the top deck which was closed off by a hatch. A door leading down into the heart of the boat.

He tried the door. Buffeted it with his shoulder but it was firm. He decided to try the windows and clambered out on to the railing which ran round the boat. He eyeballed through the window and could see all this gear like a recording studio: two TV screens and rows of navigational gear and a steering wheel. It was awesome. He went over the other side, peering down through what was like a plane's windscreen. Tried the windows on the other side, rootled in his thigh pocket for the chisel, worked it into the rubbery surround between the window and the frame and tried to get it loose. There was a catch on the window: if he could get it to click free he'd be able to get a hand inside and release the window. *Click*, it came free. Hand in, open window, shinny in on belly, pooch-muncher catching as his legs come in after him. Up on his feet, window shut behind him. In.

He looked around him. This was clearly the superb luxury air-conditioned lounge area referred to in the magazine. It was well crucial – better than the lounge area in most people's houses. He took in the gear – the cream-coloured fitted sofas, the CD, the video, the mini-bar with all the glasses and bottles secured in racks against glistening mirrored panels. He went walkabout: down into a small kitchen with fridge-freezer, microwave, everything. Down a ladder and into the faint smell of oil and fuel. The engine room at the back. A corridor past a bathroom with a Jacuzzi, a bog, the two bedrooms at the front of the boat.

He went to the drawers and the wardrobes for a rootle and

unearthed some of Dorian's clothes – trousers and shirts, jockeys and a green BC – and felt a frisson of excitement just to touch it. He traded the BC for his own and lay down on the expansive bed, luxuriating in it. Awesome. He headed back upstairs and examined the fridge: took a cold beer from it and crashed on one of the sofas. Glugged on the beer, and surveyed the room with proprietorial ease.

His reasoning went like this: Dorian's my dad, he hasn't got any other kids, ergo it's all going to be mine one day anyway. He took another slug on the can. Stands to reason: it's gonna be mine one day, so I might as well start helping myself now. It's pretty well mine already, right? I've got a right to it. I got a fucking right. He crushed the empty can. He went to the fridge for another, ripped the tab off, took a good glug, belched heavily. Decided he'd go and see if he could get up through that hatch on to the bridge. Then he could stand there with his hands on the wheel and pretend he was steaming through the water at fifty knots.

He was in the passage when he heard the voices. He stopped dead. Felt the thump of a foot above his head. Someone was getting on to the boat. He was about to reach for the mutt-mangler to challenge the intruders: 'Get off my fucking boat or I'll crush you.' Then it occurred to him that in the strictly technical sense it wasn't really his boat either. What if it was some friend of Dorian's? What if it was Dorian himself?

Which it was. He heard a parental sound-byte and belted down the ladder. He stood by the door of the bog and listened intently. A door opened and he caught more paternal vocals:

'. . . by Herman Melville. Coming down here always makes me think of it.'

There was a girl's voice: he ID-ed it from before: the chick in the Porsche. 'I did that at Poly. Module 7: the American Novel. It's the very long one, isn't it? About a whale. I don't think I finished it actually. I read *The Great Gatsby* – have you read that? Robert Redford was in the film.'

Dorian sounded like he wasn't too interested. 'So that was how you wasted the taxpayer's money?' he said.

'That's not fair,' the girl said. 'It was very interesting.'

'Yeah. I'm sure it was.'

'Anyway, I didn't waste the taxpayer's money. Daddy paid the fees because I didn't get very good "A" Levels.'

'You didn't get any.'

'I got a D in Art.'

The girl was moving out of range. She said something but he didn't get much of it except the word *Jacuzzi*.

'Not yet, love,' Dorian said irritably. 'Wait till we're out on the water for Christ's sake. You can spend all afternoon in the thing if you want. Get me a drink then come up here and have a look at this view. Fuck, I always get a hard-on when I've eaten oysters. Was quite embarrassing walking back to the car in these shorts.'

'If you hadn't eaten five dozen – '

'They were good. Anyway, there's some oil or something in them that's good for your kidneys or your liver or one of those bits. I'm just going down to have a dekko at the engines.'

Still clasping his beer, he edged back towards the bedrooms figuring a place to hide. He stood in the doorway of one of the rooms and saw Dorian's feet emerging down the ladder. Dark hairy legs. He's my dad: maybe I'll have tons of hair like that one day.

Dorian opened the far door and switched on a light. He was humming to himself. It seemed like he was in a really good mood, unlike last night. He peeked out from behind the door: his revered pater was toodling with some bits of this massive engine, then he came out again and pushed open the door of the bog. He listened to the paternal piss streaming into the bowl. Horse's bladder.

'Fuck, that's better,' he said, almost like he was talking to him it was so near. Then he went back up the ladder. 'Where's that drink?' he called. Gaz returned to the ladder to hear what was said. 'Look at this,' he said. 'Crushed fucking beer can. How childish.' His heart leapt into his mouth. 'That'll be Colin fucking Nutter. He was drinking this piss last time I came down here. He's probably got a beer can mountain in his house. Idiot . . .'

He resolved to dispose of his own nascent beer can mountain the moment he returned home. Obviously it was not *de rigueur*. Not if Dorian said so.

Now there was a sound of roaring engine, the vibrations humming through the body of the boat. He went to the port-hole and saw the water and the pontoon moving past. The boat hummed over the surface like Thunderbird 2. It turned slowly and rolled over the calm water. This was awesome. The *Hustler* weaved out into the estuary, gathering speed as it nosed towards the sea. You could feel it in your stomach. He took another glug on the beer and wondered if he was going to get seasick. It would be a pain if he boked all over Dorian's awesome boat. Looking down he could see white surf spraying up from the hull. The last fingers of land hovered away out of view. Massive.

How fast can this fucker go? he wondered. The engine roar was heavy now, thrumming in the walls, doing weird things to the beer inside his guts. He wanted to piss but daren't use the bog for fear of apprehension. He had a good idea: he'd finish the can in his hand then point the python into the can and stash it somewhere for later disposal. He went through into one of the bedrooms, glugged the remain-der of the can, leant against the wall to steady himself, pulled his cock out and carefully targeted it at the pear-shaped hole. He zipped up and hid the can in the bottom of the wardrobe.

He looked out of the door, saw the girl's legs coming down the ladder at the other end of the passage. Well tasty. He pushed the door shut, leaving a thin crack to watch from. She went into the bog. The door was open but he couldn't hear the sound of her pissing above the engine roar. She came out of the bog carrying her trousers and panties; in the dim light from the port-hole he was sure he caught a glimpse of bush. He started getting a hard-on, felt the beer swivelling round his brain. The light went on in the bathroom. Sound of rushing water: the Jacuzzi. She came out again and was walking down the passage towards him. He should have made a bolt for the wardrobe but just stood frozen to the spot, wiped out by the whole situation. This time he got a definite, unqualified eyeful of the gingery pubic triangle.

She pushed her way into the other bedroom, inches away from him. When she came out she had a red towel wrapped round her. She went back up the ladder; he waited; she came back down the ladder with a Walkman in her hand, the earphones plugged in her ears. As she dropped the towel he caught a fragment of *tss tss tss*. He got a full load of her firm white bum and a partial side view of tit.

He waited a few minutes, then edged the door open and crept down the passage. Over the engine roar he could detect the burbling of the Jacuzzi water. He remained concealed in the shade and angled his head round until he saw the Jacuzzi in the wall-length mirror. The girl's head was leant back against the edge, and her eyes were covered with what looked like two slices of cucumber. Her arms were stretched languidly over the sides. The Walkman was hissing. He stepped into the doorway and peered at the erupting surface of the water. Tantalizing, momentary glimpses of tit and cunt flashed off the lurching bubbling water.

A clonking sound from above disturbed his erotic reverie. He looked at the ladder. Froze. Saw his father's loafer-clad foot. He beetled back down the passage and pulled shut the bedroom door. Dorian was approaching with a couple of flight bags. It was all right: he'd take them into the big bedroom where the girl had gone. Wouldn't he? No, he wouldn't. He pushed open the door. He was now standing in the doorway. Dorian was standing two yards from him. They were looking at each other. Father and son.

'What the fucking – '

Dorian dropped the bags.

'You little cunt – what the fuck are you doing here?'

'I – I come down like – '

'Shut up! Don't speak.'

Dorian grabbed at his head, clasping the thin tuft of hair which protruded from the rear of the BC. He wrenched. The pain shot right through his teeth. Dorian was behind him, levering his head forwards, shunting him out of the door. They went the length of the corridor. His nose collided with the cold metal of the ladder and a new jolt of pain fired up his sinuses.

'Up,' Dorian said. 'Up the ladder. Now.'

He clambered up, the dutiful son. He was in the superb luxury lounge area. Dorian came up behind him, grabbed at his hair again and pushed out through the open door on to the deck. He fell on to the deck. Dorian was standing over him, bronzed hairy legs sticking out of white socks and blue deck-shoes. There was murder in his eyes.

'How did you get on the boat?'

'Window. I – I – '

'You broke the fucking window?'

'No, I – '

He was trying to get up; he was on his knees when Dorian kicked him in the chest and he fell back. His head hit something. He felt sick and thought he was going to chunder. Dorian kicked him again. He was shouting at him.

'I've had it with you, you little turd!'

He carried on; Gaz couldn't hear what he was saying. Dorian kicked him again, really hard this time, right in the stomach. Then something happened in his head, and he was on his feet and dimly aware that he had the pooch-pounder in his hand and Dorian was backing away from him into the luxury lounge area. He was swinging the mutt-mangler at his father, but it was as though he was watching himself from a distance, like a seagull. He was aware of the sparks spraying all over the place when the dog-destroyer missed Dorian and smashed into a load of electronics. There was a mashed metal sound.

He was chasing his father back out on to the deck. Dorian was grabbing at a long white pole with a hook on the end. He was turning towards him. There was a speck of blood at the corner of his mouth. His eyes were black with hatred. Gaz crouched and swung the pooch-pounder wildly. It was just senseless violence, a whole load of it stored up inside him and now spewing out randomly. He felt the pounder make contact with Dorian's head. A weird sensation of crumpling. It all happened in a split second: Dorian just suddenly wasn't there any more. He was there one moment, and then he wasn't. He had gone overboard. Like.

He dropped the pooch-pounder, grabbed hold of the rail. White surf was pumping out from the back of the boat like a fountain. The engines were roaring. He could feel the sea air blasting the back of his head where Dorian had wrenched the hair. He stared into the white wake. He saw Dorian. Dorian was just a little black blob maybe sixty, seventy yards away. Then the black blob disappeared.

Then he realized Dorian was dead. He had killed Dorian. He had killed his father.

Oh fuck.

It was a few minutes before he could get his head at all straight. He stood gawping at the rushing sea. All he could think was: now I'll never know him. Now I'll never have a proper dad. Cos I killed him. I blew him away.

He backed slowly towards the superb luxury air-conditioned lounge area. Then he went up the steps to the deck. He didn't know where he was going. There was a smell of burnt plastic. He looked at the mutilated electronics. A little grey mouthpiece dangled on a coil of wire like a telephone's. Of course it was like a telephone's: it was the fucking radio. He'd mashed up the radio.

Some of the other stuff wasn't looking too happy either. Lots of red lights were flashing and a bleeper was making a quiet deathly moaning sound. Still, he supposed the damage couldn't be too extensive: I mean, the boat was still going, wasn't it? The boat was still trundling through the sea. He could see it – rushing at him from the other side of the windscreen.

Then he panicked. His guts churned and his head spun. The boat was roaring onward and he was standing here at the scene of the crime. The murder. He knew what he had to do. He ran back down to the deck and looked at the inflatable swinging from the davit. He grabbed the pooch-pounder off the deck and stuffed it into his pocket; changed his mind and hurled it overboard. He saw it plonk into the water. He grabbed hold of the ropes which supported the inflatable. Which one did you pull? He tugged different ways. How the fuck were you supposed to do this? The inflatable came loose. It dropped like a dead weight on to the foamy wake, wobbled on the waves. He looked at it. It was already twenty yards distant. He dived into the water.

Swimming was not one of his strong points, being as how he hated going to the Leisure Centre because everyone stared at his puny white body. But he had a grasp of the basic idea, and started flailing with all limbs the moment he was under the water. He came up gasping for air, shocked by the cold. A wave hit him straight in the face and he choked. It tasted like the crap he had seen the man eating. He bobbed up in the water, coughing his lungs out, trying to see the inflatable. It had disappeared: it had sunk: he was going to drown. Drown or be eaten by sharks and octopuses. He bobbed higher, pumping his feet. They were like lead. A wave crashed over him and then he saw it twenty, thirty yards away.

He knew he had to lose weight or he'd never reach the inflatable. His feet were heavy: the Yaks. No, impossible. Unthinkable. Anyway, it took about five minutes to undo all the laces in normal circumstances. He dug down into the thigh pockets and heaved everything out: chisel, knife – shit: the cash. He'd just turfed the best part of £200 into the water.

He started towards the inflatable. The waves kept coming at him. He did not know how long it took. Maybe ten minutes, and then he was grappling with the side of the inflatable, trying to get in without capsizing it. When he finally got in he lay flat at the bottom sucking in the air. He boked a load of sea-water and lay with his face in the puke. There were gravelly bits of peanut from the Snickers in it and gelatinous splodges of McRib.

Some time passed. When he came round he looked about him. There was sea everywhere he looked. Then he remembered about the sun setting in the west and figured that would be the way to go. He tugged on the cord protruding from the engine and the inflatable lurched up in the water and started whirring round in circles. He got his head round the rudder and zoomed off into the sunset. He hit land on a stretch of empty marshland. There was a power station in the distance. The sky was turning gun-metal grey. He walked two or three miles down a track. Cows peered malignly at him from a field. He came to a village where he found a phone booth and vandalized it for cash. He nicked a bike and got on to a main road that took him to Southend. He dumped the bike and got a train. He was back in Shepherd's Bush by ten, walking down Uxbridge with a double whopper cheeseburger.

'Where've you been, dirt-box? You stink. You honk like a fucking cesspit,' Dog said.

'Fuck off.'

'Where've you been?'

'France.'

'Fuck off.'
'You fuck off.'
'Fuck off.'
'Fuck off.'

CHAPTER NINETEEN

COLIN WOKE UP EARLY and wondered about the fate of the £1000 which had mysteriously disappeared the night he got pissed with Richardson.

It had been nagging at him for over a week, and there were only two ways he could account for it. Either someone had stolen it (only how had they managed to inveigle it out of his wallet and replace the wallet in his trouser pocket where he had found it the next morning?), or he had lost it in the snooker game with Richardson. He did not recall a great deal about the snooker game with Richardson. He had a faint remembrance of a blue he had potted, and then a rather distinct impression that he had not potted much at all after that.

He had to find out what had happened. He would contact Richardson, suggest another beer and get out of him precisely what had happened that evening. He probably wouldn't get the money back, but he wanted to assure himself that it had been lost in the manner he supposed. Who knows? Maybe he could challenge Richardson to a game of darts (at which he fancied himself extremely proficient) and win back at the okky some of what he had lost on the baize.

Over breakfast Kate said, 'What are you doing today?' She meant, 'Are you going to manage to find a job today?'

'Got a few appointments,' he said vaguely.

'Oh . . .? Where?'

'Round the place.'

He was ostentatiously eating a huge plate of egg, bacon and sausages which he had had to buy for himself, and reading something in the *Mail* about football. Sylvester was battling with a pound of prunes and dried apricots. Jessamy was shovelling a bowl of bran and Ultra-Lo goat's milk round a dish.

He lit a Bensons and Kate gazed at him with that strange, other-worldly expression she had developed of late. In the wake of the Richardson/snooker/pissed-out-of-brain night she had not displayed her customary hostility, but seemed rather to have remained entirely indifferent to his every action. She rarely spoke to him, spent great swathes of time up in the bedroom engaged in secretive reading, went out on two or three occasions and returned with no shopping, and was so preoccupied she seemed hardly to register it when he spoke to her. She had not once alluded to the Richardson evening.

He found all this very disconcerting. Then a thought occurred to him, and it struck him it was a thought he should have had a long time ago. Was it not obvious that his wife was displaying all the symptoms of a woman engaged upon an affair with another man?

When the thought did finally surface he put down his coffee and gazed at his wife with an expression of stunned incredulity. It had never crossed his mind before: he just did not think of Kate as the sort of woman who would do a thing like that. He resolved to investigate. He got up and took his coffee through into the living room where he smoked three more Bensons. He waited until she took the children to school, then phoned Castle Security.

'David Richardson, please.'

'He's not here,' a brusque voice replied.

'Can you tell me when he'll be in then?'

'No.'

'You must have some idea.'

Pause.

'Who is this?' the voice asked curtly.

'Friend of his.'

'You don't know where he is?'

'I wouldn't be asking if I did, would I?' Fucking moron.

'Look, I'm sorry, mate,' the voice said. 'Only he's not been in for a few days. Hasn't phoned or nothing. I went round to his place yesterday and no one had seen him there for a while. I was getting a bit worried about him in fact. You haven't got any idea where he might be?'

'No. I can't help.'

'Maybe he's just done a bunk, only that don't seem his line at all. I've never had any problems with him. Very reliable employee, matter of fact. Never sick. Never late. That's why I was thinking maybe he'd had an accident or something.'

'Yeah, well. I don't know.'

'You let me know if you hear anything, all right? You can always get me on this number – ask for Reg Castle. He's a good man, David, I don't want to lose him.'

'I'll do that,' Colin said. 'Can you tell me his address? I'll go and knock him up.'

'Sorry, I can't give out employees' addresses, mate.'

'Why the hell not? I'm trying to help you here.'

'Company policy, mate.'

'For Christ's sake – '

'Look, mate . . . No, listen, I can't go breaking the rules just for you. You get my drift? If I make an exception for you then – '

He dropped the receiver, lit another cigarette. Bureaucracy: it was what was ruining the country. Dorian had said so many times. Then he recollected himself and remembered that he now hated Dorian's guts. It was a problem: he kept thinking of Savage opinions and pronouncements, approving them in his own mind, and then remembering that he hated Savage's guts.

He went out before Kate returned. Aimlessly he drove

round for a couple of hours, sat in traffic smoking and watching other drivers. It passed the time. Down to Hammersmith, out to Chiswick where he stopped and went and sat by the river and smoked three cigarettes. Then it approached eleven and he returned to Shepherd's Bush and proceeded to the Stumbling Block where he ordered a pint of Dopplerbrau and some peanuts.

'Seen that bloke David Richardson in the last week at all?' he asked the barman.

The barman, a morose, pink-eyed twenty-stoner, peered suspiciously at him.

'Don't know him,' he said.

'Tall bloke – comes in here quite a lot. Sort of brylcreemed hair, normally wears a dark overcoat, smokes those cheroot things – '

'Don't know him. Two-fifteen.'

'I know the man,' a man at the bar said. He spoke in a soft Irish brogue.

'Yeah?'

'Always talkin about guns and tings. Military man.'

'That's the one – yeah. Has he been in last week or so?'

'Not to my knowledge,' the man said ruefully, shaking his head.

There was a pause. Everyone looked at the bar. Then the Irishman's companion said, 'He's a fuckin loony if ya ask me. Headcase.'

'He likes to spin a yarn for sure,' the other, more tolerant, replied.

His friend, the hostile one, retorted, 'He talks out of his fuckin arse.'

'Very generous man though,' the other riposted. 'Always buy you a drink if you're a little short.'

'So he can bullshit at ya,' the second ejaculated.

'There's worse crimes than being a little fanciful,' the first rejoindered.

Eventually he ascertained that neither man knew Richardson's address and bade them farewell. He moved on to the Goose Green and the Withered Arms and the Dead Eagle in each of which establishments he met with no more success. At two-thirty he called it a day and returned home. Kate was out. He went up to the bedroom and initiated a comprehensive search of her belongings. After five minutes he found a bundle of papers concealed at the bottom of the drawer which contained her sewing and dressmaking equipment.

They were not what he had feared they would be. They were entitled: *Awake!*, *Now Is the Time for a New World*, *Proclaiming God's Kingdom on Earth*, *Look! I am Making All Things New*, *Life – How did it get here? By Evolution or Creation?* There were ten or twelve copies of *The Watchtower*, each heavily thumbed. He sat on the end of the bed, his brow puckered, and puzzled over this development for a goodly period.

Dog knew Gaz was up to something. The way he was on the Friday night when he came in, red-eyed, unusually belligerent, choked up with emotion. Whatever it was, it was something to do with his supposed father. He resolved not to get excessively pissed and to have an early night so as to be in a position to monitor the boy's activities on the Saturday morning. He persuaded Christie to bed, rogered her, drank one more can of Wobbler and smoked a joint, rogered her once more, then set the alarm clock the way he did on the rare occasions he had to get up before noon for paid employment.

As anticipated the boy rose early and was out of the house ten minutes later. There was no point in following him: like all young thieves, toe-rag was highly sensitized to surveillance, checking behind him every twenty yards, scanning every intersection as he went about his thieving and other nefarious doings. Deduction was the thing: he'd have to work out what the boy was up to. He started in on shit-box's room immediately he saw him through the window, loping off down the street, head twisting automatically back and forth. It took precisely one minute to find the tattered, grease-stained copy of *Boot!*, its margins doodled with inept pictures of boats and the ill-formed words HUSSLER and BRADWEL. He inspected the words and grinned knowingly, then became aware of his bare foot resting on something damp. He craned down to inspect it: it was a freshly spunk-filled sock. He flushed the sock down the bog and washed his foot thoroughly in the basin.

After another hour's kip and breakfast (he was now extending his culinary range to button mushrooms cooked in garlic, grilled Lincolnshire sausages and four slices of black pudding), he took the Transit east along the river and out into Essex. It was a leisurely journey: he stopped for a pint in the General Lee, another in the Fortunes of War. At the marina there was no sign of toe-rag. He parked the Transit in a back street in the town where the boy would not see it, bought a six-pack of Jack Hattersley's Authentic Yorkshire Bitter (another new development, this interest in real ale), located a well-concealed spot in some long grass, and lay basking in the sun while he watched the marina below.

He was on his fourth can, starting to feel the pleasant warm alcohol infusion, when events took a highly unexpected turn. The sinister, dark-coat-clad figure he saw hovering on the distant pontoon – unmistakable in the preposterous sunglasses – was that of Richardson, his occasional employer.

What's he fucking doing here? was what he thought. *What's his fucking game?*

It was like a character from one film showing up in another. He lit a Marlboro and toyed with his ear-ring, scratched his ear, wrenched some mucal matter out of a nostril, balled it up between two fingers and flicked it into the dune grass. He was thinking, punishing the grey stuff. He took another long pull on the Jack Hattersley's.

Richardson knew about the boats at Bradwell – it was from Richardson that he had heard of them. So what was Richardson's angle on this? How did he fit into the picture? Maybe, alternatively, it was just chance: maybe he'd come down to do some boating with Nutter or something. He finished the can and opened a fifth.

Richardson stood looking at a boat for a minute, then started walking down the pontoon, shuffling, looking intently about him. He had a quick dekko down one of the other pontoons, then left the marina and disappeared out of view. Dog stood to piss into the brush and watched him wend his way up towards the town. He waited. He was on the sixth can, dangerously near now to the necessity for renewing supplies, when the gangling figure of his girlfriend's little brother went loping down the pontoon, head still swivelling, legs encased in the ridiculous potato sack strides, disjointed hips attempting their pathetic imitation of a black's walk. He knew where the boy was going.

Sure enough. Here it came. One last scan, and there he went: on to the boat. It would be the boat of the supposed father, and it was the same one Richardson had shown such an interest in ten minutes earlier. He finished can six, was beginning to feel quite pleasantly pissed, and thought now was the time to roust toe-rag, the time to shake him down, hold him upside down and bang his head on the floor until some information dropped out. Anyway, it would be a good laugh to catch him red-handed, right in the middle of his plundering of the vessel. Bang on the door and shout: 'Open up! Police!' Make the little cunt shit in his potato sacks. There was certainly enough room in there for whatever came out.

He started off down the hill, took the concrete path leading to the pontoons, and fell in step behind some twat in shorts, Hawaiian shirt and baseball cap with a delectable bit of blonde crumpet at his side. He stayed in lane to scrutinize the bird's astoundingly well-proportioned arse.

He overheard something about an old man and the sea, then realized they were boarding precisely the same boat: the *Hustler*. *That*, he realized, catching a glimpse of the face, is the bloke the boy reckons is his dad. *That* is about to get a very nasty surprise. Without breaking step he continued to the far end of the pontoon, sat concealed behind some orange lifebuoys with his feet dangling over the water, and awaited developments. A few minutes passed; no sound of disturbance; then the boat pulled out seaward.

A moment later he saw Richardson running down the pontoon. Richardson wasn't looking very clever. He seemed to be looking right at him but he showed no sign of recognition. He waved his arms in the air, like a bird; took a Teachers bottle from the pocket of his overcoat, spun the cap off and swigged. He started walking back up the pontoon. Dog thought: He's pissed. Pissed or mad. He still couldn't get a handle on what Richardson was doing here.

He found a pub in the town, had a few pints, played some pool with the locals, had one more swift pint, and returned to the car-park of the marina late in the afternoon. Richardson was still sitting in the Avenger, cheroot smoke funnelling from the crack at the top of the window, his red eyes gazing out to sea like a crazy loon.

He pondered. He thought about this. Something weird was going on here. Something he needed to know about. While he drove back to town he pushed the grey matter to the limit of its tolerance.

He got in some beers and returned to the house. No sign of shit-box. At ten-fifteen he heard steps and boomed out into the hall. Toe-rag looked like shit and an awful waft came off him.

'Where've you been, dirt-box? You stink. You honk like a fucking cesspit,' he said.

'Fuck off.'

'Where've you been?'

'France.'

'Fuck off.'

'You fuck off.'

'Fuck off.'

'Fuck off.'

Toe-rag retreated to his pit. Dog thought hard: what was happening here? What the hell was happening? He sat up late downing cans at the kitchen table, trying to figure things out.

He was back on the Benzedrine. Sustains you through long nights in the jungle. His whole system was brittle with electricity. He thought if someone touched him they'd probably get burnt. He was sitting in the Avenger with the empty whisky bottle at his feet. He was trying to piece together the events of the last three days. They were important; they were very important, if he could just be absolutely sure what they were.

Friday evening.

He had returned from Savage's house, back through the garden and over the wall, through the rain to the Avenger cocooned in Barrett Meadows rhododendrons. That much was certain. He sat looking at the rain snaking down the screen in the dim white light from a garage entrance. He smoked a cheroot and found the bottle of Teachers in the glove compartment. He realized if he had gone into the house ten minutes earlier he would have killed Savage and there would have been an end of it.

He stayed all night in the Avenger, sipping the whisky, plotting, thinking, remembering. The rain abated during the night. He wound down the window and the clean night air, tinged with rhododendron, shifted the smog of cheroot and scotch. He took two bennies, and returned to the tree as dawn rose on Saturday morning. There were no stirrings until 10.07 when he glimpsed Savage at the kitchen window in a floral get-up. An hour later Savage and the girl were placing bags in the rear of the Porsche. He returned to the Avenger.

He tailed them around the M25, pushing the Avenger's motor as far as it would go. He lost them somewhere in the vicinity of Woodham Ferrers but knew by now where they must be bound, and drove on to the marina at Bradwell. They were not there. He paced round the marina in his sunglasses inspecting the boats. Located Savage's clean-keeled *Hustler*, and Nutter's barnacled, paint-chipped *Dealer*. Had a good shufty at both, then moved on, fearful of rousing suspicion. The Benzedrine was wearing off and he was hungry. He walked up the road and found a seafood stand where he dined on giant prawns, mussels and oysters – high protein food: he thought he was going to need it. He walked a short way into the town and bought another bottle of scotch and forty cheroots, returned to the Avenger. He took some more bennies and sipped at the bottle. Some more time passed.

It was around here that he started to lose hold of things. For one thing he was pretty certain the whisky and the amphetamines weren't altogether agreeing with him. System wasn't what it was when he was a younger man. He was not at all sure what had happened. He could remember this: Savage arrived, with the girl in tow. He remembered the lurid hue of Savage's shirt. Turquoise and orange, with parrots on it. Distinctly remembered that. He waited a few minutes, his fingers in his pocket curling round the cheese-wire, then followed them down to the water. He could not recall how he got on to the boat, nor where he concealed himself.

The real point was this: he had a complete blank on killing Savage. He had absolutely no recollection of killing Savage. No matter how hard he dredged round his memory he just could not locate it. He remembered something he'd read in the *Encyclopaedia Britannica* in the Uxbridge Road library.

It was a mine of information, that book. You could spend a lifetime with that book and still there'd be things you didn't know. What he had read on this occasion was something about how the mind erases traumatic events it can't handle. How the memory dumps the horrors it can't bear to go through again and again. And that, he concluded, must be what had happened to him.

He knew he had killed Savage, he must have killed Savage. He had objective evidence to indicate as much. It was sitting here in front of him now, on Monday afternoon, as he sat in an underground car-park in Chertsey. It was in black and white in the *Staines Sensation*:

LOCAL MAN MISSING OVERBOARD

Savage feared dead as police step up search

Police and coastguards were last night increasingly concerned about the fate of local businessman Dorian Savage.

Savage was last seen on Saturday afternoon when he took his exclusive luxury yacht from its moorings at the Bradwell Marina, Essex. Later that afternoon Dutch coastguards were alerted by radar as the boat, the *Hustler*, sped uncontrollably towards the coast. They were unable to contact the boat by radio and it collided with the coast, disrupting the sleepy seaside town of Monster, near Rotterdam.

On board was Miss Natasha Stansfeld, believed to be a friend of Savage's, who now lies in a coma in a Dutch hospital in what doctors

> describe as a critical but stable condition. Essex police have flown to Rotterdam hoping to question Miss Stansfeld when she regains consciousness.
>
> Preliminary examination of the wreckage of the boat, which collided with a concrete sea-wall, has revealed that the inflatable dinghy which usually hangs at the rear of the boat is missing. Police are speculating that Savage may have used the dinghy to flee the boat, but an extensive two-day search of sea and coast has failed to locate the dinghy.
>
> Police are also investigating Savage's financial affairs. Savage, Managing Director of his own life assurance company, Savage Life, may have staged his own death in a Reggie Perrin-style attempt to collect his life assurance under another name. A police spokesman would not be drawn on this speculation last night.

Stansfeld – it was a name he recognized. The other woman had been called Stansfeld. He pondered it. He pondered it while he circled the Chertsey one-way system. He stopped for a pint in the Terrier's Hackles, and pondered it more. The two women had looked similiar. Then he figured it out. Savage had been rooting two sisters. He was not sure what this development signified; he thought it probably signified very little.

There was one thing he had to do now. He had to work out for his own satisfaction how it was he had done away with Savage. You couldn't go round being completely clueless about stuff like that. He would piece it all together, like a jigsaw puzzle. How he had killed Savage, how he had got back to the shore and the Avenger, what he had done all day yesterday – Sunday – and how he had arrived here in Chertsey, now, on Monday afternoon.

It was important he know all this. The client would doubtless want to know all the details. He would have to have a good account of events for the benefit of the client. Yes. Definitely.

CHAPTER TWENTY

'BUT YOU CAN'T believe all that crap!' Colin shouted. 'I just don't believe it.'

'I don't want to talk about it if you're going to be aggressive,' Kate said.

'You don't mind talking to complete strangers about it, do you? You don't mind knocking on complete strangers' doors and behaving like a fucking loony – making a complete idiot of yourself.'

'I said I don't want to talk about it. Anyway, I've only been door-to-door once. I didn't feel fully comfortable with it yet. Rose said – '

'Fuck Rose. Fuck what Rose said. I've had it up to here with fucking Rose.' He took an angry slurp of the beer he happened to have in his hand. 'Now you listen to me, and you listen good. Are you telling my kids all this crap?'

'Your kids, Colin?'

'Oh. So they're not my kids now? Someone else's are they? Jesus's maybe. Immaculate conceptions were they?'

'That's not what I meant. You know perfectly well what I meant. They're our children.'

'All right then – I'm not having our fucking children indoctrinated by your loony friends. Have you got that?'

Kate sighed. She looked pityingly at her poor benighted husband, clinging to his beer can, fidgeting with his cigarette. His props; his raft. What was it Peter had said about rafts floating through the turbulent sea of life, but only one of the rafts was the true boat that came home to the shore?

She couldn't fully recollect the complicated metaphor, but it had struck her as very perspicacious.

Rose and Peter had explained to her how uncomfortable people often are when they are confronted with the truth, especially firmly opinionated people like Colin. Rose's husband had reacted in a very similar way – he had, in fact, left her. Susan's parents had never again spoken to her. Gladstone's father in Grenada had threatened to come to England and kill him. This was one of the prices which sometimes had to be paid. Colin, she supposed, might be one of the people who would never be able to understand, however much you explained to him. There were people like that: people Jehovah could never get through to, however much you tried to guide them.

'Why do you think they're "loonies", Colin?' she asked, with infinite patience. She found it so easy to be patient now. She was patient and calm and unruffled. When you had beheld the infinity of His patience, His never-ending patience as He waited for His children to come to Him, it was so much easier to be patient.

'Why do I think they're loonies? This is unbelievable. They think the world was made in six days – '

'Not six literal days. If only you'd listen to me for a change. The word "day" in the original Hebrew can mean a much longer period of time – '

'Shut up! I've heard all this. You want to read that Charles Darwin book I've got upstairs. Very interesting.' (This despite the fact that he had never got past page one.) 'You might learn something.'

Kate smiled sadly and shook her head.

'A few weeks ago,' he continued. 'Listen. Please listen to me. I'm not trying to attack you here. Just listen. Say a month ago, imagine I'd told you that in one month's time you would be knocking on people's doors – '

'I was different then – '

' – telling them the world's about to end cos it says so in

the Bible. Can you imagine that? Can you imagine what your reaction would have been if I'd come home from work one day and told you I was a Jehovah's fucking Witness? Can you?'

'Please don't use language like that – '

'I'll use what fucking language I like. Listen to me. If I find you've been putting all this crap into the children's heads I'm going to take them up to my mother's – all right? I can't stop you thinking whatever fucking lunacy you want to but I'm not having you getting at the kids. Particularly Sly – he's very suggestible. Believes anything you tell him.'

'Perhaps he's closer to the truth already. Perhaps you could learn from him,' Kate said.

He spoke very calmly now. It was necessary to take a firm grip on this situation. 'If you don't shut up I'm going to hit you,' he said.

'Violence is your only recourse,' she said smugly. 'The only thing you understand, the only way you have of expressing yourself. I feel sorry for you, Colin. Really. I really do feel sorry for you. I want to be able to help you, but you won't let me in, you won't let love in. You're barring the way. You're putting up a wall around yourself because you're afraid. I understand that fear. Really I do.'

'You heard me. I mean it.'

'I heard you, Colin,' she said. 'I hear everything you say. It's you who won't hear what I'm trying to say to you.'

'I've had enough of this. I'm not pissing round any more,' he said.

'Oh, that's exactly what you're doing. If only you knew how much, if you knew what was at stake.'

She just sat there with this benign, idiot grin on her face. This reminded him of something Dorian had told him once, about the time he was trying to flog a policy and suddenly twigged the guy was off his rocker.

'One more word,' he said. 'Just one more fucking word.'

'Is that how much you fear the truth, Colin? Why are you

so frightened to listen? Why aren't you prepared to just listen?'

He carefully placed his beer can on one of the nest of occasional tables, rested his cigarettes on the edge of the ashtray. He walked the three paces to where she sat and slapped her hard round the face.

'I warned you,' he said.

She smiled. 'I know, Colin. But I want you to know that I'm prepared to keep talking to you so that one day you might begin to understand.'

He hit her again, with knuckles this time.

She kept smiling. 'You can't hurt me,' she said.

'You stupid fucking bitch,' he said. 'You silly fucking bitch.'

He went up to the little room on the first floor which he had once pretentiously dubbed his study. There was a spare bed in there (which he was now sleeping in), a desk with a dilapidated laptop PC, a couple of filing cabinets, a collection of fifteen or twenty books such as *Deregulation: The Implications for Your Business*, the *Rothman's Football Yearbook 1988* and the unread copy of the *Origin of Species* purchased long ago at the instigation of Dorian. There was an ashtray with about two hundred stubs in it, three milk-scummed coffee mugs, a bottle of Glenlivet, and a telephone which he had dragged through from the adjacent bedroom.

He lit another Bensons and was about to start making some calls pertaining to his efforts at finding work when the phone rang. He snatched at it. If it was one of Kate's religious loonies he was going to savage them, he was going to issue death threats.

'Nutter?' a deep, quiet voice said.

'Who is this?'

'Your dog may be sick.'

'*What . . .?* What the fuck is this? Who is this?'

'I repeat: the dog may be sick. We must talk. The business is concluded as per our arrangements.'

'What business? Who is this?'

'Snooker,' the voice said. 'Remember?'

'*You?* What do you want?'

'To conclude our business.'

'I see. Well, I've been trying to get in touch with you as it happens.'

There was a silence.

'The World – three o'clock?'

'The world?'

'The World Turned Upside Down – Chiswick, by the river.'

'I know it.'

'Three?'

'I'll see you then.'

He put the phone down. What had Richardson meant about a dog? He pondered, he deliberated. Dog, dog and bone, phone. Sick = tapped. Your phone may be tapped. This process of deduction took fifteen minutes, two cigarettes and a Glenlivet. Why, he wondered, would anybody bother to tap his phone?

Maybe the blokes in the pub had been right: maybe Richardson was barking mad. One thing was certain though: he could not possibly be as mad as Kate was at the moment. He reckoned Kate was heading for Broadmoor if she carried on at this rate.

By two he'd had enough of the day and felt a thirst coming on. Kate had gone out, doubtless to reinforce her fledgling faith with the Jehovah's Witnesses. Perhaps she would be able to boast to them: 'My husband punched me this morning.' 'Well done, Kate. You are doing Jehovah's work! Next week you must endeavour to provoke him to a violent axe attack.' Perhaps they had these meetings where they all sat round hallelujahing and weeping and bashing tambourines as each Witness stood up and gave a triumphal account of how many people they'd managed to provoke to mindless violence in the last week. Then the one who had done best (been shot at perhaps, or carved up with a razor) was nailed to a cross and they all drank tea and ate doughnuts and sang hymns. Just thinking about it made the veins in the side of his neck stand up and twitch.

He drove out to Chiswick and managed to find a parking space on the Mall. He walked down the river to The World and ordered a pint of Führerbrau. There was a faint suggestion of sunshine on the river and he sat at a table outside. Predictably, he started thinking about Kate; the subject depressed him so much he downed the lager in two goes and went back for another pint.

He mused over the second pint. Kate had done this sort of thing before. Her diets. Her morbid fear of certain foodstuffs. Her obsession with allergies. Her flirtation with radical feminism when she had hung out with a crew of man-hating dykes. Her ludicrous educational theories about the children. The time she ate nothing but carrot and alfalfa for a fortnight. The month she smelt like a cross between a skunk and a hippy on account of something called aromatherapy. The time she joined CND. The visits to an acupuncturist. The pile of books about Buddhism and Stonehenge. Her yoga. The visits to a hypnotist. Her abandonment of tea and coffee. Her fortune-teller, Madame Zoroastra, or whatever she'd been called. The time he found a vibrator in the bathroom and she calmly explained she was working on her sexual responsiveness by wanking herself off three times a day.

Nor was it only her. It ran through the entire family – Julia the mad piss-artist sister; Olive the loopy mother who threw wobblers over Christmas dinner; Hester the crazy aunt who kept locking herself in cupboards and car boots and lavatory cubicles; Rupert a distant cousin who hanged himself from a tree in the garden because he failed an 'O' Level retake. There were no two ways about it: he had married into a family blighted by congenital madness. The one consolation with Kate, however, was that none of the manifestations of her insanity had ever lasted very long. At least, they had not done so to date.

Richardson arrived at precisely five-to-three. This was not quite true. Richardson came along the path by the river at that time, stared blankly through him and continued down the path. He wondered if he was supposed to follow. The guy seemed crazier with every moment. Perhaps he had not noticed the last time he saw Richardson. It seemed likely considering how pissed he had been. Five minutes later Richardson came back from the same direction, presumably having circled the block.

'Mr Nutter,' he said, putting out a hand.

When he had sorted out the drinks he sat down opposite Richardson. Richardson lit one of his cheroots, and his bloodshot eyes darted back and forth between the river-path and the door of the pub. He had three or four days' stubble.

'The job has been done,' he said. 'On Saturday afternoon. It went according to plan. There were no hitches.'

He lit a Bensons and took a sip on the Führerbrau. There was no question about it: Richardson was a loon. 'Good,' he said. 'That's good then.' *Humour them*, that was the thing. Never let on you know they're round the twist. Richardson, at any rate, seemed like the harmless sort of lunatic. At least he wasn't going to try and persuade your children that the world was about to end and they were going to be spirited up to heaven. He was just your standard sort of mad pub bullshitter. For Christ's sake: this was good fun compared to Kate. He was really quite enjoying this. 'That's great then,' he said.

'You saw it in any of the papers?' Richardson asked.

'No, I didn't as a matter of fact. Haven't looked at a paper recently.'

'There wasn't much in the nationals. A couple of small paragraphs in the *Telegraph* and *Independent*. Nothing in *The Times* – it's a terrible paper these days.'

'Yeah. Don't read it myself,' he said.

'Plenty in the local papers up that way though. Don't worry. We're completely in the clear.'

'Good. That's good then.'

There was a pause. Both men sipped beer.

'It's good to do business with a man like you, Mr Nutter. I respect a calm man, doesn't get flustered under pressure. A lot of men would start cracking up now, thinking twice. I knew you were reliable though.'

'Yeah, well. I'm used to pressure from my line of work. You get accustomed.'

'You're not in a hurry?' Richardson said, on a slightly more jovial note. 'Time for another one?'

'Yeah. Thanks.'

Richardson went into the pub. Colin grinned: this was the first light relief he had had in weeks. He would play along with Richardson for a bit, with whatever it was he was talking about, see if he couldn't find out what had happened to the grand, suggest a game of darts. He knew there was a board nearby in the One-Eyed Raven.

Richardson returned. Colin noticed his hands were shaking as he held the glasses. He looked like he'd been on a bender for a few days, which was good news as far as the darts was concerned. Richardson put the glasses on the table, ashed his revolting cheroot. 'Did you have any luck with finding a job yet?' he asked.

'No. Something'll turn up though. There's always something in the sales game. Might have to take a cut in salary, but something always turns up. I'm not really in a hurry to find something else just yet. Thought I'd take a bit of a holiday for a few weeks.' He sipped at the Führerbrau.

'You seem more relaxed than when we last discussed the matter,' Richardson said, his voice again subtly altered.

'Oh shit, yeah,' he exclaimed. 'I must have been pretty wound up then. Nah, quite honestly I was never any great shakes at insurance. I think things'll work out better in another line of business. I've been talking to a guy about time-shares, and another bloke who's got this satellite dish franchise – that could be a big growth area, lot of money to be made there, I reckon.'

Richardson's mask remained impenetrable. 'I trust this doesn't herald a change of heart regarding our arrangements, Mr Nutter?' he said. It sounded as though he was joking, but it was difficult to tell with Richardson.

'Course not!' he declared. *Humour them*, he reminded himself. 'I tried ringing you at work the other day, matter of fact – your boss didn't seem to know where you were.'

Richardson looked suspicious. 'I told you not to try and make contact,' he said coldly. He had that fierce, crazed look in his red eyes again.

'Sorry,' he said. 'I was very careful.'

'You only spoke to Castle?'

'Yeah.'

'It's probably all right then. I had to take a few days off to get the job done. It took longer than I'd thought it was going to. There were no problems though.'

'Fine . . .' he said expansively. He wondered if it would be bad form to ask precisely what this job was. Perhaps it would be better not to. Both men were silent for a moment, ruminative. Colin watched a boat scudding by on the silver river, four muscular oarsmen pumping at the water.

'You're not like most people,' Richardson said. 'You don't seem at all curious to know the details. I like that.'

'I always figure someone'll tell you something if they want you to know about it,' Colin said merrily.

'That's a wise sentiment,' Richardson said. 'People who ask too many questions are liable to get hurt.'

He cleared his throat. 'About that snooker we played,' he said. 'I can't remember – how many games did we play in the end?'

'Two.'

'That all?'

'Yeah.'

'And I – er – lost both. Must have done.'

Richardson smiled, an occurrence rare enough that it was worthy of note. His thin lips peeled back to reveal small, sharp, cheroot-stained teeth. 'I thought you were a bit the worse for wear,' he said in an unusually jocular fashion. 'Still, it doesn't hurt once in a while, does it? A man needs to let off tension sometimes. I like a massage myself, good go in the sauna and then a once-over with the birch and a good massage.' He maintained the weird grimace and peered into Colin's eyes. 'I suppose you'd already had a few before we met up.'

'I had,' he said. 'Christ knows – a few gins, three or four pints before you turned up.' He always liked to impress people with his intake capability.

'Well, that explains it then,' Richardson said. 'I can't play at all if I've had too much. Still, no harm done, was there?'

Colin laughed. 'Except my fucking wallet!' he exclaimed.

'What's a few quid?' Richardson said.

'Yeah,' he said ruefully. *A few quid*: the guy was being pretty blasé about it. It seemed odd to him that a burglar alarm installer who drove round in a beaten-up old Avenger could treat the matter of £1000 so lightly. 'You a darts man at all then?' he asked. 'I thought maybe we'd have a game some time.'

'It's better if we don't see each other again, Mr Nutter.'

'Call me Colin, for Christ's sake,' said Colin. 'Why's it better then?'

'Come on,' Richardson said sternly. 'Play the game. Neither of us wants to take unnecessary risks. It's very unlikely they'll ever put us together, but it doesn't pay to be careless.'

Here we go again, he thought. It was one of the interesting things about lunatics, the way they lurched back and forth. Perfectly normal one minute, mad as a cuckoo's arsehole the next. Certain things seemed to trigger them off. He supposed the secret was to work out what things it was that had this effect on them. Or, alternatively, maybe it was just that Richardson didn't fancy his chances at the okky and didn't want to part company with his winnings from the snooker. Colin had other ideas about that.

'Get you another?' he said. 'Guinness again?'

'All right.'

He walked through into the bar of The World Turned Upside Down. The theme was nautical (reflecting its position upon the river) and antipodean (reflecting its name). Early maps of the world, naval paraphernalia, paintings of whales and other more fanciful creatures of the deep littered the crowded walls. There were telescopes, sextants, compasses, globes, Toby jugs of grinning sailors, and a vast ship's wheel above the bar. The juke-box displayed a strong nautical bias ('Sailing', 'In the Navy', 'Yellow Submarine', 'Surfin' USA', 'The Boat That I Row', 'Bridge Over Troubled Water' etc.). Netting filled with plastic lobsters and crabs was strung over one piece of ceiling.

Waiting for the Guinness to be drawn he limbered up the wrist of his right arm, preparatory to the darts. Get that smooth action going. He had also taken the precaution of downgrading his drink from a Führerbrau to a less punitive pint of Norseman. He returned outside with the two pints.

Richardson was smoking another cheroot and rifling through a bundle of newspaper clippings which he must have produced from the recesses of his overcoat. Colin sat down and took a sip on his Norseman.

'Thought you might be interested to look at these,' Richardson said.

'What's that then?'

'The newspaper stories I was telling you about.'

'Oh. Of course,' he said; his hand reached out and took the proffered sheaf of newsprint. He choked on the next sip of lager.

REGGIE PERRIN MAN MAY BE IN SPAIN

Detectives investigating the mysterious disappearance of businessman Dorian Savage would not yesterday rule out the possibility that Savage has done a bunk to the Costa del Crime in Spain.

Colleagues of Savage's dismissed the suggestion, however. 'Dorian would have taken the boat with him, wouldn't he?' said Tony Cockerel, a long-time friend of the missing man.

'It isn't his kind of scam at all,' Cockerel continued. 'And you reckon he'd just leave that poor girl on the boat like that. Dorian isn't that sort of bloke.'

An *Egham Event* reporter in Spain reports seeing a man answering to Savage's description in a bar favoured by the criminal underworld.

Coma girl speaks to police

Last night detectives investigating the disappearance of local life assurance millionaire Dorain Savage were able to speak to Natasha Standfeld as she regained consciousness following her crash ordeal aboard the missing businessman's luxury yacht.

'I'm afraid Miss Standfeld wasn't able to be very helpful,' Chief Detective Inspector Dave Newsome said, following his interview with the injured girl. 'Apparently she was in the jacuzzi and had no idea that Savage wasn't on the boat. When she got out she looked for Savage all over the boat and couldn't find him.

'The boat was travelling at consider-

able speed and she tried to radio for help but the radio had been smashed up. She was unable to bring the boat under control.'

DI Newsome believes the damage to the radio may be a significant clue in unravelling what happened on that tragic afternoon.

Miss Standfeld was rescued stark naked from the icy seas by intrepid Dutch seamen. She was unconscious and if they had been a few seconds later she would have drowned.

SAVAGE BODY FOUND!

A Middlesex Monitor EXCLUSIVE

Last night police rushed to the scene when the body of missing insurance mogul Dorian Savage was found washed up on the windswept beach close to Foulness power station.

From the condition of the bloated body it was impossible to tell what might have befallen the dead businessman. 'He could just have fallen overboard,' Detective Inspector Dave Newton said. 'You'd be surprised how often that happens, even to experienced mariners.'

The Inspector used the occasion to warn members of the public about the hazards of the sea. 'If he'd been wearing a life jacket this might never have happened,' he said.

'Of course, this scenario still doesn't account for the inflatable being missing. I am now convinced that the inflatable holds the key to this investigation.'

A thorough search of the coast has started in four countries – Britain, France, Belgium and the Netherlands where the powerful yacht collided with a sea wall. 'This is an example of how the police forces of different countries can cooperate together,' DI Newcome said.

Savage dinghy recovered

Police were last night examining the motorized inflatable found a few miles up the coast from the holiday resort of Southend-on-Sea. The boat has been positively identified as coming from the ruined yacht the *Hustler*, linked to the death of financial tycoon Dorian Savage.

Detective Inspector Dave Newton who is heading the investigation said last night, 'This is very significant. Someone landed this boat and we want to talk to that someone.'

Newton refused to rule out the possibility of foul play. 'This is starting to look very nasty,' he said. 'The radio smashed up, the boat going at considerable speed, Savage overboard and drowned, and someone bringing the inflatable into shore. My team are now treating this as a murder investigation.'

He stared at a photograph of the dead man which accompanied this last article in the *Staines Sensation*. The caption beneath the picture of a grinning Dorian: *Savagely murdered?*

As he read through the articles he began to receive some intimation of what was going on. A chilling trickle passed down his spine. He looked up at Richardson, whose face maintained its impenetrable façade.

'I'm sorry about the girl,' Richardson said. 'I didn't know about her. Sounds like she'll be all right though.'

He now knew that Richardson had killed Dorian, and he had the strongest possible feeling that Richardson regarded him as an accessory to the murder. Why, after all, would Richardson kill a man whose existence he had not even been apprised of until he, Colin, mentioned him that drunken evening ten days ago?

He now realized he had been incorrect, massively incorrect, in his original assessment of Richardson as a harmless maniac. It was now very clear to him that Richardson was an extremely harmful maniac.

He noticed that his own lower jaw was wobbling. He felt sick.

'Why . . .?' he said quietly.

'I figured the boat was the easiest place. A lot of nasty accidents happen on boats – I looked up the figures in the library. I was thinking about that little tractor thing he had in his garden – you know it? – but when he went down to the boat I reckoned on that as the best opportunity. I weighted the body – I don't know what happened there. Some fish must have chewed through the ropes or something. I wasn't expecting him to be washed up. It's a shame, but not a disaster. There's no cause for worry on that count.'

At this moment he would gladly have embraced the Jehovah's Witnesses. He would gladly have spent the rest of his life beating on a tambourine, knocking on doors, kissing fat Gloria, singing hymns. He did not need to be told: he now knew why Richardson had been so off-hand about the game of snooker; he now knew what it was he had done with the £1000 that night in the Athenaeum Snooker Club. It was not exactly that the events of the closing stages of the evening were coming back to him in lucid detail, just that he was remembering enough to piece together the rest of it and make the obvious, the unavoidable deduction.

The words 'I could kill that cunt' which had been on his

lips a number of times in the last ten days now took on a terrible new significance.

Richardson had noticed his silence. He repeated, 'Don't worry about the body. There's no way they can pin it on us. I wasn't seen. I told you. I'm a pro. I've done this kind of work before.'

You walk into a pub; you have a few too many drinks; you casually strike up a conversation with a bloke you've met once before; you have a few more drinks; the day wears on. Ten days later you discover you are implicated in a murder.

'One more?' Richardson said. 'You seem to have slowed down a bit.'

He nodded mutely, which action Richardson appeared to interpret as a positive signal *vis-à-vis* the drink. He disappeared into the The World Turned Upside Down. Colin stared at the newspaper cuttings, at the picture of Dorian, his erstwhile best friend, now a corpse, a cadaver, a water-bloated carcass washed up on a desolate beach. He felt dizzy. He felt like jelly. He felt the world spinning out of control, himself plummeting down into a dark abyss of unnamable horrors. Suddenly he was seized with paranoia: he was sitting here outside a pub with a pile of newspaper cuttings about the man he had killed. He turned them upside down and reached for his lager like an automaton.

A violent blow on the back pushed his nose into the drink. The dark figure of Richardson was towering over him. 'Drink up,' he said. 'Weather's turning out all right, eh?' The sun was glittering on the low tide of the grey Thames. 'Got some nuts,' Richardson said. 'Felt a bit peckish.'

He drank his lager on autopilot. His mind was whirring like a tumble-drier. He remembered with extreme clarity a film he had watched late one night. A man discovers that his friend is the Devil. He looked at Richardson's pinched red eyes, at the sinister, brown, pointed teeth. The resemblance was uncanny. Richardson was the Devil. The Great Beast.

'What d'you reckon to all this global warming business

then?' the Beast said. 'Couple of hot summers and everyone thinks the world's coming to an end. I can't see it myself.' The Devil took a swig of Guinness.

'I dunno . . .' he said. 'Probably a load of bullshit.'

'I can see their point about the countryside though. Driving out to Essex at the weekend, it really struck me. Countryside's a fucking disgrace. Wasn't like that when I was a kid.'

'No.'

'I always try and buy those green things though. You know, like that shaving foam without TCP, whatever it's called – you know the stuff – and that biodegradable washing-up liquid. You never know, best to be on the safe side. You don't want to fuck up the environment if you can help it, do you?'

'No, no. My wife gets all those things.'

'Right. Very nice woman, your wife, by the way. Funnily enough I was talking about all this stuff to her when I was doing your system. We had a nice chin-wag. Extremely pleasant woman, I thought. You're a very lucky man to have a wife like that.'

'Yes.'

'I never married myself. Never met the right woman I suppose. What with being in the services and that, you don't get much opportunity. I had some good times though. You bet. Those chicks out East. You ever been out there?'

'No.'

'You ought to, mate. Coo . . . I've seen some action out there, I can tell you. Those Asian chicks know how to please a man, you know what I mean.'

He was experiencing a sense of cosmic dislocation. He was sitting here talking about the environment and the whore-houses of the Far East with a murderer, with a hired killer.

'I don't like to be pushy or anything,' Richardson said. 'But there is the small matter of the other half of the fee.'

'The other half?'

'The other grand.'

'The other grand,' he said. 'Yes. Yes. I haven't got it today. I – er – '

'Too short notice. I understand,' Richardson said. 'There's no hurry. If you could let me have it in the next week or so. Clear things up. Not nice to have debts hanging over your head.'

'No. No, I'll have it next week,' he said.

'How about here? Same time next week,' Richardson said.

'Yeah. Yes, I'll do that.'

'I've got to shoot,' Richardson said.

Shoot. Shoot me if I don't pay up. Shoot my knee-caps off. Shoot my children. Come on – we're dealing with a psycho here.

The killer quaffed the rest of his Guinness, gathered up the press cuttings – his reviews – and put a hand out. He found himself shaking it. It was damp and hot. 'Next week then,' Richardson said.

'Yes.'

When he returned home some time later – he really wasn't sure what time it was; he really wasn't sure what he was doing – there was a gathering of Jehovah's Witnesses in his living room. Fat black Gloria, grinning Susan, radiant Peter, and more he did not recognize. Jessamy and Sylvester were sitting on the floor with rapt expressions on their faces. Everyone welcomed him. 'Hello Colin!' they chorused and beamed their happy smiles at him. They were so friendly these people. Why had he gone out? Why had he not stayed here, drinking drinking chocolate and talking about God's paradise on earth?

'Hello,' he said. 'Hello. I've just got to pop upstairs. Some things to do. I'll let you get on.'

'There are some letters for you,' Kate said.

'You don't look well,' big Gloria said. 'You under the weather?'

'No no. I'm fine. Fine, thank you.' What a nice person.

What a sweet, normal respectable, well-balanced sort of person Gloria was. Why wasn't everyone he knew like Gloria?

He took the letters from the phone table, stumbled up to his study and ripped open the envelopes. He did not register much. It was all bumph – bank crap, mortgage threats, credit card rubbish, HP shit. He had more important things to think about. He didn't have time for this. There was just one letter which tore him out of his absorption in the matter of Richardson. It was postmarked Saturday. He read it slowly and thoroughly with a rising sense of disbelief. It was as though a cold hand had reached out from the grave and clasped his heart in its grip:

> Col,
> I made a mistake. I'm sorry about it, just a bit of a misunderstanding, mate. If you're interested your old job's still available. Apologies. Give me a bell and we'll meet up for a beer or something.
>
> D.

CHAPTER TWENTY-ONE

'LETTER FOR YOU,' Christie said.

Dog looked suspicious. He did not get many letters, and those he did get generally heralded bad news – National Insurance gyp, Poll Tax gyp, non-payment of fines gyp. He was standing over the cooker tending to some boil-in-the-bag kippers, black pudding and six fried eggs. Christie sashayed in in her dressing gown and dropped the letter on the table, went back out. He looked at the large brown buff envelope, picked it up and ripped it open with his teeth.

Flesh flashed at him, a colossal pair of tits. It was the new edition of *Grunt*. A letter and a sparkling new fifty-shot dropped from the pages.

> Dear Mr Barber,
> Here is your complimentary copy of *Grunt* and the £50 gratuity for the photo-set featured in the Readers' Wives section.
> I would like to take this opportunity to thank you for your valued contribution to the magazine and to say keep those photos coming in!
> Yours with a kiss
> Selena

He held the fifty up to the light and confirmed the presence of the watermark. His brain hastily converted it into the currency he best understood – about thirty pints of lager at today's exchange rates. He grinned. Well, there it was – in print like. Official. He pushed the eggs round the pan and flicked the busy pages in search of the Readers' Wives. Here they were: Katie from Shepherd's Bush. Beautiful. Bernard Matthews. They had done a very tasteful job with the photographs. Laid out at different angles against a pink and turquoise background which set off the hues of the duvet. A real interior decoration job. And there was nothing wrong with the snaps – he reckoned Nutter could get a job doing this if he was ever looking for a new line of work. They were first-rate pix. Christie was just jealous, jealous of Katie, jealous of Katie's firm, neat model's tits. He wondered if he mightn't pop down the road and show the Nutters the happy outcome of his entrepreneurship. Thought maybe that wasn't such a great idea.

'Oi!' he shouted. 'Come ear!'

'I'm washing my air.'

'I got something to show you.'

When he had finished breakfast she was still in the bathroom so he left the magazine open on the kitchen table so she would get a load of it when she finished. Passing the bathroom door on his way out he called, 'Something on the table in there you'll wanna see.'

He proceeded to the Goose Green with the fifty and splashed out on a £2.50 can of that imported Japanese lager which he invariably referred to as 'Kamikaze'. Everyone thought that was fucking funny. It was early and there was no one about, which allowed him to take up residence in a corner snug and get on with some thinking.

There was a lot of stuff to think about; a lot of thinking to get done.

There was Richardson and his presence at the marina – the way he sat in the Avenger with mad red eyes staring at the sea. There was toe-rag stowing away aboard the *Hustler*, coming home late smelling like a shit-house.

The boy's behaviour had been well on the weird side in the six days that had passed since then. He had stayed barricaded in his room all Sunday. Monday he sneaked out when no one was looking, straight out without even pissing or washing (not a toe-rag strong point, admittedly) or eating anything. He had managed to corner him on the Tuesday but the boy was completely spaced out. He decided it was going to be a necessary sacrifice of principle to break with all precedent, with all received tradition, and express sympathetic feelings towards the boy:

'You feeling all right? Got the flu or something? You don't look too clever.'

'I'm awright,' the boy mumbled and looked away evasively.

'I'm just making some breakfast – bangers, eggs, black pudding, tomatoes. D'you want some?'

'No.'

'Not hungry? You gotta eat, you know, build yourself up.'

He was standing blocking the corridor so Gaz couldn't get past without barging him out of the way. He looked like a trapped animal, cowering away. 'No,' he said.

'Come on,' Dog said, 'what's the problem? Something's bugging you. You in trouble with the police? That it?'

'Why d'you wanna know? What's it to you? You never give a shit about me before!' he blurted.

'All right, I'm a bastard. I'm trying to be less of a bastard now, trying to make up. Look, come and have some sausages.'

'I don't want your fucking sausages. What d'you want wiv me?'

He backed off, showing his palms, as though to say, 'You're a big bloke – I don't want no trouble.' That was a fucking laugh. It was a serious strain this being-nice-to-Gaz business. Executives keeled over and died from less strain than this.

'Nothing,' he said. 'Just concerned cos you don't look too good. Just showing a bit of common humanity.'

The boy said nothing. He generally did not if you deployed a long word like that. He looked confused and suspicious.

'Tell you what,' he said, 'd'you wanna make some cash this afternoon? I got a job clearing out some rubbish into a skip. Twenty quid in it for you.'

'I don't want nuffin from you,' Gaz said.

He gave up, went and ate all eight sausages and the rest of breakfast on his own.

There had been no further developments since then, and a search of toe-rag's pit had turned up nothing except the absence of bits of the arsenal: that truncheon thing he made out of the lead he nicked from the Transit, the knife and chisel. He was not at all sure what this signified.

He finished the Kamikaze and went for a pint. Put Nembutal Wakefield on the juke-box then sat and thought some more. The Gaz avenue was proving fruitless, and he suspected that confronting him directly with the Bradwell expedition might prove counterproductive, might force his hand too soon. He had to bide his time – play the long game.

So there remained the Richardson avenue. He had to go and see Richardson, which he would do on the pretext of seeing if there was any work going.

He finished the pint, left the Goose and cut through the bus station towards Mondaugen Mansions, the collapsing Victorian pile where Richardson kept his abode. He hit the buzzer – no response. Looked up and down the road – no sign of the Avenger. A Paki woman emerged out of the door. He grinned savagely, said, 'Just going up to see David Richardson,' and shoved her out of the way.

Richardson's rooms were on the third floor at the end of a dank passageway which always smelt of cat piss. He knocked on the door. 'Oi! David. It's me. Dave,' he called. There was no answer. He had a quick squint back down the passage, took a step back, and put the size 12 Doc Marten through the panel of the door. The door proved even less resilient than it looked and his foot disappeared through the plywood, followed by the whole of his leg up to the knee. He was standing there on one leg with the other ensnared in Richardson's door. It was not going to be much of a result if it turned out Richardson was in after all. Richardson was mad enough to get a meat-cleaver and hack the protruding leg off at the knee. Spurred on by this thought he went at the task of withdrawing the leg with an urgent determination.

When he got the leg out he punched the loose ply free and got a hand in to the handle. The room stank of cheroots and Old Spice. Unwashed takeaway curry containers were piled up in the sink under the rust-stained geyser. Richardson had always been partial to the kind of curry that ripped the lining off your guts. Said it was from his days out in Pakiland. A tin teapot, packet of Red Label and tin of black shoe polish sat on the tea-stained Formica.

He went through into the dark bedroom, found a light switch, flicked it and one of those green poker table lights came on. There was Richardson's stark pallet-like bed, a tartan rug neatly folded at its base. He didn't reckon Richardson could see much action, other than of the self-administered variety, on that thing. The small table with a pile of his military magazines, an old radio and a quarter-full Teachers bottle. He was about to take a belt on the bottle, then thought he didn't really fancy drinking out of the same receptacle Richardson had wrapped his laughing-gear round. You'd catch rabies or something. He went through the drawers on the chest, had a quick dekko inside the dark wardrobe, flicked through a pile of newspapers. He noticed there was something funny about the newspapers: there were bits cut out of them. That was interesting. He looked round the room, then it struck him what had happened. There were neat rectangles of newspaper pinned to the far wall. He thought he'd go and have a little squint at those.

SALESMAN FEARED DEAD

REGGIE PERRIN MAY BE IN SPAIN

COMA GIRL SPEAKS TO POLICE
SAVAGE BODY FOUND
SAVAGE DINGHY RECOVERED
HUNT FOR SAVAGE KILLER
Police search for ruthless assassin
SAVAGE AUTOPSY REVEALS BLOW TO SKULL
LIFE ASSURANCE MAN HAD NO LIFE ASSURANCE
No kids and he hated family
Ashamed of humble origins
POLICE SEARCH FOR MYSTERY MAN IN TREE
Neighbours saw man with binoculars
SAVAGE LOVED TWO SISTERS
Tasha and Becky fought for his love!
THREE IN A BED
I LOVED MY LITTLE BOY *EXCLUSIVE!*
Heartbreak of Viv Savage
DOGS HAD VOCAL CORDS CUT OUT
Neighbour speaks of Savage cruelty
SAVAGE BOAT MISSED FERRY BY INCHES
100s Could Have Died

Well, this was very interesting. This was extremely interesting. And it was going to require even more thought, a lot more very careful thinking out. He thought he must have had to put in more thinking in the last week than in the previous twenty-two years of his life. It was little wonder he was eating so much: you needed extra fuel if you had to think this much.

He went along the wall ripping the cuttings from their pins, bundled them all up, shoved them in his pocket and got out of Mondaugen Mansions in eight seconds flat. It was not a place you wanted to hang about in; not when you started thinking about the possibility of a grinning Richardson emerging out of a dark doorway with a meat-cleaver in his fist. The guy did judo, karate, ju-jitsu, tai chi, lo wok, hai so – he'd learnt it all out in Slanteyeland. He knew so: Richardson was forever telling him all about it over pints.

He got back to the Goose Green, pushed his way through to the bar and shouted for a pint of Dopplerbrau.

'Not buying me one?'

He looked round. He let out a little screech. Felt his bowels drop.

'Seen a ghost?' Richardson said.

'No. No . . . Sorry, mate,' he stuttered. He looked at Richardson's sinister red eyes. 'Just wasn't expecting to see you in here, mate. That's all.'

'Were hoping you wouldn't see me in here, perhaps?' Richardson said slowly, nastily, like he was really savouring this.

'Course not. Why wouldn't I want to see you?'

'Because you know I'm very angry with you.'

He knew. How could he know? He was a ghoul. He had that ESB, whatever it was called.

'Why's that, Mr Richardson.'

'You know. Don't piss about with me, Dave. I don't take kindly to it.'

'I know . . .?'

Richardson's smile revealed those cruel black teeth. 'My spirit level, Dave. I lent you my spirit level two weeks ago and you were supposed to return it next day.'

He felt an overwhelming sense of relief. The spirit level! Of course. He would gladly have purchased Richardson ten new spirit levels.

'Shit. I'm sorry, David. Look, I'll get you a pint, fetch it straightaway. It's in the back of my van. I just forgot about it. Guinness is it?'

Now he had the dubious pleasure of sitting and drinking with Richardson. Drinking with Richardson was a harrowing experience at the best of times; it was doubly bad when you had just ransacked his room and carried the evidence in your pocket. He could feel the scrumpled-up bundle of paper bulging from his side. It rustled every time he moved. He had a sudden nightmare vision: Richardson reaching over, casually enquiring, 'What you reading then?' His transformed visage as he clocked the content of the reading matter.

They discussed a job Richardson had coming up, a security system on a place up in Holland Park. While Richardson discoursed on the technicalities of the job, Dog speculated on how odd it was that the rich denizens of W11 entrusted the safety of their homes to a psychopath like Richardson. Curiously, this was a thought which had never before occurred to him.

After three or four pints Richardson started acting weird. He started chewing on the end of his cheroot. He fixed Dog with his black slit eyes. He was twitching and grinding his teeth.

'D'you know, a lot of people think I'm a bullshitter, Dave,' he said.

'Do they?' Dog tried to look shocked. 'No. I'm sure that can't be the case,' he said, though it did not sound entirely convincing.

'They do, Dave. They do. I've heard them. I'm not stupid, you know.' Gobs of spit kept flying out of his mouth while he spoke, flecking the table and coming dangerously close to Dog's pint. It looked like he was getting angry again. You could tell from the way his eyes tightened up into tiny little ball-bearings.

'Who said you were? I'll nut the bastard.'

'A lot of people, Dave. A lot of people think I'm a bullshitter. But they don't know. There's things they don't know about me. A lot of things.

'What, er, what sort of things exactly?' Dog said as casually as he could.

'Things I can never talk about, Dave. Bad things. Terrible, dark things.'

'Terrible, dark things,' Dog found himself repeating. 'This is like, you know, from when you was a mercenary like?'

Richardson's face suddenly twisted into a savage mask, like that of a Japanese warrior. He fixed Dog with his scarlet snake eyes and hissed through clenched teeth. 'Don't ever say that! *Don't you ever say that again!*'

Dog looked contrite and tried to divine what it was he had said that had precipitated Richardson's outrage.

'It's not mercenary, Dave. Get that into your thick head. We were freedom fighters. We were liberating oppressed people. People who were being tortured by brutal communist terrorists.'

Richardson stopped and looked dismissively into his Guinness, flicked his head. He took a mouthful of the stout and seemed to calm down a little.

'What's the point? What's the bloody point I ask myself. You wouldn't understand, you and your lot. Everything's mercenary these days. Everyone's just after the next quick buck. No one's prepared to put in an honest day's sweat for an honest wage. I look at kids like you, scrounging off the Welfare, bleating on about your entitlements and your rights, never giving a damn about anyone apart from yourself. All you and your moronic friends ever think about, isn't it? How can I get loads of money for doing sod all. Where's my next pint of pissy lager coming from. What can I wangle out of the Welfare State today. Can I get a prescription for marijuana out of the doctor. Whose spirit level can I nick. How many gallons of free orange juice have I got a right to on the NHS.'

He paused, seemingly satisifed that he had unburdened himself of his sentiments. Then he continued.

'You know, this mate of mine. Honest family man, charming wife, two delightful little children, hard-working, upright citizen, pays his taxes, works his butt off. And he goes and loses his job just like that, for no reason. Employer just decides to boot him, and there's nothing he can do about it. And that man's got commitments, a mortgage and stuff. Now that's someone I can feel sorry for. That's someone who's got a right to feel he's entitled to something.'

Dog was curious about this. His mind was making a connection. 'Who's that then?' he said.

'That job you helped me on, matter of fact. Up your way.'

'Oh, yeah. I remember. Nutter. Bloke who had a boat, right? You was talking to him about boats, wasn't you?'

Richardson hesitated. A nerve seemed to have been touched. 'Yeah. Yeah, I might have done. I don't remember. It doesn't matter.'

'What line of work was he in then? Insurance or something, wasn't it?'

'Yeah, I think so. Yeah, I suppose it was.' He grabbed at his cheroots and fumbled one out of the packet. His hands were shaking as he lit it.

'Anyway,' he said. 'The point I was making was how we were freedom fighters, how we believed in something.' He downed his pint and looked as though he was about to get angry again.

'Yeah, well I'm sorry, David. That was what I meant to say. You know me, not very good with words like. So, like these dark things. This was from when you was a mer – a freedom fighter?'

'You wouldn't want to know.'

'Er, look, I'll get you another one,' Dog said, and headed towards the bar.

This gave him a pause for thought. He knew he was on to something. He was trying to fit together all of the odd things that were happening. It seemed reasonable to assume that Richardson had conceived the idea that he had killed Savage, and that presumably he believed he had done this on behalf of Nutter. Why else would he do it? But he could not see how Richardson could have killed Savage. He had not been on the boat. Toe-rag had been on the boat. Toe-rag had come back late that evening in a distraught condition. Toe-rag had – Suddenly his mind clicked. The smell of Toe-rag had been that of sea-water. The implications of this almost overwhelmed him.

When he returned to the table Richardson continued with his weird ranting, his dark allusions. It was strange: it was as though he wanted to tell you, wanted to let slip the terrible thing he'd done, the terrible thing he seemed to think he'd done.

Then he said, 'Disposable nappies. Disposable bloody nappies!' He shouted this, very loud. People on the other tables started giving the eyeball. He couldn't figure where disposable nappies came into the picture. This was another wobbler of a development. Richardson elucidated:

'That's what's wrong with this fucking country. Snugglers, Pampers, Muzzlers, Squelchers, Botties, Babba's goo goo shit bag – little Babba wants his free fucking orange juice and his dole money and his dentures. Free orange juice. Free milk. Free drugs. Free teeth. Gimme gimme gimme. I've got a right to it. I demand my rights. Gimme my lesbian self-defence classes on the rates. Gimme my free tickets to Wimbledon and my test tube babies and my leisure centres. Get in a couple of fights in pubs think you're a hard man, think you're something. You don't know piss all. You never seen a dead man. You never seen him when he looks up at you – terror in his eyes, pleading – like a pig that's been stuck. Blind terror. Life and death. Then you know what it's all about. You know there's only one fucking thing that counts. You wanna live. That's all you know . . .'

Dog didn't normally make a point of leaving pubs early. In point of fact, he found it rather hard to leave once he'd settled in and had a few pints. It was just as well they had closing-time, because he thought if they didn't there was a serious danger you'd just stay in the pub for the rest of your natural life. It was different today though. He was unnaturally eager to vacate the establishment. He couldn't actually get his pint down fast enough when Richardson started ranting. Half of it went down the 'I Fought The Law' T-shirt – he didn't even notice.

He was going to come up with an excuse the moment he'd sluiced the Dopplerbrau down the hatch. He started saying something about a job he had to get done, but it was pretty obvious Richardson wasn't listening. He said he'd catch up with him later, got up and made for the door.

CHAPTER TWENTY-TWO

THERE WAS A GROUP of three well-spoken young lads at the corner table. He distinctly heard one of them say, 'Place is full of loonies,' and he knew they were talking about him. 'Apparently there was a big loony-bin up near Wormwood Scrubs they closed down. The loonies all sort of gravitated to round here. They wander round the Green talking to themselves.'

'It's this so-called Care in the Community. I mean, it's a load of bullshit. It's just the Tories trying to save money.'

'It's awful. I saw this thing on *Panorama* about this guy who'd been in a mental hospital for sixty-something years or something and they just chucked him out on the street. I mean, even if he wasn't mad before he went in there there's no way he can cope with ordinary life now. And he's just wandering round the streets and living in a box, completely unable to look after himself, you know, find somewhere to live or a job or anything.'

'It's terrible.'

'There's nothing wrong with the *idea* of Care in the Community, but it's completely underfunded.'

'Yeah, yeah. A lot of those old Victorian institutions were scandalous. But just chucking these people out on the streets.'

Richardson put his Guinness down, turned his head and stared right into the middle of the bloke's head with fire-filled, gimlet eyes. The guy nearly shat himself. Now they were hiding behind their *Guardian*, sniggering like schoolboys after some prank. Tee hee hee – don't look now – he's still looking at us. They didn't know he had super-sensitive hearing, finely honed by years of listening. How could they?

It started to rain when he left the pub. He was conscious of the wet on his face, the sweetness of the water which trickled down the craggy crevices of his face on to his lips. He cut through the bus station into Cormorant Avenue, took the steps up to Mondaugen Mansions. Even in the semi-dark he saw the hole in the door from the end of the corridor. The door was ajar, a crack of yellow light spilling on to the mildewed wallpaper. He froze.

He had, of course, feared this. It was not weighting Savage's corpse properly – that was what had brought it up, and brought him this problem. It had been a risk to stay here. He had known that all along.

As he inched along the corridor his hand went down into the coat pocket and the fingers curled around the cheese-wire. He listened at the door. Heard a ruffling of paper, the scuff of a foot on the lino. He eased the door open a couple of inches and caught a rear view of the intruder. He was at the table in the bedroom, riffling through the pile of newspapers in the pool of yellow light. He could not be absolutely certain, but it looked as though there was only one of them. Any other would have to be standing right against the wall by the wardrobe. He slipped his shoes off. He got the two ends of the cheese-wire firmly clasped in his hands. He worked open the bottom of the door with his foot, and crept across the murky kitchen.

The man had just begun to turn towards him as the wire went around the neck, but not far enough to be able to prevent it. With the weight of his body forcing the man down on to the table, he closed his eyes, gritted his teeth and concentrated only upon the force he was bringing to bear on the wire. The man writhed and kicked and flailed, sending the newspapers cascading to the floor. The Teachers bottle fell with a dull thud. He was quite a small man, not more than five-six, eight or nine stones, but he discovered hidden strength now, strength he might never have known he had. Richardson was aware of his blows, of his arm as it reached round and scratched desperately at his face. He knew the thing to do was to ignore all this and just concentrate on the wire. That way the man would desist soon enough. The man was trying to get his hands up under the wire, but it was a futile endeavour. That was always the worst thing to do. He supposed it was just a last despairing instinct. The man was making a terrible gurgling sound and his head was flopping about. Then he was still, and Richardson knew that he was dead.

When he turned the carcass over, laying it on the table under the light, he was surprised to recognize the face of his landlord, Mr Pond. This was not what he had had in mind at all. It was a shock. Had he been late with the rent? Was that why Pond was searching round in here? No: he was always on the nail with the rent. He could distinctly recall giving Pond the £190 on the first of this month. Pond saying, 'If only everyone was like you, Mr Richardson. Always on the nail. Never even need to be reminded. My life would be simplicity itself.'

He had always enjoyed a very amicable relationship with Pond. Pond, like himself, held a low opinion of the drunks and drug addicts and students and dolehounds who occupied the building. From time to time they had discussed the matter. Sometimes Pond had invited him into his little sanctuary on the ground floor, taken his bottle of Chivas Regal out of the safe behind the bookshelf, and offered him a small glass. He was impressed with the fact that Pond trusted him sufficiently to let him see where the safe was. He was sure Pond vouchsafed this knowledge to none of the other tenants. His regard for Pond went up. He regarded their relationship as extremely cordial.

He went back and collected his shoes from the passage and shut the door. Things were beginning to make sense now.

Pond would not have put that hole in the door: he owned the door, and had a master key if he wanted to start going through people's rooms. No: he must have been doing his rounds, seen the hole in the door, and come to investigate. Which meant someone else had put the hole in the door.

He reflected that it was a terrible thing to have mistaken Pond for an intruder and to have had to kill him. Back in the bedroom he looked at Pond's body. He seemed to be doing rather a lot of killing this week. Savage, now Pond. The thought of Savage prompted him to look at the wall, and he noticed for the first time that the cuttings were missing. He linked this event to the hole in the door. Whoever had put the hole in the door had also stolen the cuttings. That made sense. But who was it? That was the question.

He patched up the hole in the door with the side of a cardboard box and some Sellotape. It would not now be immediately visible to the casual passer-by. He walked down to the Supasava store on the Goldhawk Road and bought three packets of black bin-liners, a pint of milk and an ample supply of cheroots. On the way back he took his tool-bag out of the boot of the Avenger. There was a good robust metal-saw and a plentiful supply of Stanley blades. They would probably do the job as well as anything. He felt completely calm. Workmanlike. He supposed this was not surprising. He'd been getting a lot of practice at this sort of thing recently.

Gaz stayed out of the house as much as possible. He kept getting gyp from his mother for not going to school. More worryingly, he was being subjected to Dog's attentions. Dog was prying, trying to find things out. He didn't know what he was going to do if Dog found out about Dorian being dead and put two and two together. He didn't see how Dog could find out, but Dog had a way with these things. Hadn't he managed to find out about the picture and that it was his dad? Once he got you talking he could find things out. So the obvious thing was, just don't talk to him. Stay mum. Don't give nothing away.

He was up at the stash-point on the Scrubs. It was raining and the whole expanse of muddy land was deserted under the cavernous grey sky. He sat in the bushes and it rained all over him but he didn't care. He stared at the prison, the four ocean liners. Thought: I'm going to go there if they ever find out. He wasn't ever going to let that happen. He would run, keep running. He would kill himself before he let them take him. Take No Prisoners, he thought.

Dorian had deserved to die. He should never have hit him, kicked him in the chest. He didn't have a right to do that, not to his own son. He wondered where Dorian was now. What had happened to him? Guessed he was fish food by now.

He lit a Marlboro but a heavy drop of rain fell from the dark heavens and extinguished it. He chucked it into the bushes. He didn't really want it anyway.

He had been giving this a lot of thought. He reckoned he was now the heir to Dorian's estate. He could go and live in that big house and maybe even have Rebecca there. That would be fucking great. He could just say: 'Why don't you carry on living here? I don't mind.' He could live in that house with Rebecca and no one could ever come there. Not Dog or his mother or Christie. They could all fuck off. He'd be able to see them on the TV thing at the gate. He could just say 'Fuck off!' into the microphone and they wouldn't be able to get at him.

Sadly, he could foresee all sorts of nasty complications arising, and like maybe they'd be able to pin the murder on him and then it wouldn't be worth having all the money, would it? That was a bit of a downer.

It carried on raining, but he didn't move.

It rained all into the early evening. The sky went gun-metal grey. He ate a packet of Dextro NRG and started walking up Scrubs Lane and along the canal towards Kilburn and Maida Vale. There was the cemetery on his left, full of spooks and weirdness and dark shadows, the car-dump on his right full of trashed-up motors.

He climbed over the railings into the cemetery and wove between the dripping trees and the gothic headstones. There were dead flowers and these little pictures of the dead guys on the new kind of headstones. **Michael McManus (Dad) In Loving Memory.** Some red-faced fat cunt who looked like he got pissed every night and beat his wife and kids up.

He moved on into the darker, older recesses of the cemetery. The leaves of the trees dripped with rain. It was totally horrorshow, but it was like he was feeling. The place was a buzz cos it was cold and dark and creepy which was how he felt. He sat on a slab of cold wet stone and started crying, buzzing like a fucking kid.

Everything had gone wrong. Everything had fucked up. It was unfair. Why was it always him? Why did everything always go wrong when it was him? Why couldn't he have a dad and loads of money and everything like other people had? Why couldn't nothing ever go right? It could only happen to him. Not anyone else. All you want to do is just get to know your dad and you end up fucking killing him. It was totally unfair.

Richardson had chopped up Pond's carcass by nine o'clock. It had been harder work than he had foreseen and he was sweating feverishly. He had packed all the bits into four bin-liners, then placed the bin-liners in further layers of bin-liner so that everything was now securely packaged up. The blood had been the chief problem. There had been gallons of it. It had insinuated its way into every corner of the flat despite his most careful preparations. You would not have thought a man as small as Pond could produce so much. He had lifted Pond up on to the draining board and bled him into the kitchen sink, severing each of the major arteries and allowing the blood to course into the tea-stained hole. It was as well he knew about these things from the *Encyclopaedia Britannica*. Still there had been a considerable surplus when it came to butchering the carcass. Each time he started in on a new limb further reservoirs of blood were untapped, little founts that jetted over his trousers or the front of the stove. He spent over an hour wiping up the spillage from the lino and the façades of the kitchen units. Now he had changed all his clothes and bundled up the bloody garments into a fifth bin-liner which he would dispose of at the same time.

He went and sat through at the table in the bedroom with a mug of tea and a cheroot and thought about how he was safely to get rid of Pond's carcass. He thought about the canal. Didn't like it: it was too reminiscent of the sea where he had ditched Savage. He thought about marshlands, gravel pits, bogs, mine-shafts and landfill sites. Maybe he should just do the obvious thing and put the parts of the cadaver in the dustbin. No. The police were wise to that sort of thing. They would dig up the landfill with sniffer dogs.

He reached down to the floor and picked up the fallen Teachers bottle. Unscrewed the cap and took a belt out of the neck. He had to think hard about all this, and he had to get on with it. Someone had come and taken the cuttings away. They would come back, probably with the police. It was imperative he was not here when that happened. Imperative. That meant clearing out tonight, and taking Pond with him. Pond had made things so much more complicated. Silly Pond, silly old Pond – why hadn't he kept his nose out of this? Why had he had to go and get involved? He was about to go back through into the kitchen to ask Pond, then he remembered he had already dismembered Pond, so there would not be much point.

He poured whisky in the tea and thought he might as well

start packing his suitcases. He travelled light, had always prided himself on being able to up camp in a few minutes. Everything fitted into the two suitcases: the pile of shirts, the spare pair of trousers, the handful of paperbacks, the austere range of toiletries, the kettle (that was his; it had not been on the original inventory; he had bought it for himself and didn't see why he should leave it behind for Pond to profit from). Sundry other accretions of a lifetime.

When the cases were packed he put them by the front door. He would take the bags containing Pond's remains to the car first, put them in the boot, then put the suitcases on the rear seat. The whole operation took five minutes. He took one last look at the old room, pocketed the Teachers bottle, locked the door and went downstairs. He returned the door keys through the slot in Pond's door, pulled the front door shut behind him, and climbed into the Avenger.

The cemetery was totally unreal. It went on for miles and miles and the great thing was there was no one else here. Apart from the stiffs of course – but they didn't count. What's more there were these old-time geezers who, when they pressed the snooze button, weren't happy with just a lump of stone or a carving of an angel – they went and had this little mini-house built for themselves with their coffin stuck in there. Given the fact that there was supposed to be a housing shortage, this struck him as well on the selfish side. I mean, it wasn't as though they were making much use of the gaff, was it? Just fucking lying there for a couple of centuries.

He had located one particular vault belonging to some guy called General Sir John Chudleigh KG, GCB, DSO. It was like a pretty weird name. The hut was called his mausoleum and was bricked up like no one even bothered to come and see him no more. He found a loose bit of stone and some crumbling mortar which allowed him to hack a hole and get in out of the rain. He kept lighting matches to get a dekko at the inside of the place and quickly came to the conclusion that it would make a pretty useful crash-pad.

He remembered seeing an old mattress dumped on the railway siding off Scrubs Lane; he could fix that up in here, dry it out, put it on top of DSO's coffin in the middle of the room just like a bed, bring the Tosh and his tapes down here with some batteries, fix up a new torch, get in a few cans of Iso, rig up some kind of shelf to keep his clothes on, even put a picture of Norman on the wall. It would be great. Then he could just come down here and crash out and no one would know where he was. Basically, he could live here. This would be his house. He couldn't see that old DSO was gonna kick up too much.

Outside an owl hooted. The rain had stopped and a full moon illuminated the necropolis. He took the path through the headstones leading back to the railing by the canal. Under cover of dark he would nick the mattress, then, when it was dead late and there was no possibility of Dog still being awake (it was a Friday night – he'd be pissed by two or three) he'd go back to Esterhazy and grab what he needed. He'd probably never go back there after that. Wouldn't be any point. He could really fix up DSO's old pad, make it like a proper home.

CHAPTER TWENTY-THREE

THE MORNING AFTER he had seen Richardson, after a night of strange terrors during which he twitched and writhed on the spare bed, Colin rang Tony Cotterell at Savage Life.

'Tone, it's me, Col. I just heard about Dorian – saw it in the paper.'

'Yeah?'

'It's terrible. What happened?'

'I was gonna ask you the same, mate. Everyone round here reckons you done it. Surprised the police haven't come round to your place yet.'

'What you talking about, Tone?'

'Motive, means – I thought it must be you, mate. Don't take it personal or anything, mate, but it don't look too good, does it? Dorian chucks you out, next week he takes the big swim off the side of is boat down the same marina where you've got a boat. I wouldn't like to be in your shoes, I'll tell you that for nothing, mate. Did you do it? Well, I s'pose you're hardly gonna tell me if you did.'

'Course I fucking didn't!' he bellowed. 'How can you think that?'

'Sorry, mate. Didn't mean to upset you. I'll tell you what, it's been right fucking chaos round here since it happened. Don't look like the company's gonna survive. You were pretty smart getting out when you did. You always were a slimy cunt when it came to getting out of the shit though. Remember that time Dorian set up this meet with – '

'Tony. Tony, please. Listen to me. What are the police saying? Have they been asking questions?'

'Routine stuff. I dunno. Something about some guy who was stuck up a tree near Dorian's gaff like he was watching im. I expect they'll get round to seeing you. Course you've got nothing to worry about, have you? Got an alibi and all that. By the way, mate, d'you see that paper that called me Tony Cockerel?'

'I don't know, Tone. I'm not sure.'

'Yeah, well I'll tell you what. I'm gonna put that bastard's bollocks in a wringer. *Tony Cockerel!* Can you fucking credit it? I gave im a right earful yesterday, I'll tell you that. If he thinks he can pull that kind of stunt he's got something else coming. Find a fucking car tool in is face if he don't . . .'

When he finally got off the phone he did some hard thinking. Running wasn't going to solve any problems. He would sit tight and avoid Richardson. If the police picked up Richardson he would not deny having met the man – would not even deny having discussed the fact that he'd been sacked by Dorian. What he would totally stonewall on was any suggestion that he had commissioned Richardson to kill Dorian. It would be one man's word against another's: respectable mortgage-holder and family man against Shepherd's Bush pub-hound and certifiable lunatic.

The building society withdrawal. This was a problem. He would insist it was a gambling debt he had discharged to Richardson.

But what about the second half of the money? Should he give it to Richardson? The answer seemed to be affirmative. Richardson had killed once. Why should he not do so again? The imperative thing was to get rid of Richardson, never to have to clap eyes on the man again.

£2000 for a couple of frames of snooker seemed improbable, but he thought he could front it out. People did stupider things, after all, especially when they were pissed. People certainly did stupider things: they did things like hiring maniacs to kill their friends. They did things like actually killing people. Every time he thought about this he felt a vertiginous rush of nausea.

The thing to do was to continue to behave in a perfectly ordinary manner. He therefore resolved to get a job. He telephoned Peter D'Angelo about the satellite dish sales job, and D'Angelo said, 'Glad you got back to me, Col. Doing anything for lunch tomorrow? Why don't you pop down, bout one say? We'll talk then.'

Things were looking up; everything was fitting into place. By tomorrow afternoon he would be masterminding the sales operation for satellite dishes over the whole of North-West London. What could be more normal? He would be a totally respectable citizen once more, beyond any suggestion of suspicion.

He waited in all day on tenterhooks. There was no sign of the police. On Saturday morning he left the house at eleven, allowing himself an hour or so to sit in the car somewhere and bone up on satellite dishes. 'Seeing Peter about that job,' he told Kate, but she didn't seem remotely interested. Doubtless she was absorbed in thoughts of Armageddon. He thought: Behave in a perfectly ordinary way. What if the police came round and questioned Kate in his absence? Would it not be suspicious if she knew nothing about Dorian's death?

'Oh,' he said. 'Something I meant to tell you. Terrible. Dorian's dead. Boating accident, but apparently there are suspicious circumstances. The old bill think he might have been knocked off by someone. It's in all the papers.'

'Oh,' she said. 'Good. That's nice for you, Colin.'

Jesus. You couldn't say he hadn't tried.

He drove the BMW to the end of the road, pulled up to wait for the oncoming traffic. He heard a door opening. Looked round. Richardson was climbing into the rear of the car. He looked more crazed than ever, and smelt strongly. He could not identify the smell.

'Keep driving,' he said hoarsely.

'What do you – '

'Just keep driving. Don't talk.'

He pulled out into the Uxbridge Road. He could see no alternative.

'I didn't come to your house. For obvious reasons,' Richardson said. 'I've been waiting for you all night.'

'Why? You said next Thursday – '

'There have been complications.'

They were driving past the police station. Over near the doors he could see a couple of bobbies. He could slam the brakes on, jump out, cry: 'Police! There's a murderer in my car!' But he did not do so. He kept on driving. He looked up into the rear-view mirror. Richardson's satanic gaze bored straight into him.

'We've got to take care of a couple of problems,' he said. 'And I'm going to need the money ahead of schedule.'

'What – what are these problems?' He kind of knew they were not going to be minor problems.

'A body. A man was on to us. I had to take care of him.'

They were driving around the one-way system on the Green. He had forgotten where he was going. Why he was in the car.

'Body,' he said, like a distant echo. 'There's a body?'

'You don't need to know the details. I'm going to have to lie low for a bit. We'll be all right. Don't worry. What's your bank? We can stop up in Notting Hill, get the cash.'

'You've killed someone else? I don't want anything to do with this. It's nothing to do with me. It's your body – your business.'

'It's *our* business, Colin. Don't go wet on me now. I'd figured you as tougher than that.'

There was a cacophony of car horns. He noticed he had just narrowly avoided collision with an articulated lorry. The car was circling the roundabout.

'Keep your eyes on the road,' Richardson said.

He blurted: 'I never wanted you to kill Savage, you fucking madman! I was pissed. It was the drink talking.'

'You gave me the money, Colin. You paid up front. And I've got it in a little plastic bag with your fingerprints all over it. That's a common precaution in my profession, you know. Now, don't start bottling out here. We can see this thing through together. I've got it all planned out.'

He stopped at the traffic lights on Holland Park Avenue. His head was spinning. Richardson was making a rustling sound in the rear of the car. He was leaning forward.

'Something you might be interested to see,' he said.

Instinctively Colin put his hand back to take hold of the proffered object, the way he did when Jessamy wanted to show him her crying doll or Sylvester to show him his clever watch which told you what time it was in Perth. He looked at it. For a moment he could not think what it was. Then he realized what it was. It was a severed finger, encrusted with a rusty patina of dried blood.

It was Saturday lunchtime in the Goose Green and Dog was curiously introspective as he contemplated the bizarre possibility that toe-rag had killed his own father.

'Patricide,' Nige said.

'Who?'

'It's a thing. When you kill your own dad.'

'Yeah?' Dog said. 'And what's it when you kill your girlfriend's kid brother? Cos that's what I'm gonna do if he keeps on winding me up like this.'

'Bratricide?' Nige said. 'I don't know. I don't think there is a word.'

Dog's thoughts returned to the disappearance of his prey. He turned it round in his mind, inspecting it from various angles, but could make no progress with it. He sipped at his lager and his consciousness slowly drifted away to the other vexatious matter, that of Richardson. He scratched at his nose, lit a cigarette, and mulled further upon the dislocation of the world. After a further stretch of time he decided that he would visit Richardson under the pretext of returning the spirit level. He collected it from the van and he and Nige set off through the bus station.

Halfway down Cormorant Avenue they became aware of unusual developments. There were six police cars blocking up the road, and a cordon of red and white plastic surrounded the vicinity of Mondaugen Mansions. A gaggle of twenty or thirty spectators were peering at the open front door and the group of officers there assembled.

They shuffled to a halt on the edge of the gathering. Neighbours were standing outside their front doors speaking in low tones. Others were craning out of adjacent windows gawping at the spectacle. Dog lit a Marlboro, surveyed the crowd, and picked out a likely informant.

'What's going on then?' he asked.

The man looked frightened, as people were wont to do when addressed by Dog. 'I don't know . . . sorry . . . Mr Capriatti says Mr Pond's missing and there was blood all over the kitchen.' The last part of the sentence was delivered with ill-concealed glee.

'Who's Mr Pond then?'

'The landlord. Mr Capriatti thinks he's been murdered. One of his tenants apparently.'

'Which one?'

'I don't know. I'm sorry.'

'Where's this Mr Capriatti?'

'They arrested Mr Capriatti. I'm sure he couldn't have done it, not Mr Capriatti.'

Dog grinned. 'No, I don't think Mr Capriatti done it either. You know Mr Richardson then?'

'Sorry, no . . .'

'One of Mr Pond's tenants.'

'That's the one!' a middle-aged woman screeched. 'It was

in his flat. Where they found the blood. All over the place. Mrs Papaspyrou found it – she was just taking some letters up there for him. Mrs Stodel saw him last night, putting bags in the car. The police have taken her in for questioning.' She uttered this last remark in a tone of reverential awe.

'I see,' Dog said. 'So let me get this straight. Pond's missing, there's blood all over Richardson's flat, and Richardson was sticking bags in his car last night. Is that right?'

'Yes. Yes, and Mrs Bergander says she heard – '

He had stopped listening. He looked at Nige, nodded, and they proceeded up Cormorant Avenue.

Richardson was severely disappointed with Nutter. The man had gone to pieces on him. It was not what he had expected. They had collected the £1000 from Nutter's bank in Notting Hill, driven the length of Ladbroke Grove, and were parked in a secluded spot in Kensal Green when Nutter suddenly broke down behind the wheel of the car. He wrapped his arms round the wheel and started banging his head on it and blubbing uncontrollably, rambling on about Savage and a letter he had received from him.

'He was my best friend – I loved that man,' he howled. 'That man taught me everything I know. He was my mate.'

'You should have thought of that before you put a contract out on him then,' Richardson said sternly. Some people – can't make their minds up.

Nutter burbled on: 'He was gonna give me my job back . . . It was just a cock-up. He didn't mean it. I was the best salesman he had. He told me that once . . . I loved that man . . .'

Richardson was in the passenger seat of the BMW. He'd had enough of this. He turned angrily to Nutter. 'Get a hold on yourself, man. What the hell's wrong with you?'

Nutter's pink, contorted face looked at him. 'You fucking

lunatic!' he shouted. 'Why did you ever get me involved in this? Why did I ever meet you?'

Something snapped in his head. He had to clamp his teeth shut on his tongue to stop himself doing something he would regret. He had had it with people accusing him of being a lunatic. The three lads in the pub yesterday, now Nutter – not once but twice.

Nutter started hitting his head on the steering wheel again. The horn hooted.

'*Stop it!*' he shouted; he grabbed hold of Nutter's jacket to drag him off the wheel; tried to get his arm round to slap Nutter's face, but the seat-belt prevented him.

'Get a grip on yourself, man!' he instructed.

Nutter carried on blubbing and moaning. After a few minutes he calmed down a little. He flopped back in the seat with his eyes shut. There were tears dribbling down his cheeks.

'Come on, man,' he said. 'The worst of it's over. Have a cigarette, steady your nerves.' He picked up Nutter's Benson & Hedges packet off the dashboard and lit one for him. Pushed it into Nutter's mouth. Nutter took it like a baby accepting a dummy.

'Come on, man,' he said more gently, the sergeant-major offering solace after the dressing-down. 'There's no need to feel bad about it. I've seen men crack under less pressure. It's nothing to feel ashamed of. Come on, chin up. Smoke your cigarette, you'll feel a new man.'

Nutter made a gentle gurgling noise.

He thought probably the thing to do was to take Nutter's mind off his worries, get him involved in the details of the plan. 'Everything's going according to plan,' he said. 'My car's safely hidden. We go back after dark, get Pond out and carry him into the cemetery. With the two of us it shouldn't take twenty minutes and then we're clean away. And that's all you've got to do. After that, you're free to go.'

Regrettably this speech did not have the effect he had intended. Nutter started blubbing again. The cigarette was still in his mouth but he seemed hardly aware of it. The ash fell down on to his freshly ironed white shirt. Richardson extracted the cigarette and placed it in the ashtray.

'Come on, man,' he repeated. 'Show some pluck. Spirit that built the Empire – all that.'

There was a shrill warbling sound.

Nutter lurched up in his seat and let out a little cry.

'Only your phone,' Richardson said. 'Best not to answer it perhaps.'

Nutter grabbed at the phone.

'Hello . . .? Peter? Christ, I'm sorry. I'm – I'm stuck in traffic . . . Two? I know I said I'd be there by one. I'm coming straight over – I mean, I'm on the way. Be with you in ten. You know what this fucking traffic's like. Honestly, I'm almost with you – '

He didn't like the sound of this. He didn't want Nutter saying anything he shouldn't, not in the state he was in. He pushed his gloved finger down on the receiver's rest and cut off the call.

'That was my fucking job!' Nutter howled. 'You just lost me my fucking job, you maniac! I hate you. I hate you you fucking cunt! You fucking, loony cunt!'

'Come on, Colin. You said yourself. There's always something in the sales game. You'll pick something else up. We have more pressing concerns just at the moment. It'll all be over by tonight. You've just got to sit tight. Hold your nerve. I know you can do it. Be a man. Show me what you're made of.'

And Nutter started blubbing and raving again.

It was unfortunate, he thought, but he could see no alternative. He was going to have to kill Nutter this evening. Bludgeon him by the grave they had dug for Pond and bury him along with Pond. He did not want to have to do it, but he knew he could no longer trust Nutter. He could not risk

Nutter breaking down and letting the cat out of the bag. So he was going to have to kill Nutter.

Gaz slept little. He lay curled in the duvet on top of DSO's casket and remembered years ago, when he was little and they lived up on the White City, before the council rehoused them after the neighbours complained about Adeline and her gentlemen callers, and then she went and stabbed one of them with a bread knife.

He was three and Christie was six; one of Mother's men came round, his yellow Capri grumbling on the road four storeys down, hooting impatiently. Gaz knew the man: the smell of his fierce aftershave, the vicious bristle of his thin moustache. Christie and him were sitting in front of the telly. Mummy saying, 'Ear's some money for chips. I'll be back later.' The Capri roaring away up the central artery of the estate, Gaz standing on a chair on the balcony watching, thinking I'll have a car like that one day, only bigger, much bigger, like a rocket.

Nine o'clock, ten o'clock, a film on telly, *Return of the Killer Sparrows*. He was crying and clinging to Christie's arm. Traipsing down the stairs and up the road to the chip shop, holding on to his big sister's hand. Twelve o'clock, one o'clock, he was asleep in the chair, the telly invading his troubled dreams. Dawn creeping through the blanket pinned over the window.

'Where's mum?' he asks Christie. She doesn't know. Sometimes she doesn't come back for days on end. He has wet himself in his sleep and walks round with the stickiness on his inside legs. Christie searches the kitchen for food: a few dusty cornflakes at the bottom of a box, margarine on charcoally toast. When that's gone she looks for money for more chips but can't find any. His tummy rumbles and hurts. She tries the telephone to ring Aunt Frankie in

Peckham, but the phone was disconnected when the bill wasn't paid. That's what happens. Other men – he knows they're not the same as Mother's men – come for money or to take things away. Other people come and look at him and his sister, look at his teeth and his bottom.

When the next morning comes his sister tells him they're going to Peckham to find Aunt Frankie. It is a strange odyssey, the furthest he has ever travelled. 'You just do what I tell you and stay next to me,' his sister tells him. He has no other plans; wants to cling tight to her.

At Shepherd's Bush Green they waited for a bus. It was raining, the rain seeping through the neck of his anorak, tickling his back like cold fingers. His hand clasped in hers, he jumped the step on to the bus. When the conductor came round Christie said they had no money, and they were thrown off. And on it went; eight buses and three hours, views of places he had seen on TV, and then they were standing in the middle of great flat acres of tower blocks, litter wafting in gusts, the rain blowing hard in their faces. He is hungry; the fist tightening in his guts.

Christie approaches a man standing by a looted red phone booth. 'Scuse me, mister, where's Mafyou Arnold House?'

Man says: 'You come with me, luv. I'll look after you.'

He doesn't know what happens, only his hand wrenched along and they're running over the soggy mud – *plash plash* – his feet slipping, squelching in a big dog dirt.

They stop. 'Why we running?' he says.

'That man,' Christie says. 'Dirty old man.'

In a shopping precinct, grey metal grilles on the shop fronts, his sister goes to an old woman craning over a basket on wheels. 'Where's Mafyou Arnold House, missis?'

Up flights of concrete stairs, echoing footfalls, he can feel his heart cracking at his ribs like a caged bird mad for freedom. 'One-oh-six,' his sister says, and rat-tats on the flaking paint door.

'Who is it?' muted through the door. 'Whatever it is, I don't want it. I'll call the police.'

'It's me, Aunt Frankie. Let us in . . .'

A great clanking of bolts and grating of chains and wrenching of bars; the thin slither of light where the door creaks open. Her fat pink face. 'Oh my gawd. Look at the sight of you . . .'

He remembered a day or two that seemed like the happiest of his life. He was warm and clean at night, with the taste of cocoa going sour on his tongue, like there were tiny gritty bits caught in the folds of the tongue that he could squeeze out if he sucked hard enough. He could hear the quiet susurration of his sister's breath down below on the bunk, hear the dim babble of TV voices through the wall. Comforting voices. He liked his Aunt Frankie.

Then his mother came for them and argued with Aunt Frankie. He heard the voices going like cockerels and his heart anticipated his mother's violence.

'You're a bloody hoar!' Aunt Frankie shouted. 'Way you treat those kids, you should be ashamed of yourself.'

'It's none of your fucking business.'

'It's my fucking business when they come knocking on my door half-starved, poor little things.'

'Fuck off.'

He remembered the taxi ride home through the grey streets, through the yellow lights crying in the puddles, remembered days of solitude locked in the room with Christie, sharp-edged tins of food shoved through the door. The feel of shit gone flat like a pancake in his pants. His mother's voice: 'Donchew ever fucking do that again you little git, d'you ear me?' The repeated clonk of her hand on the side of his head, so he hears a singing sound and feels his teeth jarred together.

Years later he began to understand something of where it was his mother went with the men in the growling cars. He smelt the sicky, boozey, smoky smell of her, guessed darkly at the sweaty activities behind her closed door, at the giggling and cackling and moaning. Like animals, he thought. Like *Life on Earth*. Sometimes there was violence, his mother's face splodged with purple and yellow bruises in the morning. 'Donchew look at me like that!' He hated the men, sensing that they were the root of the problem, that life might be like it was with Aunt Frankie if the men never came. Then he wanted to kill them – wanted to end them, to stop them, to finalize. He dreamt of guns and coshes. Saw blood smudged on the wallpaper . . .

After a couple of hours' uneasy sleep he woke up feeling like a bag of shit. Even with the plastic bags he had laid on the mattress on top of DSO's coffin the damp had still got at him. His strides and his jacket had a horrid mouldy feeling and his legs and his back ached. Number one priority for today was going to be to get the mattress out in the sun and give it a good drying-out.

Apart from that, everything was going well though. His mission to Esterhazy last night had been a total result. Dog and Christie had been asleep – he had been able to hear Dog's revolting snore coming through the door – and his mother had shown no signs of consciousness. Her TV was on, but that didn't mean anything. He had bundled up all his good clothes, his duvet, the Toshiba and some food which he nicked from the kitchen. A big stash of Christie's Lean Cuisines which would tide him over for a while. They were not, he discovered, particularly good when eaten cold straight out of the plastic, but they were a handy stand-by.

Outside a load of birds were going ape-shit as the sun came up over the cemetery. Shafts of the sun were coming in the slits at the top of the mausoleum so he was able to get a better recce at it. It was weird, but weird in a good kind of way. He reckoned he could get to like it. He put some music on fairly quietly, just enough to drown the birds out, and opened a can of Isotonic. He climbed up and had a peek outside, then shifted the stone and pulled himself out through the hole.

He rested the can on top of a headstone and took a leak on the side of this carving of Jesus hanging on his cross. Then he decided to go and do a bit of exploring. In the morning sunlight it was even better than it had been last night. Great expanses of stone and flowers and models of angels and Jesus all over the gaff. It completely freaked him out. He went back and dragged the mattress out through the hole and laid it in a gap between a couple of trees where the sun was shining.

As the morning wore on people started coming into the cemetery. They came and put flowers on the graves, and there were other guys with lawn-mowers and stuff. He killed the music on the Toshiba and stayed inside his new house. He reckoned it was a pretty good bet no one was gonna come and see DSO. He'd read what it said about DSO on the front of the mausoleum and like he'd died in 1948. Fucking eons ago. Who was going to give a shit about him now?

He unbagged his gear and sorted it out. There was a little stone ridge along the wall which was just the right size for his tapes. He lined them up along it. Then he noticed his N-V-Scratch tape was missing.

He racked his brain and it suddenly came back to him. A few days ago he'd been worried that Dog was going to nick it or smash it up and he had carefully hidden it behind a piece of loose skirting-board. This was a bummer. It wasn't as though it could easily be replaced. It was the special limited edition with the extended remix of 'Your Mercedes' on it. This meant he was going to have to return to the house one more time to fetch it.

CHAPTER TWENTY-FOUR

THE BLACK PLASTIC bags had a strange feel to them, squidgy, the weight unevenly distributed, as though they were filled with large chunks of offal. They were of course filled with large chunks of offal, and with bones, meat, cartilage, gristle, tendons and nerves.

Colin remembered the dog which had died, the similar means of disposal he had then contemplated. He recalled what a problem that had been at the time and considered how improbable he would then have thought it that a short while later he would be encountering precisely the same problem with a man.

'This one's lighter,' Richardson said. 'You take it. That one's got the head in it.'

They were standing at the boot of the Avenger, which was concealed in shrubbery on a narrow stretch of track running along the wall of the cemetery. The BMW was parked back at the top of the lane. The moon was behind the trees; pale orange sodium light glowed from the nearby Harrow Road.

He put down the heavier bag, the one with the head in it, and took the other, which did not seem appreciably lighter. He wondered which bits it contained: the liver, perhaps; a thighbone hacked off at the knee. Pond's penis possibly? He tried desperately to recall the relevant passages on detachment from his books on executive stress management.

Richardson slammed shut the boot of the Avenger. 'Don't worry,' he said. 'Just act normal. The thing is not to act suspiciously. Just look as though you're going about your ordinary business.'

There were a number of objections he might have lodged against this line of reasoning, but he did not do so. He did not do so because he was no longer speaking to Richardson. He was no longer speaking to Richardson because he had discovered that nothing he said had the slightest effect on Richardson. If Richardson didn't want to hear what you said, he simply blocked it out.

He had also discovered that if he said nothing it helped to maintain a certain level of calm. Every time he gave utterance he became hysterical, like a woman. He supposed it was the strain of trying to communicate with a psychopath, a man perforce beyond the reach of ordinary human discourse.

'Follow me,' Richardson said.

He picked his two bags from the ground and, in the absence of any viable alternative, complied with Richardson's demand. They were standing by the iron railings. A light breeze rustled through the leaves of the trees. They put down the bags and the brand new Spear & Jackson spade purchased that afternoon from an ironmonger off Ladbroke Grove. 'Right,' Richardson said, 'I'm going to climb over, you pass the bags over to me, then you climb over.'

The madman's tall frame straddled the railings with surprising agility. His overcoat snagged as he swung himself over and landed on the far side. He stood there, the sodium light illuminating his face, making his malign, Staffordshire bull terrier eyes glow a terrible shade of orange.

'Right. Now, Colin, be careful here. We don't want the bags catching on those spikes, spilling anything. I'm going to be very angry with you if we spill any of Pond. Have you got that?'

He nodded mutely and lifted the first bag. As he hefted it up between his two hands he could feel the bits inside wriggling about. It was as though Pond was making a last feeble protest against burial.

He felt the hot, wet touch of Richardson's flesh as he took the bag. 'There . . . nicely does it,' Richardson commented.

They repeated the procedure with the three other sacks and the bag of clothes and the spade. Holding the spade in his hands it occurred to him to bludgeon Richardson to death, but he did not do this. He did not do it, not because it was not the single thing in life he now most devoutly wished to do, but because it would not solve the problem. It would merely compound the problem: he would have to get rid of two corpses.

He climbed the railings. An owl hooted. Distantly a train rolled westward out of Paddington. Silently they picked up the bags and the spade and he fell in behind Richardson. They cut into the heart of the dark cemetery, moving through the cover of trees into the open where the moon illuminated the crowded rows of headstones and their accompanying paraphernalia.

Notwithstanding his resolution not to talk to Richardson any more, there was something he was terribly curious to know about. He said: 'Did you take his clothes off before you cut him up?'

'Of course I did, Colin. Clothes get in the way. I left his smalls on, of course. For the sake of decency. He wasn't wearing much anyway – he'd just popped up from downstairs. Just a shirt, trousers, a pair of carpet slippers.'

'What d'you mean, he'd just popped up from downstairs? I thought you said he was on to us – *you* – on to *you*. Now you make it sound like he was just coming round to borrow a mug of sugar. Who was he?'

'Questions, Colin. Questions. Don't ask too many questions.'

'I'll ask what questions I fucking want. *Who was he?* Come on.'

'Keep your voice down, Colin. He was just someone who went sticking his nose in where he shouldn't. Understand?'

Richardson came to a halt and dropped the bags and spade. It was evident that they had arrived at the appointed spot. Wilting wreaths littered the site of a freshly dug grave. A shiny plastic headstone bore the inscription **Maria Pacquette**. Richardson leant over to heave the wreaths aside. 'Mary Packet,' he said. 'Poor old Mary Packet. Only thirty-four when she pegged out. You ever noticed – they make a big do out of it, these left-footers, eh?'

'What?'

'Big send-off – for their dead.'

'Oh. Yes.'

'Right. We'll take it in turns. Five minute rota. I'll dig first, you keep watch, then vice versa. Happy?'

Happy.

Richardson started digging. The soil was light and came up easily. Colin stood by, now reconciled to the fact that he was going to spend the next twenty years in prison. After the terrors of the last week things could not get any worse: prison would be pleasant, peaceful, in comparison to this. With good behaviour, parole, he might be out by his mid-forties. He could start life over again, afresh. There would be no more drinking, no more striking up conversations with lunatics in pubs.

He could learn a skill in prison – carpentry, perhaps – to set him up for his new life. Kate would of course divorce him once he was prosecuted. It was regrettable, but there it was. There was nothing to be done for it now. Fate was going to roll forward. There was no point in trying to resist it.

Richardson was already a way down into the grave, eighteen inches or so. The five minutes had elapsed but he showed no sign of stopping. He seemed entirely engrossed in his work, heaving the soil out between strong, stertorous breaths.

Colin thought some more about his post-prison life, envisaging a small cottage in the country and his carpenter's workshop. There was a comely wench who served behind the bar in the Goat's Head . . .

His reverie was rudely interrupted.

'First bag,' Richardson said. 'Come on. Look smart, man.'

He lifted the bag and carried it to the side of the pit. Some time must have passed. The hole was now three or four feet deep, the length of a man.

'Bring it down, this end,' Richardson said.

He stepped over the pile of earth, feeling his foot slip in the soft soil. 'Drop the bag, carefully,' Richardson said.

'How can I drop it carefully?'

'Just do it,' Richardson commanded.

He dropped it, neither carefully nor carelessly, went back for the next, and continued with the procedure until the five bags were evenly distributed across the bottom of the hole.

'Good,' Richardson said. 'Phase one accomplished.'

Richardson was standing two yards behind him as he dropped the last bag into position. He looked round at Richardson. The spade was windmilling over Richardson's shoulder. He could tell immediately that Richardson was killing him. He had known all along that this was a likely outcome. It had been at the back of his mind all day, from the moment Richardson got into the car. He had known Richardson would kill him. There could not have been any other outcome.

Dog and Nige waited until Gaz returned to the house. When he came back out, glancing distrustfully up and down the street, they remained concealed behind a brown Cortina parked at the top of the road. Dog was wearing a motorcycle helmet; Nige an elaborate disguise involving a curious woolly hat, sunglasses and copious facial hair. They tailed him, one walking ahead and then pausing to inspect a shop window while the other ambled along the opposite pavement and followed for the next hundred yards. The boy was on a nicking spree: he went into an electrical shop, a tobacconist's, a hardware store; came out, went round the corner, whipped out a set of batteries, a chisel, a packet of crisps.

For over an hour they tailed him north until he came to the top of Scrubs Lane and disappeared down a footpath. He was last seen swinging himself over the railings into the cemetery. They reconnoitred on the bridge over the canal. Nige knew the cemetery from childhood drug-taking expeditions and guessed that Gaz would be holed up somewhere in there. They resolved to get hold of some torches and wait for dark before continuing the search. With the torches acquired, they repaired a short way up the canal to the Blind Bargee.

'I should have thought of it,' Nige said. 'I kipped out up there a few times when I was in trouble with my mum.'

'How big is it then?' Dog asked.

'It's pretty big but he'll be in one of the burial vaults. There's not so many of them. We'll find him if we're quiet.'

They had a few pints. At nine the sun set; Nige suggested they make tracks.

'One more,' Dog said. 'Quick one.'

One stretched to two and it was twenty-past. Dog's zeal for the quest was waning.

'One more,' he suggested. At ten they bought a six-pack, donned their respective disguises, and meandered along the towpath to the cemetery. 'Quiet,' they kept reminding each other as they clambered the railings.

'No, I'm fucking serious,' Nige said, and walked backwards into a headstone, dropping torch and six-pack into the long grass. Dog decided to piss in a vase of flowers.

At length they sorted themselves out and headed west along parallel paths. When they came to the first of the vaults they climbed up and explored the cobwebbed interior with the torches. Nige signalled to go north and they cut through the trees in silence. There was a distant voice and they both ducked down. Having crawled a short distance they could discern two figures in the moonlight thirty yards away. One was tall and wearing a distinctive overcoat. They were both carrying bags.

Dog raised the visor of his helmet. 'Richardson,' he whispered.

Nige looked apprehensive. 'This is getting a bit heavy. Maybe we should get the police.'

Dog shook his head solemnly.

They continued through the headstones, stopped when one of the figures spoke. Dog heard a familiar voice, the tail-end of the sentence – '. . . cut him up?'

A row ensued. Something to do with a mug of sugar. Dog recognized the other voice as Colin Nutter's.

They followed a short way until the two men stopped and Richardson started hurling flowers off a grave. Dog saw the spade now and began to understand. A terrible wave of sobriety descended upon him. Nige was jabbing at his arm and protesting in muted tones.

'Shut up,' Dog said. 'I'm thinking.'

He pushed his brain to the limit as he contemplated the Savage–Nutter axis and its place in the scheme of things. He remembered about Nutter losing his job, and suddenly the whole thing started to make sense. What Richardson was doing down at the marina, everything. Nutter had fallen for all Richardson's Mad Max Muller the Mercenary crap, had thought Richardson could take care of Savage. Richardson went to do the business and fucked up. He hadn't managed to get on to the boat in time which was why he had been standing there flapping his arms about.

Toe-rag was on the boat hunting down his daddy – thieving from his daddy – whatever. Savage found him and went berserk, there was a fight, the boy bashed Savage with his lead stick (the contusion on the head in the papers), Savage fell into the sea, the boy dumped the cosh and escaped on the dinghy, the boat carried on into the side of Holland. The boy came home smelling like shit.

At this point Richardson went crazy and thought he'd done it – or else the other way round. Back in his room he found Pond poking round and the cuttings missing and made the obvious deduction. He slaughtered Pond, hacked up the body, then press-ganged Nutter into helping him bury it.

Now that he thought about it, he was amazed that he had not reached this conclusion long ago.

Richardson was spooning soil out of the hole while Nutter stood watching. Dog sensed that something was about to happen. Richardson was not digging that hole for one body – he was a lazy bastard, would never dig that deep just for the one. No, he was on a killing spree now and was planning to cover his tracks by putting Nutter in there too. Nutter was standing there watching Richardson dig his grave.

Richardson emerged out of the hole and said something. There was another minor dispute. Nutter lifted the bags and walked round the grave, Richardson hovering behind him with the spade grasped in his fist.

He looked at Nige. 'You help me,' he whispered.

He felt virtuous. He felt a surge of righteous violence rush through his blood. He grasped one of the lager cans in his fist and began to run towards the grave. When he was almost upon it Richardson's crazed eyes swivelled towards him as the spade arced down towards Nutter's head. Time seemed to freeze. The spade caught Nutter a glancing blow at exactly the moment Dog's crash helmet impacted on Richardson's belly. Nutter fell into the grave, producing a hideous squelching sound as he hit the plastic bags.

Dog began to kick every available part of Richardson's anatomy and smashed the lager can down on his head. The can crumpled and exploded in a cold spray of lager. The spade fell from Richardson's hands as he collapsed. His red eyes flashed up at Dog with a bewildered, imploring look which seemed to suggest that he could not possibly understand why anyone would wish to do this to him. Blood was gushing from his head and blinding him. He made a last imploring croak, and then was still and silent.

Gaz knew trouble was coming. He sensed it following him as he returned to the cemetery. After a while he knew that it could only come in one form: Dog. He smelt Dog like a deer smells a wolf on the wind and knew that he couldn't remain here now. He packed all his gear up in two bin-bags and was about to leave when he heard the voices from outside.

He climbed up and scoped a tall guy and Nutter coming between the stones with bags and a spade. He froze in position. Nutter and the weird guy with the staring eyes he had seen down at the marina eating the revolting fish from the stand. How did he fit into the picture? What was his connection with Nutter? *What was going on here?*

When Staring Eyes started digging he had a good idea what was in the bags and his resolve to change addresses was further strengthened. People were stashing bodies twenty yards from his new gaff. He watched for a while, and then there was a flurry of strange activity. There was a sound of heavy feet punishing the ground and a man in a helmet went chewing into the tall guy. He knew in a moment that it was Dog. A display of quite horrifying violence ensued and it was all up with Staring Eyes in less than ten seconds. Nige appeared out of the shadows and was dragging Dog off, trying with little success to calm him down. Then they did a runner, rushing off into the dark of the trees.

He pushed the stone free and dragged his bags out of the mausoleum. He was about to flee when he remembered Colin Nutter dropping into the grave, so he went and aimed his torch down into the hole. The scene there revealed very nearly made him sick. Nutter was flat out on a bed of red and black, his grey suit soaking up the blood from the squelched bags. It wasn't much of a suit anyway. Not like Dorian's wicked power suits.

He took a can of Isotonic out of his pocket, shook it up, tugged the ring-pull and squirted it like champagne into Nutter's face. Nutter gasped in the darkness. He shone the torch so Nutter could see where he was; there was a whimpering sound from down in the pit. He guessed Nutter had just worked out where he was.

'Colin, like,' he said. 'We've gotta piss off.'

'Who are you?' Nutter said. 'Please. Don't hurt me any more. Oh God, what have I done? I didn't mean to do it. Please . . .' There was more squelching as he flailed about, trying to stand amidst all the bones and blood and plastic.

'No,' he said, trying to sound reassuring. 'It's all right now, but we've gotta piss off – before the police come.'

'Go away! Tormentor!' Nutter howled. 'Leave me to die in peace.'

Seeking to reassure Nutter as to his true identity, Gaz brought the torch up and shone it on to his own face. This did not have the desired effect; Nutter let out a still more piercing howl.

'Colin. Shut up! It's me. Gaz Hoskins. Like I live down the road from you.'

'Who are you?' Nutter said.

'Like I said. Gaz. You gotta get out of there. Come on – I'll help you. Hang on.'

He swivelled the torch to locate the spade, grabbed it and dangled it down in the pit standing astride the hole. There was more squelching as Nutter grasped hold of the end and pulled himself up. His shirt and suit and face were straight out of the most corrupting video you could imagine.

'Why?' Nutter said. 'Who are you?'

'It don't matter who I am. We've gotta get out of here.'

'Where's Richardson?'

Gaz flashed the torch at the mangled figure. 'That im?'

Nutter let out another little shriek. 'How did he get like that? Who did that? Did you do that?'

'It don't matter who did it. He was gonna kill you.'

'I know – I know that. Who are you?'

'You got your motor down here?'

'I don't understand.'

'When you come down with im – d'you bring your motor?'

'Car. My car. Yeah. Yeah. He got in the back. That madman got in the back.'

'Look – clean yourself up a bit and then give me a lift back to Esterhazy, all right.'

'I don't understand. Who are you?'

'I live down the road from you. Look.' He shone the light into his face again.

'I know you,' Nutter said.

'Yeah . . . come on. Get a move on.'

'Why are you here? What are you doing?'

'Don't ask questions – we gotta leg it. We just got mixed up in the same shit, right? Just get moving. You got your car keys?'

Nutter felt in his pockets. 'I'm covered in blood – I'm covered in fucking blood.'

'You worry about that later. Let's leg it.'

'The money,' Nutter said. 'Get the money off Richardson.' There was a demonic glint in his eye. 'They'll be able to trace it.'

Gaz aimed the torch at the cadaver. 'That Richardson, right?'

'Yeah. He's got my money, the bastard. Give me the torch, what's-your-name – give it here!' Nutter seized hold of the torch and jumped down on to the body. 'What happened to him? His face has disappeared. I can't believe this.'

'This guy did him over. I'll tell you in the motor. Hurry up – we gotta go.'

Nutter pushed his fingers into the inside pocket of the coat and pulled out a wallet. His bloodied fingers rifled through its contents and he emitted a small whoop of delight. 'It's here!' he cried. 'He's a madman. A murderer.' Nutter started kicking what was left of Richardson in a belated show of resistance.

'Who'd he kill then?' Gaz said.

'Everybody! You wouldn't understand. It's terrible – terrible. He killed everybody. Pond. Savage – '

'He killed Dorian Savage?'

'Yes. Yes . . . oh God. Who killed him? Did you kill him? You've done a service to mankind. They ought to give you a medal.'

'Look, it don't matter who killed him. We gotta move. Come on! Where's your motor?'

He picked up his bags and moved towards the road. Nutter glanced suspiciously at the bags and seemed momentarily confused, then started following. 'What's in the bags?' he said.

'My gear. I was living up here, but I've got to piss off now.'

'Yeah. Yeah, I see. I suppose you would . . .'

They got to the lane and walked swiftly under the sodium light the hundred yards to the BMW. Gaz shoved his bags on the rear seat and climbed in the front. Nutter was shaking – he could hardly get the key in the ignition. The motor started. Gentle BMW purr. They pulled down the lane towards the Harrow Road. 'If we were seen . . .' Nutter mumbled.

'I don't reckon we were – you'll be all right. Who was the guy in the bags then? Guy you was burying.'

They were coming down Wood Lane towards the Bush. 'Look. Listen to me. Gaz. You've got to believe me. It was nothing to do with me. That maniac dragged me into it.'

'S'all right. I believe you.'

'Have you got any cigarettes? Please . . .'

'Yeah. Sure. You want me to light you one?'

'Thank you. I still don't understand what's happened . . .' They circled the Saturday night Green and turned into the Uxbridge Road. Drunks were wobbling back from the pub, people on the hoof ingesting fast food. 'I can't go home,' Nutter said. 'Not like this. I can't go home like this. Oh God . . .'

'Mrs Nutter wanna know what you'd been up to, eh?'

'Yeah. Yes. Oh God . . .'

'If you drop me, I could go round and tell her you're not coming home yet. Bit late or something.'

'No. I – I've got to go away. I can't stay here. Where d'you want to be dropped?'

'Anywhere here. Just up there will do.'

The BMW pulled up outside the chemist at the top of Esterhazy Road. Nutter looked at him, terrified. 'You won't tell anyone what you saw – please. Please promise me.'

'No way – you think I wanna get involved in that shit?'

'Thank you. Thank you,' Nutter said. There was a note of pathetic gratitude in his voice.

Gaz decamped with his two bags. 'See you then, mate,' he said, as the door slammed and the car surged away towards Acton.

He let himself in up the road. Dog and Nige were drinking in the kitchen. Dog's helmet was on the table between them.

Dog looked up. 'Where've you been, toe-rag?' he said savagely.

'I saw you!'

'What d'you see?' Dog was up out of his chair.

'Saw you kill Richardson. Murderer!'

Dog's fist balled up and he came at him. Adeline was standing in the door. 'What d'you call im?' she said.

'Murderer.' He turned to Dog. '*Murderer!*'

'You get out of this!' Dog shouted at Adeline. 'Out!'

'I'll leave it to you boys then,' she said calmly, and returned to her TV.

'What d'you see?' Dog said as he grabbed him and pushed

him into the wall. 'What d'you see, shithead?' There was a great wave of sweat and Dog's breath.

'I saw you kill im. He's dead. Give us a beer.'

Dog let go, looked distrustfully at him. Nige pushed a beer across the table. Dog grinned slowly and threateningly. 'I saw you kill Savage.'

This completely fazed him. This was a total turnaround. A knockout. He couldn't – he couldn't know. 'How d'you know about that? You can't!'

'I come down to Bradwell. I sees you get on his boat.'

'But . . .'

'Dad-murderer,' Dog said. 'You killed your dad! You killed your own fucking daddy.'

Gaz glugged on his beer. Nonchalant. Insouciant. 'Might have done.'

'Might have done!' Dog grinned. 'You pushed im off that boat, didn't you? Then you were scared shitless and you does a runner on that dinghy. I've got you well sussed.'

For the rest of his life Gaz would wonder how it was Dog could know all of this. It was like Dog was sitting in the sky watching everything that happened everywhere on a TV screen. He glugged on the beer and felt the most profound consternation.

'Got something for you,' Dog said. 'Where's it gone?' He rootled round on the table and found the copy of *Grunt*. The Readers' Wives page.

'How much d'you get for that then?'

'Fifty.'

'That's mine. You should give me that. I nicked them. I just got a lift with er husband. He's alive.'

'Yeah?'

'I got him out of that hole. Covered with blood.'

'Yeah?' Dog said, looked thoughtfully at him with his fat pink eyes. 'Look, toe-rag. You don't tell no one about me doing in Richardson, I don't tell no one about you and your dad. All right?'

'All right.'

'Cos I'll kill you if you ever open your mouth. I mean it.'

'I'm not gonna.'

Dog pulled the tab on another beer and smiled.

'Toe-rag,' he said, suddenly friendly. 'D'your dad have any other kids at all?'

'How d'you mean?'

'Finished your beer? Have another one. We got plenty.' He went to the fridge, pulled more Wobblers from the stockpile and threw one over. Things were really changing round here. Amazing what a couple of murders will do.

'Fanx . . .'

'I mean, he wasn't married, your dad, was he?'

'What's it to you?'

'Just interested, mate. No need to get aggressive. I give you a couple of beers and you act like I've just nutted you. Calm down a bit. Have a seat. Be a bit sociable for a change.'

He eyed Dog uncertainly and took the seat.

'Was he married then?'

'Nah.'

'So he wasn't married. But did he have any other kids – like apart from you obviously?'

'Why d'you wanna know?'

'Come on – tell us. I'm just asking. Have a smoke.' He offered his own fags, a total first.

'All right. No, he didn't have no kids. Not as far as I know. Part from me.'

'So all his dosh . . .' Dog looked at Nige. 'What d'you know about inheritance?'

Nige looked thoughtful. 'Well, far's I know if there's only one kid . . . yeah, I see what you're driving at. Tell you what, I know this lawyer lives up in Willesden. He'd know all about it.'

'When can we see him?' Dog said. 'Can we give him a bell now?'

'It's midnight on Saturday – I don't think he'd take too kindly to it.'

'We can give him a bell in the morning then.'

'*We?*' Gaz said. 'What's this we? Whose dad was he anyway?'

'We're just trying to help out, mate. Legal advice and so on. Can get very complicated, legal stuff. Have another beer. You eaten? Nige was just going to get some kebabs.'

'Right . . . Yeah.'

'What's yours then? It's on me. Large one – chilli sauce?'

'I don't like chilli sauce.'

'No chilli sauce for Gaz, Nigel.'

'Fine.'

Gaz thought about it and began to appreciate the huge leverage given him by his new status as heir apparent to the deceased managing director of Savage Life. His world was suddenly and subtly altered. 'Get us some chips as well,' he said.

'Get him some chips, Nigel,' Dog said calmly.

'Salt and vinegar?'

'Yeah – and one of them rum doughnut things.'

'Ones with cream? Fine.'

'Have another beer,' Dog said.

'S'all right. I haven't finished this one yet.'

'Just help yourself when you fancy one.'

'I will. And what about that fifty? That's mine.'

'Who sold them, eh? I got my expenses to consider – commission like. What say we split it fifty-fifty?'

'Eighty-twenty.'

'Sixty-forty. I can't say fairer than that.'

'Seventy-thirty.'

'Sixty-five-thirty-five.'

'Sixty-nine-thirty-one . . .'